What was she doing here? She was supposed to be with Takashi. They had both taken sleeping medicine at the same time and had lain on the ground clasped in each other's embrace. He must still be asleep, even now, right here with her!

She struck a match and felt a shudder run through her body the moment she looked at the wooden object she had been holding in her hand. For a moment she thought she must still be dreaming. Takashi's body was lying beside her in a somewhat twisted position. The thing she had been grasping when she first regained consciousness was protruding through his jacket and the shirt beneath on the left side of his back. It was a large knife.

Also by Shizuko Natsuki
Published by Ballantine Books:

MURDER AT MT. FUJI

THE THIRD LADY

THE OBITUARY ARRIVES AT TWO O'CLOCK

INNOCENT JOURNEY

Shizuko Natsuki

BALLANTINE BOOKS • NEW YORK

Library of Congress Catalog Card Number: 88-92834

ISBN 0-345-35645-4

Manufactured in the United States of America

First American Edition: May 1989

1

A Sinister Invitation

Within the bright pool of light cast by the standing lamp, Takashi Sato was slowly, gently caressing the nude body of Yoko Noda. It was almost as though he were carefully and minutely going over each part of her body in order to verify its reality. She began to perspire, and the man's fingers responded to the moisture with even greater gentleness.

Yoko closed her eyes against the glare of the light and in a transport of ecstasy murmured urgently, "Turn off the light."

But Takashi had never yet conceded to her wishes in such a matter. Instead he responded with impatience and resumed moving his fingers with even greater concentration. Then, still in the glare of the light, his lips slowly moved to her flesh. A look of intensity burned in his eyes, but a hint of sadness as well. Even with her eyes closed, Yoko could tell this.

1

"Please, turn the light off."

After half a year's experience, she knew he would pay no attention to her request, but the words came automatically to her lips. The sound of her voice seemed to stimulate Takashi, and he devoted himself single-mindedly to his efforts.

This was the usual pattern of their sexual encounters, their unique ritual for lovemaking. As the man touched his lips to her moist skin, he began to lick. It was time to relax a little.

Beads of perspiration formed on Takashi's narrow forehead, and he gazed at Yoko with a detached expression on his face. Yoko felt a change in the way he moved his hands, a different manner of caressing her than before.

"Oh, it's good tonight," she murmured.

"What?"

"That *thing* is really disgusting. Let's not use it tonight."

As she spoke, Takashi's hand was already reaching for the condom on the night table. He stopped midway and turned to Yoko. He tended to be rather domineering during foreplay and was always deeply conscious of the halt that had to be called on account of "that thing." Yoko always had the condom laid out in advance, ready for even the slightest chance that she might get pregnant. Takashi, however, knew that she would have preferred to make love without having to stop for safeguards.

A look of suspicion clouded Takashi's face. "But surely you're not still . . . ?"

"Of course not, but it's all right tonight."

"What's that supposed to mean?"

"The pill, silly. Haven't you ever heard of the pill?"

Suddenly Takashi's narrow eyes opened wide with astonishment, an angry glint in them. This surprised Yoko.

"You mean you're on the pill?" His voice seemed strained.

"Yes. I got them from a friend who has a pharmacy; I thought I'd try them and see if it's better this way. I'll ask her for more."

"Don't. I don't want you to." He closed his eyes and shook his head as he spoke.

"Why not?" Opening her eyes, Yoko saw that Takashi had pulled away and was looking at her.

"They're not good for you."

"Oh, really?"

"Think about it. The pill is basically an ovary hormone. If you take it artificially, your body will stop producing it naturally. Eventually your body will stop ovulating altogether. That's how it stops conception. You're barely in your twenties, and I don't think that sort of medicine is good for you."

Yoko, somewhat confused, looked steadily at Takashi and felt a chill run up her spine. She was surprised that he was so well informed about the pill, and it gave her a queer feeling to think he was so concerned about her well-being. It's appropriate for two lovers to be concerned about each other's health, even if they're not married to each other; still, this didn't necessarily apply to Takashi and Yoko. In fact, their affair had always seemed casual and temporary even though it had already lasted for some six months. Takashi was thirty-eight and Yoko was a college student who worked evenings as a bar hostess.

Takashi's lips were pursed in irritation as he reached across to the bedside table for a cigarette. He propped his chin on his left hand, where his wristwatch indicated nine o'clock. They were in a hotel room at the foot of a small hill in the Kanda district of Tokyo. The room was warm and quiet and shut out the noise and bustle of the city beyond the window.

Perhaps the pill was not so important after all.

Noticing that his face had grown gaunt in the months she had known him, Yoko began to think things over. Clearly he was upset about something. Maybe he was not being so unreasonable after all in asking her to stop using the pill.

Takashi Sato was president of Sato Metal Industries. It was an old company and he represented the third generation as president. Sato Metal Industries was a wholesaler of nonferrous metals including copper, aluminum, nickel, and tin. It was an individually capitalized company with its head office downtown near Tokyo station and its warehouses in the suburbs. Yoko had heard that the company employed some one hundred and fifty people. Recently, however, business had been very poor. Some two months ago, in the early summer, Takashi had alluded to the fact that he might not be able to avoid bankruptcy.

"Things today aren't like they were in my father's time. Now they have consolidated the distribution channels, and we wholesalers really have our backs to the wall. We're not as bad off as they are in the iron and steel industries, but more and more, the makers are selling directly to the users. Also, the big trading companies are making inroads, and wholesalers like me will really have to scramble to survive. To make matters worse, the economy as a whole is shaky, and the price of metals is fluctuating wildly. It's very easy for a medium-sized company like mine to be swamped by the larger economic waves." Having explained all this to Yoko, he concluded, with a self-deprecating smile. "I guess I really am not such a great businessman after all."

Seven years ago Takashi Sato had fallen in love with the only child of the previous president of Sato Metal Industries. When he married her, he was adopted into the Sato family and became its official heir. His father-in-law was already an invalid at that time and soon passed away. Takashi had thereupon succeeded him as president of the company. Three years later his wife Misako had an abnormal pregnancy and both she and the baby had died.

Two years ago Takashi had married his present wife, and continued to run Sato Metal Industries, but it was not easy for him being alone among the foremen and family members who had worked for the company longer than he had. This, too, was one of the causes of his present business difficulty.

The old saying tells us that when it rains, it pours, and

Takashi's problems had been further compounded one evening in early August, about a month ago. While he was driving along a street near his office, a little girl had darted out in front of him, and he had struck her with his car, killing her. The court had ruled that the accident was primarily the fault of the girl, and the matter had been settled when the insurance company paid the family. Nevertheless, the little girl's family lived directly behind the warehouse, and every day Takashi had to endure their dark looks and their mutterings, as well as those of the people in the neighborhood.

Takashi was a regular patron of a bar called the Jugon located in Roppongi, one of the busiest pleasure districts in Tokyo. About six months ago he had taken up with Yoko, who worked there. Maybe she had just taken pity on him after listening to him recount all his difficulties. Recently he had become especially haggard and worn looking.

Yoko gently ran her fingers across his forehead as he lay on his stomach, smoking. "It doesn't matter," she said. "I won't take the pills anymore if you don't want me to."

Takashi's eyes were hard under the bright light, and he made no reply; it was almost as though he had not heard her. He seemed preoccupied.

The curious silence continued. It was hot, and Yoko was beginning to grow impatient at being ignored. "What's the matter with you tonight? Is it because I'm taking the pill?"

"There's nothing wrong with me—" But suddenly Takashi seemed to think of something and said, "No, actually there is something wrong, but I guess in this case I can go either way."

"What are you talking about?" Yoko asked, staring at him. Takashi suddenly turned to face her, then grasped her shoulders with his strong hands and pushed her over backward. Before she could even cry out in surprise, his lips found hers. At the same moment, he reached out and switched off the floor lamp. Everything went dark and he clasped Yoko in a firm embrace. In silence they sought each other with renewed vigor and quickly came to a climax. A great, rolling wave seemed to take Yoko, and for a time she felt it well up deep within her and gradually subside.

Takashi looked at her with compassion and drew a deep breath. As he let it out, he asked, "Will you die with me?"

Yoko moved her head slightly, and he continued softly, "I'd like to die with you. I'm tired; I feel I just can't go on any longer. I don't care if they call me a coward or a quitter. Suddenly I just can't handle it anymore. Lately, even when I try to care about things, I find that everything seems meaningless and stupid. It all seems unreal. Maybe I've been too much influenced by your schizophrenia." A slight chuckle came from his lips, which were close beside Yoko's ear, but it was a cold laugh, and a humorless one.

"They say I have a tendency toward depression and schizophrenia." Although this self-diagnosis was unpleasant, Yoko had described herself in these terms for the "mama-san" of the Jugon bar, and for the other hostess who worked there. Yoko had used the term long before she had taken up with Takashi. It must have been at least a year ago, she thought now, recalling a discussion they had once had at the bar.

"A psychology professor was talking to one of my friends yesterday after class, but for some reason he kept his eyes on me the whole time he was talking to her. I had the feeling he was making a clinical observation. Later, as we walked down the hallway together, he asked a lot of questions, and even though he made a joke of it, I think he was trying to analyze me."

Yoko Noda was a third-year literature student at a private women's college in the Yoyogi district of Tokyo. She was twenty-one. Although she was officially enrolled as a student, she only attended classes sporadically and was not involved in any of the clubs or other student activities. Needless to say, she had little interest in student activities. She was an indolent student, and on those days when she did make the trip from her apartment in Shibuya to the college campus, she might perch on a windowsill in the classroom listening to a lecture she thought would be of some interest. Afterward she'd go to a certain coffee shop she frequented and spend her time listening to records.

Yoko had not always been this way as a student, and undoubtedly all sorts of reasons could explain why she had become so disinterested. Her mother had died when she was five, and she had been raised single-handedly by her father in the city of Shizuoka, about a hundred miles west of Tokyo. She had been shocked when her father had suddenly remarried shortly after she had left home to attend college. Then, the school itself had been something of a disappointment. She had enrolled with great hopes, but the college really seemed to provide little more than an opportunity for its students to obtain a "Mrs." degree. The teachers were mostly a bunch of old maids who read the same dry, old lectures from their dusty notes year after year. The same was true with the clubs and student activities. Yoko had checked them all out when she first enrolled, but none of them inspired her at all. So it was natural that she gradually began to find things to do away from the college.

During the summer vacation of her sophomore year she had been introduced to the bar called Jugon by a friend she met at the beach. The bar hired her to work part-time as a hostess. The money her father sent covered her expenses, and she had no great urge to have such a job just for the experience it might provide. The fact is, she took the job on a whim, simply because it provided a way to pass the time. It was during this same time, roughly her second year in college, that she lapsed into laziness and indifference.

The mama-san at the Jugon was an openhearted woman in her forties. Besides her, there was one other young hostess and a bartender. It was a neat, cozy little bar, and Yoko felt comfortable working there. She worked from six until ten each evening, and it was only during those hours that she was able to escape her loneliness and self-consciousness. Consequently she rarely missed work and before long became an established part of the bar.

"You call yourself depressed and schizophrenic; isn't that the classic condition of all modern, urban people?"

The mama-san was an intelligent woman who seemed to understand, but Kanako, the other hostess, who was three years older than Yoko, looked at her in amazement. "What does that mean? Schizophrenic?"

"According to my professor, it's a condition that evolves easily from neurosis and depression. In the simplest terms, its chief characteristic is that one loses the will to live. One's surroundings seem more like a movie or a painting than reality. You also become acutely sensitive to time and space. You don't feel that you're actually doing the things you do. In other words, a person's response to life becomes minimal. In recent years there's been an increase in this problem among city dwellers, but while everyone recognizes the problem, no one seems to be doing anything about it."

For her liberal-arts elective, Yoko had chosen to attend a certain young instructor's psychology lectures. They had been interesting from the very beginning, and she'd made a point of attending the class regularly; as a result, she had an opportunity to get to know the teacher quite well.

"In any case, both depression and schizophrenia present certain symptoms that can be detected before the person is severely afflicted. Frequently such people are extremely methodical and obsessive. Sometimes they're very lonely, and this causes them to cling dependently to certain things."

Reviewing her professor's lectures, Yoko recalled the example of a person who loses a parent during childhood. The child's emotional pain stays with him even into adulthood and is often manifested as emotional dependency. When the person is betrayed by the object to which he is clinging, he becomes emotionally disturbed, and this is when the symptoms of depression and schizophrenia become manifest. Yoko had been greatly shaken when she first heard this theory expressed; it seemed to fit her own condition perfectly.

Her father, who operated a saw mill in Shizuoka, had lavished all his love and affection on Yoko, his only daughter, for more than ten years after her mother died. The household had consisted of her father and a maid who had been with the family for many years, so Yoko had grown up surrounded by a warm, full family life. At least until she had graduated from high school she had believed that she was the sole object of her father's love. When she left home to attend college, she was separated from her father for the first time in her life, and then, before she'd had time to adjust to living alone in her own apartment, her father had suddenly married a widow who worked in a small restaurant in Shizuoka. It had been a terrible shock for Yoko. Naturally her father had come to Tokyo to tell her about his plans before he married the woman, but the idea of him remarrying was completely unexpected. On top of that, when Yoko learned that her father had been carrying on an affair with the woman for nearly five years, she suddenly felt he had betrayed her. She realized that he must have been waiting eagerly for her to reach adulthood, and that he had actively encouraged her to leave home so he could get rid of her.

I suppose I have been emotionally damaged ever since, Yoko thought.

As the psychologist pointed out, Yoko was only now responding to this situation emotionally, and she had mentioned nothing about it to her friends at the Jugon before this, nor did her behavior suggest it.

Yoko suddenly stopped herself in the middle of what she was saying, and the mama-san frowned, giving her a sharp look. "So what happens? When a person has this depression or schizophrenia, how does it affect his daily life?"

"In an extreme case such a person would have to be put into an institution, but I'm not such a severe case. I only have tendencies in that direction."

"Do you suffer this depression every day, Yoko?"

"Yes, pretty much. But of course it's not too severe."

When anyone asked directly about these things, Yoko laughed brightly to cover her true feelings.

"Dying isn't such a dreadful thing. Whenever people like me die, they don't feel any regrets or lingering affection for the things they leave behind."

"Oh my," said Kanako with widened eyes. "What a dreadful thing to say. You're still three years younger than I am, and even though I lead such a miserable life right now, one of these days I'll find a cute guy who'll give me lots of money. I won't die unless I can die happily."

Everyone laughed at this and the matter was dropped, but afterward, whenever the subject of neurosis was bantered about with customers, Yoko was always the example they used, but they were careful to say things that wouldn't be hurtful to her.

Now, when Takashi suddenly mentioned dying, he also murmured to himself, "Perhaps this suggestion will trigger her schizophrenia." He had clearly learned of her condition somewhere, and it was even possible that she had told him about it herself.

This fact of her condition was curiously present in the air between them. In March Takashi had offered her a ride home from work to her apartment in the Shibuya district of Tokyo. On the way he had suddenly suggested that they go to a hotel, and since that time, they had continued their relationship. Yoko, of course, felt that this was something she wanted to do. She had definitely fallen for him. But still, he already had a wife, so there was no hope of ever marrying him. Also, he'd never said anything about trying to improve the circumstances of her life. Or, to put the matter another way, theirs had been a limited and limiting relationship.

"What was that you said just now?" Yoko asked, rolling over to face Takashi. His words brought back all her old apprehensions as though a fog had cleared in her brain.

"I said I wish we could die together," Takashi murmured in a hoarse whisper. "We've talked about this before. I feel that Sato Metal Industries has gone about as far as it can go. The makers won't give me credit anymore, and even the banks I've dealt with for years—although they'll give me guarantees—won't lend me any money. Last time I applied for credit, I found that there was none to be had anywhere. If this continues, I won't last until the end of the year."

Yoko said nothing.

"And think about old man Sakura. If I died, he'd be pleased, that's for sure." Takashi rolled over on his back, took a deep breath, and stared up at the ceiling.

Yoko suddenly realized that her heart was beating faster, and she reached out, her hand groping for the light switch.

"Don't turn that on," Takashi said sharply. "It's more comfortable in the dark."

"You said Mr. Sakura would be happy. Is he Yoshie's grandfather?"

"Yeah, that's right."

Yoshie was the child who'd been hit by the car a month ago in the street behind Takashi's warehouse. The child's family were textile wholesalers. In addition to the two parents, there was a sixty-five-year-old grandfather who was retired but still active. The old man had dearly loved Yoshie, his first grandchild. Ryoji Sakura was still healthy, and he was gaining something of a reputation in the neighborhood for his daily walks through the streets, following the same route he had always taken when he walked Yoshie to her kindergarten.

It was generally agreed that the accident occurred because Yoshie was playing by herself that evening and had darted out into the street chasing a ball. Since Takashi had been driving no more than five miles over the speed limit, he had gotten off with a fine and no jail sentence. The damages claim lodged by the child's parents had been settled out of court. Nevertheless, the grandfather was still angry over what had happened. He had nearly gone insane at suddenly losing the one thing that made living worthwhile for him in his old age. Even after Takashi had reached a settlement with Yoshie's father, the old man had made a point of hounding Takashi, confronting him in public and telephoning him at home in the middle of the night. One such episode had occurred a week ago. Takashi had just entered the Jugon bar when the drunken Sakura showed up and began heaping abuse on him. The mama-san had tried to pacify the old man, while Yoko hustled Takashi out the back way and sent him home.

Takashi could understand how the old man felt and knew that he was a legitimate object of Sakura's wrath. The combination of his company's financial problems and the difficulties caused by the accident seemed to have driven Takashi to the breaking point.

"I tell you, if things go on the way they have been, that old man is liable to kill me. Every time I see his crazed, bloodshot eyes, I can't help thinking that is what he has in mind."

"Really?" Yoko murmured, and suddenly a cold shiver of fear ran up her spine. She recalled that in addition to Sakura, there had been a man named Tanaka who had recently telephoned twice at the Jugon asking for Takashi. On both occasions Yoko had relayed the message to Takashi, but he had only looked grim and said, "Just tell him I don't come around here anymore."

Yoko wondered if this other man was also threatening Takashi for some reason, but she felt it would be cruel to begin questioning him about this now.

After a long silence, she heard him take another deep

breath. "Yoko, I feel totally burned out. Usually a person only feels this way if he needs a divorce. Midori and I have been together a long time now, and at this point our marriage is only a formality."

Up until now he had never said much about his wife Midori, whom he had married two years ago. He was the sort of man who rarely discussed his domestic affairs. But with a kind of feminine intuition Yoko had realized that Takashi and his wife had a complicated relationship. She had heard somewhere that he had no children.

"Midori owns a condominium that brings in a fair amount of income, so she'll have no trouble getting by if I kill myself. Even if my company goes under, the courts will still recognize the condo as her private property. Even my lawyer assured me they couldn't touch that."

Yoko merely listened to him talk without making a reply.

"Frankly, I made up my mind the other day that I would kill myself." Takashi's voice seemed almost disinterested as he spoke. "It's funny, but once I made up my mind to do it, I suddenly felt as though a great burden had been lifted from my shoulders. At first, of course, I had intended to die alone. I reminded myself to be sure to say good-bye to you. But while we have been here together, I suddenly had the feeling that I wanted us to die together."

Do I really want to die with Takashi? Yoko asked herself. The whole idea seemed unreal. This was just the condition the psychology professor had said they would expect to find in a schizoid person.

"After all," he said, "people are weak creatures; when the time comes, we're afraid to do something like this alone. Maybe I just feel lonely, but I want to be accompanied by the person who is dearest to me."

Hearing this, Yoko thought vaguely to herself, I wonder if I'm really the person dearest to him?

Thinking back over the last half year, she felt no great surge of feeling that showed she was deeply in love with this man. In fact, she couldn't deny that she had lost the burning passion she'd once felt for him. It was true that at one time she had been much attracted to him. What had she seen in him? she now wondered. Probably it was just that at thirty-eight he had seemed an urbane and sophisticated man, but now some dark and indescribable shadow seemed to hang over him. She felt there was more to it than the impending failure of his company and the automobile accident. It seemed to Yoko that some sort of complicated shadow had been hanging over him even before these things happened. Still, when she stopped to think about it, it seemed entirely possible that she had indeed become the person who was dearest to him.

"When do you plan to die?" The question came naturally to her lips.

"Will you join me, then, so we can die together?"

"Yes. I guess I don't mind dying." Even as she spoke these words, she wasn't sure which had come first, her answer or her decision.

New strength seemed to fill Takashi's arms as he embraced her again. "Thank you. It makes no difference to me whether we do it tomorrow or the next day, but I guess that now that we have decided, we might as well do it sooner than later. It feels kind of weird, doesn't it? I'd always supposed that when a person killed himself, he first put all his affairs in order so there would be nothing to worry about after he was gone. But now that I find myself ready to die, all my affairs seem too trivial to bother with. I don't care what happens. Besides, my problems are not ones I can handle; that's why I want to die in the first place."

As Yoko listened in the darkness to his voice she realized for the first time how dry it sounded. She thought to herself, Even if I reject his offer to join him, I expect I'll just go ahead and kill myself anyway. Besides, the problem of putting her own affairs in order didn't seem important, either.

The more she thought about it, the more there seemed to be no reason at all why she shouldn't die with him.

Up until today she had lived an ordinary life. Tomorrow, at an instant when no one was expecting it, she would suddenly disappear from the face of the earth.

Takashi was gripping her right arm, and she softly stroked his hand with her finger. A strange and long-forgotten feeling of self-sufficiency gently rose within her like a tide.

2

A Lovers' Suicide

The following day—September 13, 2:30 P.M.

YOKO NODA WAS WEARING HER FAVORITE OUTFIT, A PALE olive-green dress, and carried a matching shoulder bag. It was a clear, early-autumn day with only a trace of summer heat still present. The bright sunlight filtered through the thin curtains that had already been pulled closed across the windows.

Yoko lived in a small, Western-style apartment, minimally furnished with a bed, a desk, and a Western-style chest of drawers. Attached was a tiny kitchen with cooking facilities. Although this had been her home since she entered college two and a half years earlier, it still lacked a very lived-in feeling. It had been freshly swept and had the casual appearance of a room that could be quickly and easily set in order.

When all is said and done, Yoko thought, the days and months I spent in this room were rather empty and pointless. Taking one last look around, she had to admit that she felt no great sorrow at leaving, and yet there was a lump of emotion in her throat because of what she had now committed herself to do. She had promised to meet Takashi at three-thirty at Tokyo station on the platform for the Bullet Train.

Takashi had not informed his wife of his intentions, nor had he left any notes behind. He had simply left the house saying he would be in Osaka for four or five days on a business trip. Yoko, likewise, had confided her feelings to no one, not to her father, her school friends, or the mama-san at the Jugon. After several days someone's curiosity would eventually be aroused. And of course more time would pass before her body was discovered beside that of a middle-aged man deep in the mountains far from Tokyo. Her death would be a painful shock to her father more than anyone else. But for her, at the moment of death, there would be only a feeling of blank amazement followed perhaps by regrets and self-recriminations. As she recalled her father's sharp jaw and red face, she felt a deep pang of regret. It was tempered by a wish to get back at him for remarrying, and this was the way to do it. These conflicting feelings left a strange, dull ache in her heart.

Yoko had already borrowed the apartment manager's telephone and called Kanako to say she was not feeling well and was taking a few days off work. Kanako agreed to pass this information along to the mama-san. Kanako was a naive girl and seemed to accept this story at face value.

The only person for whom Yoko wanted to leave a written note was Fumiyo Chino—this thought crossed her mind again as her gaze came to rest on her desk. Fumiyo was her closest friend; they had been classmates from elementary through high school. Fumiyo had not gone on to college; rather, at the age of twenty she had had an arranged marriage with a businessman in Tokyo and was now the mother of a one-year-old daughter. Her quiet life as a housewife was very different from the world Yoko knew. About once a month Yoko went to her friend's house in Shimo Kitazawa just to visit.

Yoko felt she wanted to leave a parting message for Fumiyo. Still, she hesitated, fearing such a letter might later cause her friend problems.

Through a gap in the curtains the streets of Shibuya could be seen bathed in afternoon sunlight. Yoko's window looked out on a building that was under construction. She occasionally watched its enormous skeleton gradually change shape. She wondered how the building would look when it was completed, and realized she wouldn't be around to see it.

Good-bye, Yoko said to herself as she stepped out into the hall and closed the door of her apartment. She tried to smile. The apartment building was engulfed in midday silence.

Even on the platform of the Bullet Train at Tokyo station, the hot sun bore down. It was a weekday afternoon and the station was relatively quiet. Yoko walked to the place where people lined up for the first-class car. As she took her place in the line, she saw Takashi hurrying toward her. As always, his black hair was precisely combed, and he wore a neat, gray-striped suit she remembered having seen before. The only thing different about him was that he carried a small overnight bag and wore light brown sunglasses. When he reached Yoko, he grasped her arm firmly and said, "I knew you'd come. Thanks. That's the only thing I was worried about." He spoke all this in a low voice and sucked in a deep breath. Even from behind the sunglasses, his eyes seemed to shine brightly, and the truth of his words was clear from his tone of voice.

Now, for the first time, a warm feeling began to spread through Yoko's breast. "Do you think your wife has any idea of what's going on?"

"No. I told her I was going to Osaka to talk to two or three acquaintances about borrowing money. All she said was, 'Oh, I see.' I think she resents the fact that I am so involved in my own affairs, with the collapse of the company and all. You didn't tell anyone what we're going to do, did you?"

"No. I just asked a friend to tell my boss that I'm taking a few days off."

"Good." Takashi nodded twice. Even though they had agreed the previous night to tell no one of their plans, he appeared relieved at this reassurance.

The couple boarded the 4:05 limited express. There were many vacant seats in the first-class car, so they sat down facing each other beside the window. Occasionally they told each other how much they were in love. For a time Takashi talked about a trip he had made overseas some years back. Yoko looked out at the passing orange groves and spoke of her faint memories of her mother and how they used to go into the hills near Shizuoka and pick oranges. No doubt any casual observer would take Yoko and Takashi for a married couple, or perhaps a pair of lovers off on a fling.

It was just five o'clock when they got off the train at the resort town of Atami. A fairly large number of people debarked with them, even though it was not a weekend. The setting sun bathed the festive stores and shops of the hot-springs resort in red.

They hired a car in front of the station and followed the crest drive along the ridge of the mountains to an inn on the lower slopes of Mount Amagi. The previous night Takashi had suggested waiting at the inn until night and then setting out for the mountain peak. Yoko had agreed.

From Atami Pass to the foot of the Amagi massif, the highway runs south along the crest of the mountains, providing spectacular views. Beneath the vast and rapidly darkening sky waved broad fields of silver pampas grass, and beyond that rose the wall of mountains. As the light faded from the sky, the distant mountains grew more intensely black. Inside the hired car Takashi removed his sunglasses and, placing Yoko's hand on his knee, stroked it gently.

"Autumn has already begun," she said.

"Um. The air is very clear."

Outside the car, the wind was beginning to pick up. In the

high meadows it was already quite strong. Soon the alpine meadows could no longer be seen from the crest drive, and the surroundings were becoming more mountainous. The thick forests of cedar that covered the slopes pressed in on both sides of the road. Down in the trees it was already very dark, and the guardrail could only be seen as a faint, white blur. Before they knew it, the once distant peaks seemed to soar up near at hand.

From the time they had entered the mountains Yoko turned occasionally to look out the rear window, for she had realized that a barely visible gray sedan was following them, never quite letting them out of sight. The crest drive has only three interchanges throughout its entire length, and since traffic on it is never heavy, it is not unusual for one car to follow another for a considerable period of time. Still, it made Yoko wonder. The driver of their hired car was an older man who drove slowly, and most of the cars that approached from behind soon caught up and passed them. Only the gray sedan showed no sign of passing, and it did not even come very close behind them but continued to maintain a fixed distance. That in itself seemed unusual. Once she started thinking about this, it began to prey on her mind. I wonder if someone is following us? was the odd thought that floated through her head.

"What's the matter?" asked Takashi, who noticed each time she looked back. Suddenly Yoko felt it would be awkward to explain what she was really thinking. Besides, what did it matter? They were soon going to die. In a few hours they would be completely beyond the pale of social concerns. Anyway, there was no reason why anyone should be following them. Perhaps it was simply that her nerves had become abnormally sensitive.

"Nothing is the matter," Yoko said, shaking her head. But Takashi seemed to be aware of her agitated feelings. He was holding one of her hands and now squeezed it tightly.

The landscape around them had been dyed in the colors

of night. The high peaks surrounding them, cutting off the view, had grown black, and the oppressiveness of their surroundings increased. The stars began to pick out sharp, glittering points of light in the night sky. It was only the shining of the stars that distinguished the black of the sky from the black of the mountains.

The headlights cut a harsh white swath through the darkness of the highway, and from time to time a bug would splatter on the windshield. Here and there among the mountains they could see distant spots of burning light.

"We're almost there," was Takashi's solitary utterance as the drive through the mountains came to an end.

Takashi shifted slightly in the bed, apparently trying to get a look at his watch, and Yoko instinctively responded.

"What time is it?" she asked.

"Nine. Quarter past nine," Takashi replied softly.

Yoko got up from the bedding that was spread on the floor in the traditional Japanese manner. She had been lying beside Takashi the whole time, but despite her exhaustion, she had not really been asleep, and had been keenly conscious of the passage of time.

Following Yoko's lead, Takashi threw off the light quilt and got up. Their eyes met once as though to confirm their resolve to go through with their plan. Yoko felt reassured by the cold light she saw in his narrow eyes.

In silence they changed from the sleeping kimonos provided by the inn to their Western clothing. After touching up her makeup, Yoko glanced at her watch—it was past nine-thirty. The inn where they were staying was called the Amagi Hotel and was situated in the Amagi Meadows at the end of the scenic highway. It served as a boundary to the primitive forests of the mountain peaks beyond. Three hours had elapsed since their arrival at the hotel. They had been served a dinner of local trout and fresh mountain greens, but neither of them had felt much like eating. By the same token, they had only consumed a single bottle of beer between them. Nevertheless, there was a resolute look of determination on Takashi's face that was surely not the sort of courage derived from a bottle. After bathing, they made love for the final time. They abandoned themselves to their ecstasy for a long, slow time, forgetful of both self and circumstance. Both devoted themselves heart and soul to this final act of lovemaking. It was as though they were determined to purge every fear, hesitation, and uncertainty from the depths of their souls.

They planned to leave the inn at ten.

"The fog has begun to rise," said Takashi, pulling back the curtain and looking out. In the darkness outside the window floated a pale, white mist. "They say the mist rises on the slope of Mount Amagi all year round." Then he turned to her and asked, "Why don't you fix some tea?"

"All right."

They stood facing each other as they sipped the hot tea. Even at six-thirty when they had arrived at this traditional Japanese inn, it had not been too busy, and now everything was completely silent. Not a sound could be heard anywhere.

"I think we should leave about ten," said Takashi, lighting a cigarette.

"Yes. I think that will be fine, don't you?" Yoko intentionally looked at him with a smile in her eyes.

"Sure."

Again they were silent as they drank their tea. Yoko happened to notice a black plastic letter box that contained a variety of writing materials in the corner of the room. Depicted on the envelopes and postcards was the same design of a wild boar in colors clearly suggesting autumn.

Seeing these, Yoko again felt the urge to write a farewell to Fumiyo Chino. She quickly made up her mind and said, "I want to write a note to my dearest friend." She had hesitated before speaking, but finally put the thought into words.

She had hesitated for fear that Takashi would think her overly sentimental.

Takashi considered the matter for a moment, then with surprising gentleness nodded his assent. "You're right. I, too, ought to leave a note behind for my wife. No one really knows where I've gone, and my wife might be embarrassed if they search for me and can't find me."

They sat on opposite sides of the table, facing each other as they wrote their final messages. Yoko used simple sentences, explaining that for certain reasons she had decided to come to Mount Amagi. If one simply read the letter casually, it was quite straightforward, but should any doubts be raised about their deaths, it would provide some clues. Yoko didn't see what message Takashi wrote to his wife.

"Shall we each write a will, too?" he asked, laying down his pen and looking across at Yoko.

"A will? What for?"

"No, I don't mean we should bequeath our belongings to someone, but it did occur to me that it would be a good idea to explain clearly what our intentions are."

"I guess you're right."

"We can just write out something simple and I'll put it in my pocket where they'll be sure to find it."

"Okay. I guess it doesn't really matter."

Taking out a fresh sheet of paper, Takashi quickly scribbled three lines and silently handed the paper to Yoko. He had written simply that what they were about to do was inexcusable, an act of willful selfishness on their part. He had signed his name but wrote no date or address. Part of the sheet remained blank, providing space for Yoko to write. She thought for a moment, but no suitable words came to mind. Finally, all she wrote was, "Good-bye, Yoko."

Takashi folded this last testament into quarters, put it in an envelope, and slipped it into the inside pocket of his suit coat. Then he picked up the two letters he and Yoko had already written and stood up. "I'll call the front desk and pay our bill."

It was just ten when the couple left the front entrance of the inn. A fifty-year-old man in a *happi* coat who was the chief clerk, accompanied by the young maid who had served their dinner, were there to see them off. The inn was located at the bottom of a slope, at some distance from the toll road. Its front garden was groomed in a natural manner like the yard of a farmhouse, and in the darkness they just could see the leaves on the trees. Typically, a light fog hung over the landscape.

"It's quite an uphill walk to the golf course from here," said the clerk, placing the small overnight case beside them as Takashi put on his shoes.

"Yes, we've made reservations for the night at the golf course. Our friends plan to meet us there with the golf clubs, but we wanted to come here first for a while because we'd heard that you prepare a very good meal of fresh mountain greens. You have quite a reputation." This was the explanation Takashi had invented to account for their brief stay at the Amagi Hotel. Normally a couple had dinner at the hotel where they spent the night, but if he and Yoko arrived in the evening, and then set out on foot toward the mountain, they would arouse suspicions—someone might even call the police. For this reason Takashi had contrived his clever explanation.

"Well, thank you very much for saying so. Enjoy your golf," the plump clerk replied with professional cheerfulness. He seemed to have no suspicions about Yoko and Takashi's plans.

"I suppose it takes five or six minutes to walk to the golf course from here?"

"Your wife probably doesn't walk too fast, so it may take ten minutes or so. But the road is good, so you won't have any trouble."

Electric lights lit the path from the inn to the road, but

once they were back on the highway, they had only the light of the stars. The sky had begun to cloud at nightfall, and the stars shone only dimly and distantly through breaks in the cover. Takashi and Yoko could easily differentiate the pale white of the sky from the intense black of the mountains that loomed above them. A ground mist rose to about shoulder height, smothering everything in silent obscurity.

"Are you cold?"

"No. Not at all."

The road they followed was wrapped in solitude. Takashi gently took Yoko's hand as they walked. From time to time a hired car passed by, bringing late guests from Atami to one of the mountain resorts. Each time, once the car had overtaken them, the couple was again shrouded in silence. It was strange the way the insects, which had been so noisy early in the evening, were utterly silent now that it was the dead of night.

"Do you remember that incident sixteen or seventeen years ago when two students from the Peers school came here to the Amagi mountains and committed a love suicide by shooting themselves?"

"Yes. I remember reading about it in a book somewhere. The girl was a Manchurian princess or something."

"That's right. She had some sort of imperial blood. They came up here into the Amagi mountains from the other side. They took a taxi at midnight to the entrance of the Amagi Tunnel and climbed the slope from there through a heavy growth of bamboo. Later, when people found out what had happened, the police blamed the taxi driver for not being suspicious of two young people who got out of his taxi in the middle of a winter night deep in the mountains for no apparent reason."

Yoko made no reply.

"When I heard about it at the time, I felt it was a very sad story. If only the cabdriver had called the police, those young people might have been saved."

"Yes."

"But of course when I look back on it now, I suppose it may have turned out for the best. People aren't necessarily happy just because they live long. The most natural thing is for each person to choose his own moment of death."

The paved road ended, and after they continued up the dirt road for a distance, the view began to expand. Climbing the slope of the mountain was a switchback road lined with fluorescent lights, and above them stood a tall building with lights blazing in the windows. Before them the roofs of parked cars glittered brightly under the outdoor lights. They knew at once that this was the golf-course hotel. The fairways were on the far side of the building.

Takashi stopped when they reached the foot of the private road leading up to the hotel. A large illuminated sign stood in front of a grove of trees on their right. They could easily make out the words A GUIDE TO THE CREST TRAILS OF THE AMAGI RANGE. The rest of the sign was a map showing a network of some ten miles of trails linking the three peaks of the Amagi range and leading eventually to Amagi Pass. These were beautiful trails winding through natural forests, but since there was some danger of people becoming lost in the maze of paths, the sign also cautioned people to pay attention to the trail markings.

A narrow path began in front of the map and led into a grove of trees. The trail was completely dark. Takashi looked at Yoko and gripped her hand yet more firmly. He had his back to the light, so she couldn't see his face clearly, but she could imagine the expression on it. She nodded slightly, and at that moment, hot tears inexplicably filled her eyes and rolled down her cheeks.

Clutching each other's hand, they set off along the trail. The narrowness of the path made walking side by side difficult, and the trees seemed to press in on them. The gently sloping trail was littered with branches and stones that made the footing treacherous. Once they were beyond the range of the hotel lights the trail began to slope upward, and Takashi took a flashlight from his overnight bag.

They proceeded in silence, able to maintain their footing thanks to the pale beam of light. Through the dark tree trunks they could make out the dim white of the sky and patches of glittering stars. Off the trail, however, deep among the trees, it was pitch-dark. Yoko ignored that darkness and tried to turn her mind off, to think of nothing. She felt strangely serene; she saw nothing but the circle of light at her feet, and heard nothing but the sound of twigs snapping as they walked.

The gurgling of a brook broke the silence that surrounded them, and moments later they came upon a narrow stream that they crossed on a log bridge. They continued along the trail until they could no longer hear the sound of the stream. Takashi slowed down and presently stopped. Yoko herself was slightly out of breath.

Takashi aimed the flashlight into the trees on their left. For some distance the beam of light played whitely over the trunks of the cedars. Long ago the wild forests in this area had been replanted with the special variety of cedar unique to the Amagi range.

Takashi turned and shined the light into the trees on their right. Here, too, of course, was a dense forest of cedar. It appeared that the underbrush on the right was somewhat thinner. "Shall we go off on this side then?" he murmured.

When Yoko made no reply, he stepped into the underbrush as though afraid to hesitate and pulled Yoko along by the hand. Even among the trees there was a faint light from the stars. Perhaps some light was being reflected by the white cloud cover because they could see the trunks of the surrounding trees and the branches if they strained their eyes. There were also some open places where dead trees had fallen. In these clearings they found small springs, wild chrysanthemums, and ferns.

They entered a small, level clearing containing clusters of wildflowers. Takashi released Yoko's hand and shined the flashlight around the area. Cedar trees and underbrush surrounded them like a wall. It was impossible to tell even where they had just passed through the brush. The crest trail was somewhere in the darkness directly behind them.

A faint sigh escaped Takashi's lips. Once again he pointed the beam of light at the ground and abruptly flung himself down. Yoko slowly sat down beside him. He laid the still-lit flashlight on the ground beside them. As they sat there, the mist continued to rise. Their skin was damp, but neither of them felt the cold.

"Once it becomes known that I have disappeared and no one knows where I am, I expect that both the people in my company and old man Sakura will be angry." Takashi lay on his back and murmured these words as though talking to himself. "But eventually it will become known that I've committed suicide and they'll all feel satisfied, and then they'll be suspicious, and then there will be a great outcry. It's kind of funny, isn't it, to imagine what things will be like after we're dead." He was quiet for a moment but seemed to be chuckling silently. Then he continued, "But it's a shame, really, that I'm taking a young person like you with me when I die." Suddenly he clutched Yoko violently by the shoulder and turned her to face him. "I'm sorry, please forgive me, but I really couldn't go through this without you." Takashi hung his head.

Yoko began to weep as a strange burning sensation welled up in her heart. "You shouldn't talk that way. I'd rather hear you say you are pleased that I agreed to join you in this."

"Of course I'm pleased. I guess there's nothing more to say."

"I guess not."

Between the looming treetops a single blue star was twinkling, its thin, bright light reflected in Yoko's eyes. She was enraptured by the star and recalled an old children's story that explains how when a person dies his soul ascends into the sky and is transformed into a star.

Takashi opened the overnight bag and took out a bottle of sleeping pills and a small thermos. As he placed fifty of the white tablets in Yoko's hand, clouds blotted out the single star.

3

At the Brink of Death

Yoko STOOD IN THE SHALLOWS AT THE EDGE OF THE ASH-gray lake, under a leaden sky, the water coming to just below her knees. There was no one around and the only movement was a boat floating on the surface of the lake. Soon the boat began to drift toward the center of the lake. Yoko wanted to call out to it, to make it come back, but try as she might, no words came to her lips.

She felt cold. A terrible, inexpressibly cold chill numbed her body, beginning with her legs that were in the water. She began to tremble and the lake seemed to fade into the distance.

With great effort Yoko opened her eyes. She could hardly keep them open against the deadweight that pressed down on them. But as the dream of the lake began to break up and disperse, she was conscious once more of the cruel cold that traveled from her legs up her spine. She felt the hard chill even in her head and chest. She struggled to open her eyes but was unable to move or change her line of sight. Everything was dark; she could see nothing.

Yoko had a vague feeling that she had been asleep for a time and had now awakened. And yet she was unable to focus her attention, unable to grasp reality. She felt she hadn't gotten enough sleep, but just as she was about to lapse back into sleep, her head suddenly slipped and her cheek brushed against something hard. This movement sent a tremor through her heart, her stomach, her legs—a tremor telling her it was wrong to sleep. The tremor demanded that she struggle to cleave to something hard and firm.

As her mind began to clear, she realized there was something sticky, some foreign substance, in her mouth. Whatever it was, there was a lot of it. She pushed on it with her tongue and clawed at it with her finger. She knew, as she got it from her mouth, that she had vomited.

Yoko realized the stuff was not only in her mouth, it was smeared on her face, on her cheeks and throat, and it stained the front of her dress. She felt especially cold in those places where the vomit had soaked through her clothing. Slowly her mind began to recall the events of the previous night. Vaguely she came to the realization that she hadn't died last night after all.

Dawn had not yet broken. It was truly pitch-dark; even the stars had been extinguished, and Yoko literally couldn't see her hand in front of her face. Yet gradually, dimly, she was aware of a pale white curtain floating across the surface of the darkness.

It was fog.

The fog that surrounded her and the fog in her own mind left her baffled as to where she was or how she had gotten there. Eventually the fog began to lift and she remembered, Last night, no, just a few hours ago, I was sitting here with Takashi and I ate fifty sleeping pills washed down with hot water from the thermos. Apparently I vomited the pills, and that's why I woke up. I was supposed to die, but I woke up.

I spoiled my chance to die. I wonder what happened to Takashi?

Suddenly a pang of concern jerked her alert: Did Takashi survive, too?

Yoko struggled to get to her feet. When she tried to do so, she realized she was gripping something in her right hand. Her mind had not been clear enough to notice that until now. She tried to push herself up with her left hand so she could see what she was clutching in her right hand. When she tried to open her right hand, the fingers felt thick, stiff, and unresponsive.

What was she doing here? She was supposed to be with Takashi. They had both taken sleeping medicine at the same time and had lain on the ground clasped in each other's embrace. He must still be asleep, even now, right here with her!

Struggling to focus her attention, she tried to concentrate on what she was holding in her hand. It was a round, hard piece of wood. Had she fallen asleep clutching that in her hand?

"Takashi?" The name escaped her lips without her realizing it. "Takashi!" She began to scream hysterically and shake his body, but he showed no sign of regaining consciousness. Once again the fog clouded her vision. Everything went dark. Plunged in darkness, she was aware of nothing.

The flashlight should be there somewhere. She quickly searched for it around her feet, groping through the wet grass around Takashi's feet. Surely he had placed it on the ground before he lay down, but her searching fingers could find it nowhere. Instead, she found her shoulder bag; she should have some matches in it.

Eventually she found the matches and lit one. The tiny flame illuminated her own muddy knees, and she moved to cup its tiny flame with her hand. She saw and remembered the striped pattern of the cloth—the pin-striped trousers that covered Takashi's outstretched leg. Her gaze traveled over the edge of his jacket, his back; it was clear that he had lain down beside her. Just as she reached this conclusion her match went out.

She struck a second match. One or two seconds elapsed, and Yoko felt a shudder run through her body the moment she looked at the wooden object she had been holding in her hand. For a moment she thought she must still be dreaming. Takashi's body was lying beside her in a somewhat twisted position. The thing she had been grasping when she first regained consciousness was protruding through his jacket and the shirt beneath on the left side of his back. It was a large knife.

"Takashi! What did you do?" Stunned, she lit another match. It was definitely a knife protruding from his back. A dark stain had spread beneath the wound. Takashi had been stabbed. He was supposed to have taken the sleeping pills just as she had. The object Yoko had been grasping as she slept was the handle of the knife!

"Wake up, Takashi." Once again she shook him violently. The body, as she shook it, was completely limp.

Suddenly Yoko felt as if darkness were closing in on her again, and a low moan, a moan of fear that came from the very depths of her soul, escaped her lips. Her body began to shake uncontrollably. She had to strike another match but had difficulty maintaining control of her hands. With great effort she tried to bring the match close to Takashi's face, but his body had twisted when he fell, and his face was hidden under a clump of ferns. Even without seeing his face, this grotesque form was horrifying.

Unconscious of what she was doing, Yoko lit yet another match. This time her gaze came to rest on his left hand, which had been flung out on the ground. He always wore the silver wristwatch he had received as an honors student and was very fond of. The hands were moving as usual and indicated that the time was 4:24.

It must have been about ten-thirty when they had taken the

sleeping pills and lain down. What had happened in the six-hour interval while Yoko was vomiting in her sleep? She threw away the match and grasped Takashi's wrist with both of her hands. She quickly leapt back in surprise; he was as cold and rigid as stone. Yoko felt the goose bumps rising on her skin. Feelings of revulsion and horror swept over her like a wave.

A wail of fear escaped Yoko's lips as she stared in frozen terror. Takashi had died, but she had not. Apparently he hadn't vomited up the sleeping pills as she had. No. That wasn't it! He had died from the knife wound in his back. Something had happened here that Yoko didn't understand at all.

She got to her feet and stood in the darkness, breathing heavily. Suddenly a recollection was rekindled in her mind. When they were driving along the crest highway, she'd had the uneasy feeling they were being followed. She thought at the time that it might be some cruel enemy who was observing the progress of their so-called trip, an enemy who had followed their hired car in his own gray sedan.

We were tailed, weren't we? she decided. No doubt Takashi had also vomited the medicine and had begun to revive. He probably began to revive earlier than Yoko, and the follower had been watching. When Takashi had revived sufficiently to get to his feet, he was assaulted from behind and stabbed. The killer had then closed Yoko's unconscious hand around the handle of the knife and fled.

That was the only way to explain what had happened. But wait! What if the killer were still nearby, still hiding, watching?

Yoko's body went rigid. She could hardly breathe; she felt as if a great weight were pressing on her chest. Poor Takashi! He had revived and struggled back to life only to be struck down by a vicious killer who might still be hiding out there in the darkness, watching her.

The thought that she herself might also be killed in the

same manner suddenly struck her like an icy finger, sending a thrill of terror up her spine. Instinctively Yoko was on her guard.

She had to escape this place quickly and secretly! Trembling violently, she began to grope about in the darkness. Her hand touched the empty bottle of sleeping pills, but she tossed it aside. She quickly located her shoulder bag. She still held the matchbox in her left hand, but it was almost empty. What she wanted desperately to find was the flashlight, but a light would be dangerous if she hoped to elude the enemy who might be waiting out there in the darkness. Still, the awful, impenetrable darkness was even more frightening. How could she escape and find her way to light?

Yoko's fear was overwhelming. Her mind in a turmoil, she struck another match. Fortunately, with her second match she was able to find the flashlight under a clump of wild chrysanthemums. It was cold and wet with the evening dew, but it worked. A moan of relief escaped her lips.

Yoko slung her bag on her shoulder, clutched the flashlight, and with faltering, desperate steps began to walk away, aiming the light at the ground to guide herself. She didn't have the courage to look back at Takashi. Somehow she felt that if she tried to do this, her hidden enemy might leap out at her. She kept telling herself that she would be safe as long as she kept the light on the ground. Praying for safety, she fled the site of this nightmare.

In a state of shock, she set out in the direction she thought they had come from the previous night. Desperately she scrambled over fallen trees and broke her way through the clinging vines and thick shrubs. Although the first signs of dawn were appearing along the edge of the dark sky, Yoko was oblivious to them.

Blue, yellow, red—these three colored lights systematically filled her range of vision. The red disappeared and for a time all was faintly dark, then the blue lit up, repeating the cycle.

The corner of the bookcase and the adjoining wall were cast in blue. It was now early evening and the neon light had come on in the building across the street. The flashing, artificial light found its way through the thin curtains, and nothing, it seemed to Yoko, was quite so sad as this flickering. And yet, some odd intimacy about it brought back memories.

She had been deep in the dark forest of cedar, and it was only by good luck that she had found her way back to the crest highway. It had not been all that far to the road, but if she had mistaken the direction, she would surely have lost her way in the forest. By the time she emerged from the woods in front of the sign showing the crest trails, the sky was beginning to grow pale with dawn. Everything was quiet and peaceful at the golf course, and the streetlights lining the switchback road still cast their pale glow.

With desperate urgency Yoko retraced her steps down the road they had followed last night. From time to time she still suffered attacks of acute drowsiness that brought her to a halt, and at one point she passed out altogether. Her last conscious thought was that she needed a drink of water.

When Yoko was able to continue on her way, she spotted a taxi with Shizuoka plates. No doubt it had come from Atami earlier, bringing an early-rising golfer to the golf-course hotel. When she waved an arm, the taxi stopped and the rear door automatically swung open. As Yoko tumbled into the car, a gray-haired driver said, "You're out early this morning, young lady." He looked at her in the rearview mirror as he spoke, a touch of suspicion clouding his voice.

"I was out early to climb the mountain, but I suddenly remembered some urgent business I need to take care of," Yoko replied, wiping her mouth with her handkerchief. After emerging from the woods she had taken a lightweight raincoat from her shoulder bag and put it on so the stains on her dress were concealed. "You'll take me to Tokyo, won't you?"

"Tokyo? That's much too far. I haven't even had breakfast yet; besides, it would be faster to take the Bullet Train from Atami."

"I see. Well, take me to Atami then." Yoko did not have the strength to argue with the driver and merely slumped over, resting the upper part of her body on the seat. She noticed that her stockings were covered with burrs and grass seeds. From the window of the taxi she could see that the gray sky was growing lighter by the moment.

It was six-thirty when the driver pulled up in front of Atami Station. Since all the nearby shops were still closed and shuttered, she went to the station lavatory and drank water from the faucet. It seemed that she had never in her life consumed so much water at one time.

Yoko was able to get a seat on the first Bullet Train of the day, which departed at 6:57. Both on the train and in the taxi from Tokyo station to her apartment in Shibuya, Yoko felt groggy. She wanted only to drift off into a deep, deep sleep, but all she could manage was fitful dozing. It was around eight-thirty when she arrived at her apartment. The curtains had been closed and her room was stuffy, but nothing was changed from before. It was just like all the other times when she had spent the night with Takashi at a hotel and returned home in the morning.

Yoko stripped off her dress and collapsed on the bed. Now at last her tense muscles could relax, and with that came deep, untroubled sleep.

Yoko rolled over and looked at the bedside table. According to the clock it was 7:20 and the date was September 14. As she watched, the second hand continued to sweep around. Just watching it gave her a funny feeling, but when she stopped to think about it, less than forty-eight hours had passed since the other afternoon when she had left this apartment for what she thought was the final time. Yesterday was

September 13. Now it was only the evening of the fourteenth, yet the events of yesterday seemed very far away indeed.

She wondered if Takashi was still lying in that dark forest. Surely he was. And what about the knife stuck in the left side of his back? Had that just been a figment of her imagination? No. Absolutely not. Her hand still remembered the feel of the smooth, wooden handle. Suddenly Yoko was assailed by a feeling of unease. She had to find out what had really happened.

Presumably Takashi had vomited the sleeping medicine. Before last night Yoko had never taken any sleeping medicine, so she did not know too much about it and its effects. Takashi said he had gotten this sleeping medicine from a friend who worked in a pharmaceutical company. Perhaps those pills had been outdated or defective in some way.

Then there was the matter of the phantom person who had trailed them even after they had started climbing the mountain. Someone had fiendishly watched every move they had made, right up to the very end.

Why? The first thought that came to Yoko was that perhaps someone hated Takashi so much that he would do such a thing. This person must have sensed that Takashi was planning to commit suicide and had secretly followed them to make sure he actually died. The phantom had looked on while the couple had climbed the mountain, and had watched them take the sleeping pills and lie down on the ground. Then this person had either stayed for a while and watched, or else had gone away somewhere and had come back to make sure they were dead. Whichever way it was, Takashi had unfortunately revived while his enemy was watching.

Seeing Takashi reviving, the enemy attacked and brutally thrust a knife into his heart. Besides that, the enemy had been careful to put Yoko's right hand on the knife before he made his getaway. Clearly he supposed that Yoko would not revive. If she had died, then when the two bodies were discovered, people would suppose that she had wanted to commit a lovers' suicide, and when he had demurred, she had stabbed him and then taken sleeping medicine herself. But Yoko had survived. She had fled the terrifying darkness and returned here to her apartment in Tokyo.

Yoko drew her hand out from under the covers and held it before her face, gazing at the palm. It was still stained with mud and vomit, but the blood still flowed in the veins of her five outstretched fingers, and the light reflected off her fingernails. A deep feeling of relief and an odd sense of exhilaration surged through her.

But Takashi was dead. He had narrowly escaped committing suicide only to be hurled back into the world of the dead at the hands of a cold-blooded killer! Takashi was still sleeping, lying there alone on the cold earth among the underbrush.

Suddenly tears came to Yoko's eyes and rolled in streams down her cheeks. Her feelings were in turmoil, and a moan escaped her lips as she lay in the dim darkness. She felt a gloomy sadness that was hard to identify. Did she feel sorry for Takashi? Did she still love him? Did she feel their fate was tragic? She did not know. The only thing she did know was that she could not just leave him where he was and do nothing.

With this idea in her mind, the violence of her emotions threatened to overwhelm her. Takashi had been murdered. She was determined that the real killer would be arrested.

Now that she thought about it, she should have gone right away to the nearest police station and reported the incident before returning to Tokyo. If she hadn't the strength for that, she ought to have at least explained the matter to the taxi driver. After all, that is the natural course for anyone who discovers a murder.

But wait! Even now it was not too late. There was a chance that no one had discovered the body and reported it. Yet even as she thought of this, Yoko began to feel some nagging doubts and fears. She had to suppress them. She would go to the neighborhood police telephone and make a report.

She wondered what would be the fastest way to make contact with the police who had jurisdiction over the Amagi region so they could send someone to the scene of the crime as soon as possible. But then she wondered if the police would believe her story once she told it. The instant this doubt entered her mind, Yoko felt as though her whole world had begun to spin.

There could be no doubt about the fact that Takashi and Yoko had planned to commit a love suicide together; they had left evidence of that all along their route. The driver of the hired car who had taken them from Atami to Amagi as well as the people who worked at the inn where they had eaten dinner would surely remember their faces. The two letters they had written at the inn and addressed to Tokyo could also easily be found. And there was the sheet of paper on which they had each written their final testament, which Takashi had put in his suit pocket.

The police would certainly believe what Yoko said about their going to Amagi to commit suicide . . . but after that, then what? The following day Yoko had returned to Tokyo alone. When Takashi's body was discovered, they would find that he had been stabbed with a knife, and on the handle would be Yoko's fingerprints. No doubt hers were the only prints on the handle. Under those circumstances, why would anyone believe her story about a phantom who had followed them? Certainly the police would draw the most obvious conclusions: the couple had gone to the mountains with the intention of committing suicide together; they had taken the sleeping medicine but had vomited it, and the man had decided he wanted to live after all. Realizing this, the woman took a concealed knife and stabbed him. She had planned to follow him in death but changed her mind and fled. Then, in order to avoid suspicion, she had made up the story about the phantom killer. That is what the police would think. And once the police believed this, what sort of counterevidence could she produce? The phantom had disappeared, leaving behind no tangible evidence that Yoko could use.

Under the circumstances, if she simply turned herself in to the police, she would be arrested on suspicion of murder. Once that happened, there would be very little chance that the true killer would ever be apprehended.

Yoko sat up in bed. Her throat still felt dry. She also needed a cigarette. She got out of bed, switched on the light, and, going to the sink, took a drink of water. Ordinarily she rarely smoked, but now she rummaged through the kitchen drawers, finally found an old pack of cigarettes, and lit one.

As she inhaled the smoke, she felt a wave of dizziness and nausea. For some reason her mind was occupied with thoughts of the many evenings she had spent in the course of her twenty-one years. At the moment she felt acute physical discomfort, and while her earlier experiences had not been all that great, still, she had managed to live up till now, and she was still alive. She felt she had to get revenge for Takashi and she had to do it on her own. By the time she took her second drag on the cigarette, she was determined to do this.

Once Takashi's body was discovered, Yoko would surely become a wanted person. After all, even if she did not turn herself in, they would find the note in Takashi's pocket, and when they made inquiries at the inn, they would quickly learn her identity. There seemed little chance, however, that they would find the body right away. The scene of the murder was some distance from the crest highway, and it had happened in thick brush that would keep it hidden from sight.

Takashi had said he had told his wife that he was going away on a trip for four or five days. Since he had set out on the thirteenth, Yoko could count on his wife not saying anything about the matter until the eighteenth. But once that period of time had elapsed, Takashi's wife would surely think something was wrong if she heard no news from him. The only problem was that if anything came up at the office, there would be an outcry, and they might want to know where he was.

Also, Takashi had written a letter to his wife from the inn, so she would have a general idea of where he was. So if she began a police search in the Amagi area on the nineteenth, they would surely find the body quickly. But even sooner than that Takashi's wife would read his letter and know something was wrong, and she might initiate a search even before the eighteenth.

Having thought through these possibilities, Yoko decided that she would have at least a three-day grace period; she could be assured of freedom to act for that length of time. At the same time, as long as the murder was undiscovered, the murderer would suppose that Yoko had died as well.

Suddenly there was a knock at the door and Yoko felt her body go rigid with fear and surprise.

"Hello. Miss Noda, are you in there?" It was the voice of the apartment manager. He knocked once again.

"Yes. Just a moment please," she said without thinking.

"There is a phone call for you."

"I see. Thank you." Yoko was somewhat confused, but realized that in addition to letting the manager know she was at home, she also now had to go out to answer the phone.

Yoko quickly slipped on a sweater and a pair of slacks, and went to the manager's room. The telephone was by the window, but he was nowhere in sight. When she picked up the receiver, she could hear the hum of voices and the clinking of glasses.

"Hello?"

"Hello. Is that you, Yoko?"

She immediately recognized the voice of Kanako from the Jugon. Yoko sucked in her breath in surprise and relief. "Yes."

"How are you feeling?"

Yoko remember that yesterday she had called to say that

she was not feeling well. "Thanks for calling. I seem to have caught a cold."

"Do you have a fever?"

"Not much of one."

"Have you been eating?"

Kanako was a good person and was truly concerned about Yoko's well-being.

"Yes."

"After I get off work tonight, why don't I fix something for you to eat and bring it over?"

"Thanks, but you really don't have to do that." Yoko suddenly felt there was some grave danger in this. If anything happened and the police discovered Takashi's body, they would surely show up at the Jugon, and even here at her apartment, to make inquiries. "In fact, I have been thinking of taking a little trip to recuperate. That means I won't be able to work for a while. Will you tell the mama-san for me?" Yoko used this excuse to free herself from Kanako's questions and quickly hung up the phone.

4

The Face of the Phantom

"I REALLY THINK IT WOULD BE BEST IF YOU MOVED OUT OF your apartment in Shibuya. It would be easy to find a convenient place around here." The voice belonged to Fumiyo Chino, who was sitting in her kitchen feeding yogurt to her one-year-old daughter. Both mother and daughter wore matching aprons with a pattern of strawberries. "If you found an apartment close by, you could come here and have your meals with us."

"Thanks." Yoko was sitting on the sunny veranda reading the morning newspaper. She found no mention of what had happened at Amagi. She decided everything was probably still all right and heaved a sigh of relief.

"You ought to get out of an apartment building that has weird men like that. Really, I think you should," Fumiyo said indignantly.

This morning Yoko had tossed several changes of clothing and a few other things into an overnight bag and had come here to the Tokyo suburb of Kitazawa to visit her friend Fumiyo. Yoko had made up a story about the man in the apartment across the hall from hers bothering her. She said he had tried to force his way into her apartment with all sorts of excuses and had tried to look in through the keyhole, so she had decided to go away for a while. With this story she had asked Fumiyo if she could spend the night, and her friend had innocently believed her.

Fumiyo's husband worked for a ship-building company in Tokyo; along with their child, they lived in a small, company-owned house of three rooms and an eat-in kitchen. As a housewife, Fumiyo's life-style was very different from Yoko's. Whenever Yoko took a fancy to visit her, Fumiyo always greeted her warmly. Fumiyo's husband was nine years their senior and was a pleasant man who enjoyed drinking too much.

Yoko had first realized that it was dangerous to stay at her apartment when Kanako had telephoned the previous evening. She had spent an uneasy night and early this morning had come here. She had chosen to visit Fumiyo because her friend was the only person in the city she could turn to for help, and besides, she wanted to try to intercept the suicide letter she had mailed from Amagi before Fumiyo had a chance to see it. She certainly did not want her friend to know any more than necessary about what had happened.

"I need some time to think things over. Would it be too much of an imposition if I stayed here for two or three days?"

"Why, it's no trouble at all. I'm sure Papa will be delighted. He likes to have someone around to talk to while he drinks in the evening." Fumiyo called her husband Papa just the way her infant daughter did.

Meanwhile, Yoko was left to ponder the question of who had killed Takashi. Her eyes moved unseeingly over the newspaper as she turned the matter over in her mind. Who had followed them when they went into the mountains to commit suicide? No doubt it was someone who hated Takashi very much. Surely only the most vicious and brutal sort of person could coldly watch a man and a woman go to their deaths, and then, when Takashi began to revive, stab him to death.

Under the circumstances there were two names that came naturally to Yoko's mind: Ryoji Sakura and Shuji Tanaka.

Sakura had been half-crazed with grief at the loss of his beloved granddaughter and had gone around uttering threats against Takashi. Only the week before Takashi and Yoko set out for Amagi, Sakura had followed Takashi to the Jugon and threatened him. Consequently Yoko knew what Ryoji Sakura looked like. He was not so tall but had a sturdy build, prominent cheekbones, and piercing, obstinate eyes. When Yoko saw him, he had been drinking and had looked at Takashi with a crazed glint of hatred in his eyes.

The old man may have suspected that Takashi and Yoko were trying to go away somewhere and disappear, and had thus decided to trail them from Tokyo. Perhaps he had not been satisfied simply knowing that he had driven Takashi to suicide; perhaps he had felt a need to actually kill Takashi with his own hands.

Tanaka was a different matter; Yoko knew nothing about him. All she knew was the name of a man who had called the Jugon a couple of weeks ago and asked for Takashi. When she had said he wasn't there, the caller had identified himself as Tanaka and left a message that Takashi was to call him. The following evening he had called again with the same result. Later, when she saw Takashi, she gave him the message. He suddenly got a dark look on his face and told her that if Tanaka called again she should say that Takashi never came to the Jugon anymore. She had noticed his reaction and later, when they were alone together, had asked him about it, but Takashi had only smiled painfully and said, "I'm involved in some peculiar dealings." That was all he would say about the matter. But on that occasion, too, there had been a clouded look in his eyes, as though he were being pursued by something.

Whether the killer was Sakura or Tanaka or someone else about whom Yoko knew nothing, at least she could be confident that for the time being, the killer assumed that she, too, was dead. So, if she suddenly showed up and confronted this person, he would certainly be startled, and no matter how bold he might be, he would surely betray something at suddenly seeing her alive. In addition to his fright at seeing a woman who had returned from the dead, he would also have to assume that Yoko knew of his crime.

Yoko decided that she had perhaps three days to find this person, and the sooner the better. She stood up before she could have any second thoughts or misgivings and announced, "I'm going out for a while."

"School?" Fumiyo asked.

"Um," Yoko said with a vague nod. On her way out she took another look in the mailbox, but there were no letters.

It was a lovely morning and the business districts in the heart of Tokyo were bustling with noise and activity. Everywhere she looked, smock-clad office girls carrying paper envelopes were hurrying across streets clogged with cars. Yoko walked from the subway station along the palace moat in search of Sato Metal Industries. Earlier in the summer she had gone for lunch with Takashi, and on the way back he had pointed it out to her, so it was not too difficult to find the place. She walked along under the elevated freeway until she found the gray cement four-story building that belonged to the company. In back were two warehouses.

Yoko did not approach the building but lingered on the opposite side of the street and observed it for a few minutes. Takashi had said the company was in trouble, but of course none of that was apparent from looking at the outside of the building. The president of the company was dead, but she could see the employees in the office on the first floor going about their business as usual, not realizing anything was amiss.

After a time Yoko crossed the busy street and made her way into the alleys behind Sato Metal Industries. Takashi had told her that the accident had taken place directly behind his company and that the victim's house and the family's whole-sale textile business were nearby.

The back alleys were lined with small and medium-sized businesses and warehouses, and there was even a restaurant that catered to the local businessmen. Sure enough, as Yoko walked along, she saw some private residences mixed among the other buildings. The homes were not large but were reminiscent of the old-fashioned, downtown district of Tokyo. One could easily imagine the old, traditional life-style that was lived here.

Yoko followed a black board fence for some distance until she came to a weathered wooden gate with the name Sakura painted on it. Seeing the name, she halted and her body stiffened. Suddenly she gasped and took a step backward. From the gate she could see a stone path leading up to the house, where, as she watched, the door slid open and a casually dressed old man stepped out.

The old man approached with long strides. At a glance she took in his broad shoulders, his dark blue Oshima kimono, his receding hairline, and his sharp gaze. This was definitely Ryoji Sakura.

The old man emerged from the gate and strode past Yoko, heading for the main street. His arms swung lightly at his sides and he took no notice of anything around him as he walked resolutely along. Yoko followed, and by the time they were close enough to see the freeway, Sakura began to slow his pace a little. Squeezed into a tiny space between the pedestrian bridge over the highway and the neighboring buildings was a small playground. It contained a few stunted trees blackened by exhaust fumes, some white benches that were now a dingy gray, and a forlorn-looking little sandbox.

Sakura suddenly seemed tired, and slumped down on one of the benches. The only other person in the playground was a young man sitting on one of the other benches smoking a cigarette and holding his attaché case on his knees.

Sakura drew a pack of cigarettes from the sleeve of his kimono. He sat and smoked with his gaze fixed on the sandbox. Seen from the side, his cheeks were sunken and gaunt, but he seemed serene. Yoko stood in the street for a moment to steady her breathing, then walked resolutely into the playground. She, too, felt curiously at ease.

She sat down on the bench beside Sakura and leaning over to face him directly said, "Excuse me . . ." It was only when she spoke that he turned and looked at her for the first time.

The old man's yellowed eyes gazed at her with curiosity, but there was no particular expression on his face. Yoko was wearing a bright green blouse similar to the one she had worn at Amagi. As their eyes met, she felt a sudden rush of tension. One second passed . . . two seconds. She was desperately aware that she had to read the changing expression on his face correctly, yet try as she might, she could detect no sudden change. All she could see in his eyes was a look of expectancy of the sort a person has when someone calls to him on the street. Of course he had seen Yoko on an earlier occasion at the Jugon, but from the expression on his face it was clear that he did not remember her. Even if he was merely putting on a charade, he would have shown at least some sign of surprise if he was the murderer.

"Excuse me, but I believe you are Mr. Sakura." Yoko finally continued her opening greeting.

"Yes," the old man said in a guttural voice, giving a nod.

"I wonder if you don't recognize me?" Yoko asked, forcing herself to smile. Sakura squinted at her suspiciously. "Don't you remember what happened that evening, maybe ten days ago? You came into a bar in Roppongi called the Jugon."

This time he looked at her more carefully and said, "Ah, yes," in a clear voice. Then his face clouded with perplexity, and many tiny wrinkles formed at the corners of his eyes.

"My name is Yoko and I was there at the time."

"Oh."

"I wonder if you can tell me where I can find the Sato Metal Industries Company?"

"Are you going to Sato's office?" He looked at Yoko again; this time his eyes were cold.

"Yes. He's run up too large an account and the mama-san sent me to collect the bill. She drew a map showing where the company is located, but I seem to have lost it. I was just wondering what to do when I had the good luck to run into you. Do you know where Sato's office is?"

"Sure, I know where his office is, but it won't do you any good."

"Oh? What do you mean?"

"Sato Metal Industries is just on the verge of bankruptcy. Only the other day they had to sell off a parcel of land where they store materials and supplies. When they are forced to let go of piddling little pieces of land like that, you know they can't last much longer. Even their payroll is late, so it's not likely he'll be paying off a bar debt."

Sakura did not appear to have been drinking today, and he was not quite as belligerent as he had been the other night, but his bellowing voice was sharp with ridicule and hatred.

"Oh my," said Yoko. "What shall I do? Maybe I could work something out if I talk directly with Mr. Sato."

"Sato isn't around," the old man replied with conviction. Yoko was watching him carefully again, but he paid no attention to her. He was completely absorbed in his own thoughts. "He's been away from his office for three days now. He told his staff he was going away on a business trip, but I'd say he's either run out on them, or else he's hiding at home, too embarrassed to show his face."

"Oh, well in that case I could see him if I went to his

home. Doesn't he live in Aoyama?" Yoko knew perfectly well where he lived, but she asked the question as a way of continuing the conversation.

"Um," grunted Sakura with a sneer. The ash on his cigarette had grown long and he took another drag on it.

"I suppose he lives at home with his wife; are there just the two of them?"

"He calls her his wife, but she's more like a mistress."

"Mistress? I heard that his first wife had died, and that this is his second marriage. Are you saying he isn't legally married?"

"Yes. He's been with her for two years, but they were never legally married. She is probably a disreputable woman—she has a lover. Rumor has it that she is terribly beautiful, but he has always kept her hidden away as though he was an adulterer or something."

Talking to him close at hand like this, Yoko did not notice any signs of him being crazy. All she could perceive was the stubbornness and dignity of a man who represented one generation of an old and well-established fabric wholesaler. If one listened to him with an open mind, there was no hint of his particular anger at Takashi Sato. That, apparently, was a private matter.

"Probably his company is failing because he devotes all his time to that whore. I expect the earlier generations of the Sato family are turning in their graves. All he cares about is his own pleasure, and he has just let the company go to ruin."

At that point perhaps Sakura suddenly remembered his granddaughter, for he glared furiously about and flung his cigarette butt toward the empty sandbox.

5

The Disguise

Was Sakura innocent or guilty? That was the question.

If he was the criminal who killed Takashi and made it
appear to be a lovers' suicide, how had he managed to dis-
play no surprise when Yoko showed up very much alive? It
was possible, of course, that he had mentioned the fact that
Takashi was not around as part of an elaborate plan to cover
up his crime.

Yoko sat on the subway as she pondered these thoughts
and gazed vacantly at the person sitting opposite her. Without realizing it, she was drawn to this young man dressed in
jeans and suede sports shoes. She really paid attention when
he took off a large pair of very dark sunglasses.

"Oh!" the businessman sitting next to Yoko murmured to
his companion, "Look, she's a woman."

"Yeah. You can tell when you see her face."

"While she was wearing those sunglasses I thought she

was a guy. There are so many of those delicate-looking boys around these days.''

As the subway pulled into the station, the two stopped talking and stood up to leave. The young lady opposite, who had been the subject of their conversation, rolled up her woman's magazine and also walked toward the exit.

The conversation Yoko had just overheard reflected her own opinion. She herself had been staring at that young girl and had thought she was a boy until she removed her sunglasses and Yoko saw her long lashes. The long hair hanging in her eyes, the striped shirt, the man's wristwatch, as well as the flat chest, narrow hips, and long legs all suggested a boy's build rather than a girl's. As long as the girl had kept her face hidden by the sunglasses and said nothing, she was easily mistaken for a boy. The recent unisex fashions made it almost impossible to tell the difference between girls and boys.

These thoughts came to Yoko as she sat staring at her knees, which peeped out from beneath her pleated skirt. Yoko herself was one of the younger generation, but up to this moment she had always and un-self-consciously chosen to wear feminine clothing. And yet, when she thought about it, her build was such that she might be taken for a boy if she wore a boy's clothing. She was five-foot-three, with a slight build and a dark complexion. She had a round face, but it wasn't plump, and her breasts as well as her hips were slim. Apart from her clothing, the only thing that made her look feminine was the fact that her brown, lightly waved hair hung to her shoulders. If she trimmed her hair a bit so that it only came down to neck level, she would look very much like so many of the long-haired boys one sees about today. Suddenly Yoko had an idea.

At eight o'clock that evening Yoko was walking down a street in the Aoyama district through a wealthy neighborhood of expensive homes. It was not just that they were large; they were also well tended and resembled illustrations from an architecture magazine. Many of them were Western-style homes with foreign names on the gateposts, while others looked like gingerbread houses.

All the homes were surrounded by trees and high fences so the street was dark and shadowy. Although it was not late, virtually no people were about, though one could hear the continual sound of automobile traffic on a main thoroughfare nearby.

Yoko was looking for the home of Takashi Sato. Just as in the case of his factory, they had driven past his home once on their way to her apartment and he had pointed it out to her. She had no trouble finding it this evening. She stood before the cream-colored, Western-style house surrounded by its stone fence. Though not what you would call a mansion, it was a substantial place, and yet it had a closed, deserted air about it.

There was an iron gate in the stone wall and a narrow path leading up to the front door. Yoko got as far as the dimly lit front porch when she stopped to look at a reflection of her unfamiliar self once more. She was wearing a man's gray suit with a blue-striped shirt. She had removed all the makeup from her face and wore a man's brown sunglasses. She had bought all these things this evening at a department store in Shibuya. Afterward she had gone to a beauty parlor and had her hair cut to neck length and straightened, removing the last traces of her permanent. This was the result of the inspiration that had come to her on the subway as she was returning from Takashi's factory.

Old man Sakura had seemed quite definite when he said that Takashi's wife, Midori, had a lover. If he was right, there was one more person who was a potential enemy of Takashi's. After all, Yoko could not rule out the possibility that Midori herself might want to see him dead. Also, although Yoko had no foundation for such a thought, it did occur to her that the mysterious Tanaka who had telephoned for Takashi might be Midori's lover—or someone connected with him. Yoko decided that her next target would be Midori, and here, for the first time, she began to feel the need for some caution.

The Satos had no children, and Yoko could not recall Takashi ever saying anything about having a live-in maid, so that meant Midori must be at home alone, watching the house in her husband's absence, though there was always a chance that her lover might be there with her. What would happen if they were the ones who had killed Takashi, and Yoko now suddenly showed up at their house? This concern led Yoko to disguise her own sex as she began her investigation of Midori. Also, since she did not know when the police might begin searching for her, it seemed prudent to be disguised as a boy.

Everything was quiet at the Sato home, and a faint light was coming through the curtains of one of the windows. Yoko closed her eyes for a moment, then, taking a deep breath, she rang the buzzer. After a moment she heard the sound of footsteps muffled by a carpet and sensed that someone had approached the door.

"Who is it?" came the sound of a soft, female voice. Surely this was Midori.

"My name is Onoda," Yoko said in as deep a voice as she could manage. For a time there was silence, then she heard the hinges creak as the door began to open.

The light behind the woman made her stand out in sharp relief. She was wearing a simple, deep red dress. Her dark black hair was swept up bouffant-style, and it was in sharp contrast to her white face. She appeared to be in her thirties. She had strong eyes that seemed to be slanted at the corners, though perhaps that was due to the slope of her nose. In any case, she had prominent features that emanated grace and dignity. Her taut, white skin seemed fresh and vital; she wore little makeup. She was a large woman, and even though her dress was not gaudy, her overall appearance was showy and extravagant. Yoko recalled Sakura describing her as a terribly beautiful woman.

"Excuse me," Yoko said with a slight bow. "Are you the lady of the house?"

"Yes." The woman nodded, a formal smile on her face. Obviously this was Midori.

"I do business with your husband's company, and I came to discuss some matters with him." Yoko strove painfully to speak in a deep voice, and at the same time she watched Midori's reactions carefully. Did Midori really think she was a man? It was twilight, so it would be difficult for Midori to get a clear look. On the other hand, it also made it difficult for Yoko to read Midori's reactions. "Is your husband at home?"

"No." Midori fluttered her eyelashes. "He's in Osaka on business."

"Oh, I see. When do you expect him back?"

"I think he will be back in two or three days."

"The business I have to discuss with him is rather urgent. I wonder if you have an address or phone number where he can be reached?"

"Well, I'm afraid . . ." A look of regret appeared on Midori's face. "You see, I can't help you because I don't know where he is myself. I'm sorry," she added in a soft voice, and dropped her gaze to look down at her hands.

Yoko felt exasperation rising in her breast. At first Midori's formal, aristocratic features and her large body dressed in Western clothes had made her seem aloof and cold. Yet even in the course of this brief conversation, Midori had changed in Yoko's estimation. Now all she could see was a forlorn, neglected wife, a woman who knew virtually nothing of her husband's affairs and who had no choice but to believe whatever he told her and stay meekly looking after the house for him.

Yoko remembered Takashi's anguish as he murmured, "Midori and I have been married for a long time." Sakura had said Midori had a lover. Apparently this woman who appeared so meek on the outside had closed her heart to her husband and had been deceiving him. This was the strong impression Yoko had, and she could not suppress the feelings that welled up in her heart. Perhaps it was just jealousy she felt at seeing Midori's beauty.

Yoko was suddenly seized by a violent impulse to cruelly wound this demure woman. At the same moment, however, she spotted a pair of black men's shoes in the corner of the entry hall. Perhaps they were a pair Takashi had left out, but maybe they belonged to a secret night visitor who was hiding inside the silent house, spying on the events taking place at the front door.

Quicker than thought, Yoko whipped off the sunglasses and stood where the dim porch light would shine directly on her face. Midori's eyes widened with surprise, and Yoko glared back with hatred. Midori stared at Yoko's face. If Midori was involved with the crime, she would now realize that the young man who stood before her was actually the woman who was supposed to have died with her husband.

"Mrs. Sato, my real name is Yoko Noda." As she spoke, Yoko could feel her composure desert her, and her voice became shrill. Midori's eyes grew large and her jaw dropped.

"I have been your husband's mistress for a long time. Recently I heard from a friend that he had seen your husband at Amagi two days ago. Didn't you know that is where he has gone, Mrs. Sato?" The words gushed out even though Yoko knew she should be more careful.

Midori sucked in her breath and stood rooted to the spot. Her eyes simply stared at Yoko in amazement, while the look of shock hardened on her face. Her brows came together in a deep frown and her lip began to tremble. Her expression began to disintegrate as tears came to her eyes. Midori slowly shook her head. "My husband went to Osaka on business. Now, please go away." She spoke in a small voice and, holding back her emotions with obvious difficulty, motioned for Yoko to leave.

As night wore on, the neighborhood grew increasingly still. The streetlights were on, but they were far apart, and the street was pitch-dark between the Satos' house and the hedge of the foreigner's house across the street. Rarely did any cars pass along this street, and all that could be heard was the distant hum of vehicles on the freeway.

Yoko stepped out of the shadows from which she had been watching the gate of the Satos' house and walked into the pool of light shed by the streetlight. Looking at her watch, she saw it was 10:25. She had been watching from the shadows at the side of the street for nearly two hours. It was a warm evening, so it was not uncomfortable waiting around outside, but this job required more patience than Yoko had at first realized. Still, she had been very much intrigued by the sight of the man's shoes in the entry hall of the Sato house. If they were Takashi's, there was no problem, but Yoko suspected that someone had come to the house secretly, knowing that Takashi was away. It was just possible that Midori and this man were the enemies Yoko was looking for. Midori would have told the man of Yoko's appearance, they would both have been surprised, and they would be forced to make a new plan to respond to this surprising development. In any case, if there was a man in the house with Midori, he would have to come out sooner or later. All Yoko wanted was a glimpse of his face when he did. After all, she represented a direct threat to them, and they might try to get rid of her, but she had to gamble that she might also be able to prove they had committed the crime.

Still, for the past two hours, no one had left or entered the house. The second floor was dark, but light still shone from the first-floor window, and Midori had not come out to close the front gate for the night.

Yoko turned from the circle of light cast by the streetlight and returned to her former position. When she had satisfied herself that nothing had changed within her range of vision, she heaved a sigh of relief. She was so tired she would not have minded lying right down in the street and taking a nap. By good fortune she had survived the trip to Amagi and yesterday had spent the whole day recuperating in her apartment. But physically she was still not back to normal, and since this morning the pressure on her had been terrific.

The question was whether or not the man who owned those shoes was in the house. He might not even be there. On the other hand, he might be there and decide to spend the night. And so, exhausted as she was, Yoko felt she ought to stay and maintain her vigil, but for tonight she decided she would be practical and return to Fumiyo's house to sleep. She turned away from Takashi's house and began to walk in the opposite direction. The street led down a hill, around a curve, and passed under a freeway. As she descended the hill, the only sound to be heard was the clatter of her own footsteps. Partway down the hill, the street turned sharply and became very narrow. In a few moments it would cross the main street at the bottom of the hill. Yoko hoped to find a taxi there.

There were no streetlights on the steep, narrow street; the darkness was absolute. Although the street was lined with houses, facing her as she walked were either stone walls or garages, which further contributed to the darkness. Yoko suddenly realized how dark it really was here, but inertia kept her walking along. She was so utterly exhausted that both her thinking and her movements were sluggish. It was not long before she reached a point where she could see the freeway at the bottom of the hill. Just at that moment she heard the footsteps behind her, frantic and closing rapidly.

Yoko sucked in her breath as a shiver of fear ran up her spine. Surely her enemy had been waiting for her to come into just this sort of deserted street. Damn! she thought. What do I do now?

The sound of the footsteps stopped and her wrist was seized

in a powerful grip. Yoko felt a thrill of pain and fear and she was roughly thrust back against a stone wall. All she could make out was that her attacker appeared to be a young man wearing a suit. His face was obscured by the shadows and all she could hear was the sound of his heavy breathing.

There was no time to cry out. She tried desperately to strike her assailant with her left hand, which had not been pinned behind her, and realized that the man had a knife. With his left hand he grasped her right wrist and twisted, and pressing his body against hers, he stabbed at her with the knife.

Yoko tried to get out of the way, but her left hand flailed wildly at the air. The knife slashed toward her, and as she felt a violent pain in her left arm, she finally found her voice and began to scream for help.

Within seconds a large shadow slid away from the dark background and she realized that someone was approaching her assailant from behind. Yoko felt a cry escape her lips, and realized that the pressure on her arm had been released. At the same moment she made a thrust at her assailant. Two distinct shadows emerged before her eyes. The second shadow was the larger of the two. He had run down from the street above and seemed to have the advantage.

The knife dropped from the attacker's hand, and at the same moment he broke free and began to run headlong down the hill.

"Wait!" a deep voice called after him. Meanwhile Yoko managed to stumble forward and regain the road. As her assailant reached the main street at the bottom of the hill, she heard the man pursuing him call out in an uncertain voice, "Tanaka. It's you, isn't it, Tanaka?"

6

Light and Darkness

THE NURSE APPLIED A CLEAN GAUZE BANDAGE TO THE three-inch wound on Yoko's left forearm. The middle-aged doctor had supervised the first part of this procedure but had now turned his attention to a fresh patient-information card lying on his desk. He had a scraggly beard and a thoughtful look on his face.

When the bandaging was completed, Yoko explained once again, "I really don't know how it happened. I was trying to open a can of pineapple but couldn't find the can opener, so I tried to do it with a knife. I guess I must have slipped; the next thing I knew I had cut myself."

When the doctor looked up from the card, his eyes were hooded and hollow looking. His gaze traveled from Yoko's face to her newly bandaged left arm, on to her slightly blood-stained shirt, and down to the cuffs of her trousers. Finally a cynical smile appeared on his dry, thin lips. Yoko knew what he was thinking. She had a woman's face and a woman's

61

voice, and had given a woman's name, but she was dressed in men's clothing, although she was far too slender and graceful to be a man. He most likely assumed she was a lesbian, or a denizen of an unorthodox world and had been involved in a lovers' quarrel. The wound was not really deep enough or severe enough to report to the police, so he decided just to bandage it and let it go at that.

Having appeared to arrive at that conclusion, the doctor looked at her as if she were a nuisance and rubbed his jaw. "Well, from now on you should be more careful. Come back and see me in a couple of days; I don't want that cut to get infected. We'll take out the stitches in about a week."

Yoko meekly nodded.

It was already past midnight. Yoko was in an outpatient clinic located behind some foreign legation near Fifth Avenue in Aoyama. The neighboring buildings were silent and deserted. Fortunately this clinic provided emergency care, so there was a doctor on duty even at this late hour. Since there were no other patients, the corridors were only dimly lit with night-lights. The lights in the waiting room, however, were bright and made her squint. In a corner of the waiting room, smoking a cigarette and looking out the window, was the tall man who had saved her from her attacker. He was a powerfully built man wearing a beige jacket. Yoko had been slashed on her left arm through her sleeve. He had noticed the blood even before she herself had and had brought her here.

Sensing that Yoko had returned to the waiting room, he turned away from the window to face her. He had a tense, sunburned face and appeared to be about thirty. The dominant features of his face were his heavy eyebrows and clear eyes.

The man's eyes first came to rest on her bandaged arm and he asked, "How is it?"

"The doctor had to give me a few stitches, but it's not that bad. He asked me to come back again in a couple of days."

He gave a slight nod and looked Yoko in the eye. "Do you really think it's better not to report this to the police?" On their way to the emergency room they had discussed this.

"It's over with. It wouldn't do any good to report it now," Yoko said with a vague smile.

"Why not? I have the attacker's knife." He took from his jacket pocket a large hunting knife that had been dropped in the street. While Yoko was being treated by the doctor, he had wrapped it in a white handkerchief.

"But I didn't get a good look at the man and I know nothing about him. I didn't even realize I'd been slashed. He was a bit drunk and tried to proposition me. When I turned him down, he seemed to go berserk. I really don't see what the police could do."

Even if they did finally report it, Yoko wanted to put it off as long as possible. First she had to find out who her enemy was. Until then she would be putting herself in jeopardy by getting involved with the police. After all, she could not be sure when they might discover Takashi's body and begin looking for her.

"Didn't the doctor ask any questions about how you got hurt?"

"Yes, he did at first, but it seemed too complicated to explain everything, so I just told him it was an accident. He seemed to accept it."

"I see." The man looked at her meditatively for a moment, then said, "Shall we go?"

"I really want to thank you. You've been very kind." Yoko looked at the floor.

"Where do you live?"

"Shibuya. I can take a taxi from here."

"In that case I will stay with you until we can find a taxi."

"I'm sorry to bother you like this."

Yoko's bloodstained suit jacket was draped over the back of a chair in the waiting room. She quickly reached for it with her right hand before the man could get it for her.

As they walked along the dark street the tall man asked, "Does your arm hurt?"

"No." Her bandaged arm was numb, but it didn't hurt. After all the excitement her earlier fatigue had disappeared.

They walked on for a time in silence.

"I hope I'm not being impertinent." The man spoke in a deep but hesitant voice. "But I wonder if you would mind telling me your name?"

"Onoda," replied Yoko. That was the name she had first used with Midori, and the name she had given the doctor.

"My name is Taki. My next question may also be impertinent, but . . ." Here Taki smiled a bit for the first time. "Tell me, Miss Onoda, why are you dressed in a man's suit like that?"

Yoko had been pretty sure he would ask this question sooner or later and she had been wracking her mind for an answer. "Oh, I don't know. It seems to be fashionable these days to dress so that one can't be sure if you are a man or a woman." This was the only reply she could think of. "But you shouldn't think I am peculiar or anything, if you know what I mean." She reddened as she made this hasty addition to her explanation.

Taki did not reply.

At Aoyama Boulevard, a main thoroughfare, cars were whizzing by. Yoko looked up at Taki. "I'll be all right now," she said. "I can get a taxi home from here." She was thinking what a nuisance it would be if he insisted on accompanying her all the way home. After all, she had promised to spend the night at Fumiyo's house in Kitazawa. "I really appreciate all you have done for me. Thanks."

Once again she politely bowed to him.

"All right, then, take care going home," Taki replied with surprising casualness. Then, suddenly remembering, he took the hunting knife wrapped in his white handkerchief from his pocket. "What shall I do with this?"

Yoko thought for a moment. "I can take it home with me

if you like.'' She thought it might be useful sometime as evidence.

"Well then . . ." He seemed to hesitate again as he had earlier when he had asked her name. "Would it be too much to ask your address so that perhaps I can get in touch with you again sometime? Something might come up in connection with this, you never can tell."

He fumbled in his pocket and brought out a business card. "This is how you can reach me," he said, handing her a card that said, TOYO CONSTRUCTION COMPANY—DESIGN DEPART- MENT—OSAMU TAKI.

Yoko borrowed a ballpoint pen from him and another of his cards, on the back of which she wrote the address of her apartment in Shibuya and the name Yaeko Onoda. The false name sounded good enough, but it was too much trouble to try to think up a fictitious address on the spur of the moment.

Now that she was about to part company with Taki, the bone-numbing weariness that had vanished earlier suddenly swept over her. And yet, as she handed him the card with the name and address on it, she suddenly remembered something. It wasn't a memory exactly, too vague for that; perhaps it was just a figment of her imagination, but she had to ask. "I was just wondering, Mr. Taki, if you might know who that man was who attacked me?"

He looked at her in astonishment. "What do you mean?"

"I seem to remember that when he ran away, you called after him. You called out the name Tanaka."

Taki stood blinking his eyes, and in the glare of the passing headlights she could see the look of puzzlement and confusion on his face. "I don't know. I must have called out without thinking." He fell silent for a moment. At last he said slowly, "There is really nothing to it. It was just that for a moment he seemed to resemble a guy I know." As he spoke, his thin lips twisted into a wry smile. "You be careful now. Take care," he said as a simple farewell as he put the card in the pocket of his jacket and turned away.

There is really nothing to it. It's just that for a moment he seemed to resemble a guy I know. Taki's words remained in Yoko's mind. She wondered why his name was Tanaka, and not Hayashi or Yamada or something else. Was it just a coincidence? At the moment she was too tired even to think about it.

Could it be that the man who had slashed her was Shuji Tanaka? This was the question Osamu Taki was turning over in his mind as he walked aimlessly down the street after parting from the woman he knew as Yaeko Onoda.

No matter how much he pondered the problem, Taki was unable to reach any definite conclusion. It had been so dark in the street that even when he grappled with the man and pulled him away by his collar-length hair, he had not gotten a clear look at him. Indeed, at the time his adversary had been holding the knife in his right hand, and Taki's whole attention as he struggled was to see that he didn't get himself stabbed. There had not been time to stop and wonder who this person was.

The thought that it might be Tanaka had flitted through his mind at the moment the knife clattered to the street and the man had desperately shoved Taki aside and started running. Taki had gotten just a glimpse of the cut and design of the man's suit. It had red and green checks on a blue background. It was hard to tell the colors for sure since it was dark, but his eyes had clearly seen the checkered pattern. The suit was one Tanaka had received from one of his subordinates for whom he had arranged a marriage. The subordinate had brought the suit back from a trip to Southeast Asia, and it was rather different in cut and design from ordinary Japanese suits. That's why Taki remembered it even though he had only seen it once or twice. It was just about five days ago—on September 11, in fact, at eight o'clock in the morning—that Tanaka had left the house wearing that suit. Taki had learned this from his sister.

Shuji Tanaka, about whom Taki was thinking, was, at thirty-six, some five years older than Taki. He worked in a publishing company that specialized in school reference books and business publications. Taki's sister, Reiko, was Tanaka's wife. Deciding he could come to no conclusions about this puzzle, Taki put the matter out of his mind for the time being and, pulling his cigarettes from his jacket pocket, began to smoke.

This part of Aoyama was lined with art galleries, pottery shops, and boutiques. The whole area had a rather fashionable air about it. The shops all had their steel shutters closed, but here and there were bars and nightclubs that were brightly illuminated. There were many cars on the street but virtually no pedestrians.

As he inhaled the smoke, Taki suddenly realized that his throat felt parched, so he pushed his way into the nearest bar. It was a very ordinary place with a counter and three booths, but it was nevertheless very lively. Taki seated himself on a bar stool near the door and ordered a whiskey and water from the girl who was tending bar. As the cool liquid flowed down his throat, the familiar good feeling that was a mixture of fatigue and alcohol spread through his body.

Where in the world, he wondered, had Tanaka disappeared to? Taki leaned on the bar with his chin in the palm of his hand. He tried to pursue this question, but his mind was filled with thoughts of the young lady he had just encountered who excited his imagination.

On the morning of September 12 and twice that afternoon, Taki's sister had telephoned him at the office saying she needed to talk to him. After making an inspection trip to the site of a condominium his company was building, he dropped by his sister's house. Tanaka's home was located in a suburb between Tokyo and Yokohama. The family consisted of the husband, wife, and their five-year-old son; they lived in a two-room apartment with an eat-in kitchen. It was past six o'clock when Taki arrived to find that the child, Akira, was down with a summer cold and was in bed in the inner room.

"Osamu, something terrible has happened." Reiko sat across the kitchen table from him, speaking in a low voice that was tense with near hysteria. At the same time, tears came to her already reddened eyes. Her face was pale and her skin was dry, as though it had been sprinkled with talcum powder.

When she had called him at the office and he had promised to stop by, she had said, "Please do that. I want to know if you've heard anything from my husband recently. At first I wasn't sure of the situation, but now it's clear. Tanaka disappeared last night, and I have no idea where he is."

"What do you mean, you don't know where he is? Didn't he come home at all last night?"

"No. But I supposed he had something to do in relation to his work. In the past he's rarely stayed out all night, and even on those few occasions, he always telephoned, but as of now I've heard nothing from him."

While Reiko recalled the phone conversation with her brother, she bit her lip violently. There was clearly something wrong, Taki could tell that from the way she spoke, but he remained silent for a while watching her trying to figure things out.

"Then this morning, shortly after eleven, I got a phone call from his company, saying that there was to be a company meeting and asking why he wasn't there. They said he had certain important papers they needed, and they wanted to know how to get in touch with him."

"So that was when you called me and asked if I knew anything of his whereabouts?"

"Yes. Once I knew he wasn't at work, I called your office to see if you had any idea where he was."

"I see." Taki looked at his sister with perplexity written on his face. Reiko was two years his senior but had led a sheltered life and knew nothing of the world. He wanted to do whatever he could, of course, to help her, but he didn't care much for his brother-in-law. If there was no actual hostility between them, then at least there was a mutual sense of indifference. They had little in common to talk about since one was in the building business and the other in publishing. More than anything else, Taki sensed something sinister about Tanaka, or to put the matter more strongly, that he was an ugly customer who gave the impression of being slimy and unreliable. Consequently Taki rarely visited his sister or had dinner with them. Surely Reiko must have known that if her husband had gone off and abandoned both his family and his job, he wasn't likely to have told Taki about it.

"He doesn't have any relatives in Tokyo, and I have never heard him say anything about having any friends apart from the people he works with at the office."

"So that means we really have no leads in trying to find him."

"I guess not. I even talked to his boss and asked if they could help locate him, but he said my husband left the office about six o'clock yesterday evening and no one knew where he went. He hasn't been in touch with them at all concerning work, so he's obviously not away on business."

"Can you think of any reason why he might suddenly take off?"

Reiko seemed to wince as he asked this but shook her head. "It's possible that he might have had an accident of some sort. Do you think I should call the police?" Even as she spoke, Reiko looked up at the clock. According to her version of events, Tanaka had already been missing for more than twenty-four hours.

"It's one chance in a million that anything like that happened, but it would probably be a good idea to begin a missing person search." Taki looked toward the room where Akira lay sleeping. "If you have to go out for any reason, let me know and I'll come stay with the boy."

"Thanks. I may have to call on you." Reiko nodded heavily, but the look in her eyes was still far from certain.

Taki gave her a questioning look and Reiko dropped her gaze to the table. Brother and sister remained like this for a moment, then Reiko began to speak rapidly. "No one in the company is saying anything, but I've had a feeling for some time now that something like this would happen."

"Oh, really? What made you feel that way?"

"Well, for the last couple of months it seems like he's changed somehow. He's often been late getting home from work, and there have been several nights when he didn't come back at all. He did telephone, though, each time he stayed out, but before that, the only time he slept away from home was when he was on vacation trips sponsored by his company. His work is mostly administrative, so he's really not away from the office all that much."

Hearing this, Taki was reminded of the peculiar look on his sister's face when she had first mentioned that her husband had stayed out all night.

"He said he was busy with his work, but even when he did come home, he seemed preoccupied and thoughtful. When Akira would ask him about something, he'd give incoherent answers. I couldn't help but think it was not his work, but something else that was bothering him."

Reiko apparently suspected her husband was keeping another woman.

"But isn't there anything else? Anything more concrete than just saying that he seemed thoughtful and preoccupied? For example, were there any suspicious phone calls or anything like that?"

Reiko slowly shook her bowed head. "I can't think of anything that definite, but I just knew something like this would happen. I knew from the very first that he didn't marry me because he loved me. Apparently there was a woman he had been in love with back in his hometown of Fukuoka in Kyushu. For some reason they separated and he came here to Tokyo, where he married me, but even after Akira was born, he didn't forget about that other woman. That's why I knew, I just knew, something like this would happen sooner or later.''

Reiko was sitting with her arms propped on the table, but having said this much, she hid her face in her hands and began weeping like a little girl.

Taki knew little about Shuji Tanaka's background other than that he had been born and raised in northern Kyushu and had graduated from a private university in Fukuoka. About ten years ago he had come to Tokyo after working for four years in a local printing shop.

Reiko had gotten to know Tanaka while he was working at the publishing company where he was now employed. After graduating from high school, Reiko had worked for a trading company and their paths had crossed several times in coffee shops and restaurants, and gradually they had become intimate. They had been married in the autumn some six years ago, and Akira was born the following year, but Taki had a suspicion that they had gotten married only after Reiko had become pregnant. Still, until now they had seemed like an ordinary family, and this was the first Taki had heard of Tanaka having had a lover in Fukuoka. However, Shuji Tanaka was a secretive person who rarely revealed much of himself to others.

''Did you call his family in Fukuoka?'' Taki asked after Reiko had gotten hold of herself, but she merely shook her head wearily.

''I don't know who to contact there. Both his parents are dead. I did hear that he had some younger cousins living somewhere in the country near there, but I don't know where. He has never been back to Kyushu since he first came to Tokyo.'' Reiko looked up at him and the expression on her face said that Fukuoka was clearly out of the question. After that, all Taki could do was borrow a recent photograph of Tanaka from his sister. Tanaka was of medium build and medium height, and his eyes were somewhat deep set. He appeared to be an ordinary, even-tempered businessman.

Carrying the photograph with him, Taki set out for the local police station to ask them to institute a missing person search. The recent dramatic increase in the number of people who abandoned their families could be attributed to social conditions, and so even the disappearance of a person like Tanaka, who had no history of emotional problems and who up till now at least had no criminal record, gave the police very little help in trying to locate him. This impression was only reinforced by the officer who talked to Taki. For that reason Taki didn't bother to tell the police later when he heard a report that one of his fellow office workers had spotted Tanaka on a residential street in Aoyama two days before his disappearance.

On the day the missing person search began, Taki did not return to his own apartment, where he lived alone, but spent the night at his sister's house. There was no word from Tanaka that night, either. The next morning Taki went to work as usual, but shortly before noon he received a telephone call from Reiko.

"I just got a call from my husband's boss." Her voice was husky. "The boss asked the people in the office if they knew anything about my husband, and one man named Saeki in the editorial department said that he had happened to see my husband in Aoyama four days ago. Even though they work in different departments, Saeki and my husband were pretty good friends."

"You say he saw Tanaka in Aoyama?"

"Yes. It was about four o'clock on the afternoon of the ninth. Saeki was walking along a residential street in Aoyama when he spotted Tanaka on the other side of the street walking in the opposite direction. Saeki himself was on his way back to the office from a photography studio where they had had some graphic work done. He thought it strange to see

Tanaka in that part of town at that time of day and innocently asked what he was doing there. He says Tanaka looked flustered and embarrassed and couldn't give any reasonable answer. Saeki assumed he was there on some sort of private business and didn't say anything about the matter to anyone. He's sorry now that he didn't say something sooner.''

"I see.''

"My husband's boss thinks it unlikely that Tanaka had anything to do in Aoyama that's related to his work. Apparently at around three that afternoon Tanaka complained of having a headache and left work early. But this is the first time I heard of it, and I really have no idea why he might have been in Aoyama.''

Taki thought about this for a moment before Reiko said, "I guess it would be a good idea to convey this information to the police." Perhaps because Reiko had never dealt with the police before, her first impulse was to go to them.

"Yeah, I guess so," Taki said simply as he hung up. Next he telephoned Saeki and arranged to meet him later that same afternoon. On most days Taki spent the morning in his office doing desk work and drawing up plans, and in the afternoon he would go around to visit the construction sites. As a site supervisor, he was the leader of one of the teams in the company's planning department, and his schedule was flexible enough to allow him a little time of his own.

The meeting with Saeki produced little information beyond what Reiko had already told him except that he was able to say exactly where in Aoyama he had met Tanaka. Since Saeki's firm did a lot of business with the photography studio, he was familiar with that area and was able to draw a detailed map for Taki. With that Taki set out for Aoyama. Even if he took this information to the police, they wouldn't be able to do much with it unless they had something more to go on.

Just as Saeki had explained to him, it was a residential

neighborhood that gave the impression of being very affluent.

Taki walked around for a while near the place where Saeki had met Tanaka, then went into a liquor store on the corner. It was a small but neat place with the bottles all lined up on the shelves, and a counter on the side where they sold cigarettes, and a public telephone next to it. Here Taki passed around the photograph of Tanaka and asked about him. He got an unexpected response.

"Ah yes. This man has been in to buy cigarettes and to use the telephone," was the response from a young employee with a long apron over his jeans. "Ever since about the end of August I have noticed him walking along the street from time to time. Always alone. Sometimes during the day, but more often in the evenings or at night."

If Tanaka had been hanging around this neighborhood since the beginning of August, that would be about a month and a half. It fit with Reiko's statement that he had seemed somehow changed during the past couple of months.

"I don't suppose you know where he goes when he's walking around this neighborhood?"

"Well, I did see him one evening when I was delivering beer at Mr. Sato's house. He was just coming out the gate."

"Mr. Sato? Who is that?"

"Turn left at the corner and go down a ways. It's the house with the stone wall around it."

"What line of work does Mr. Sato do?"

"I really couldn't say, but he seems to be the president of some company downtown." The young man answered all of Taki's questions readily and with no trace of suspicion.

"When was the last time you saw this man around the neighborhood?" The young man could not be sure when he had last seen Tanaka; apparently it had not been more recent than Saeki's encounter with him.

That day Taki went to take a look at Sato's house but did nothing more than that. Tanaka's flustered response when

Saeki called out to him fit well with Reiko's description of his recent condition. Still, the cream-colored walls of the house surrounded by the stone fence seemed somehow forbidding, and so, for both these reasons Taki was reluctant to simply go up to the house and ring the bell. Instead he went to a florist shop in the neighborhood and made more inquiries. After that he found a telephone book and looked up Sato's number. He called the house, and when a woman answered the phone, he said that he was calling on a matter of business and asked for her husband's office phone number. The result of all this was that he learned some things about the Sato family, namely that Takashi Sato was the president of Sato Metal Industries, a company that dealt in nonferrous metals. He also learned that the household consisted only of Sato and his wife, Midori, and that Sato was currently in Osaka on a business trip.

Before telling Reiko the results of his inquiries, he asked if the name Sato meant anything to her, but she simply looked puzzled and shook her head.

The following day he made up his mind to inquire directly at the Sato house. There was nothing wrong in doing this, and it might just turn up a clue to help find Tanaka. It was about three o'clock on the afternoon of September 14, the third day after Tanaka's disappearance, when Taki walked through the gate of the Sato house. He was pretty sure that Sato would be at work at this time, even if he had returned to Tokyo from his trip, and Taki wanted to talk to Midori alone. The man at the liquor store had said that Tanaka usually passed there during the day or in the evenings. So assuming that his destination was the Sato house, there was a strong likelihood that he was going there to see Midori rather than Takashi.

The sun was shining directly into the entry hall when he came face-to-face with Midori for the first time. His initial impression was that she was a strong and intense woman. When he rang the bell, Midori had asked his name first before opening the door, but when she did, he found her wearing a Western-style dress of pale yellow silk. He was surprised at her obvious and coquettish beauty.

"Pardon me for intruding, but here is my card," he said with a slight bow as he handed her his business card.

Midori accepted it graciously but said, "If you want to see my husband, I am afraid he is away on a business trip," in a low, steady voice.

"No. You are the one I came to see today."

"Oh, really?"

"I came to talk to you about Shuji Tanaka."

"Tanaka? Who's he?" She returned Taki's gaze with her own intense look. It was impossible to tell if her expression was one of confusion at having been suddenly asked about an unfamiliar name, or whether she was surprised at having been asked about someone with whom she was secretly intimate. Taki also had to consider the possibility that whatever connection Tanaka had with Midori, he may have used a fictitious name. In any case, Taki had his photograph ready and showed it to her. "This man. I'm a relative of his. He disappeared three days ago and we haven't heard from him since."

It was his plan to confront Midori with the facts and see her response, but she merely studied the photograph intently and did not look up.

"I thought you might know something about him. The other day I was in this neighborhood on business, and I remember that I unexpectedly saw him coming out of this house. At the time he said he was a friend of the woman who lived here. That's why I came to ask if you have any idea at all of where he might be."

Even after Taki finished speaking, the woman kept her head bent for a time, looking at the photograph. It was possible, of course, that she was thinking of how best to answer his question. Presently Midori handed back the photograph with a look of slight bafflement and a polite smile on her face. The light was not very good, but Taki did have the impression that her naturally pale skin might have paled slightly when she saw the photograph.

"I'm sorry, but I am afraid you must be mistaken," said Midori calmly. "I don't recall ever having met this person. I don't believe I even know anyone named Tanaka."

"But as I told you a moment ago, I saw him with my own eyes coming out of this house."

Midori returned his gaze steadily and asked, "Are you sure you definitely saw him coming out of this house?"

"Yes. That's right," he replied, but there may have been a faint wavering in his voice. Unfortunately he did not have full confidence in this matter since he had only heard it from the young man at the liquor store.

Midori smiled and knew that she now had room to maneuver. "Pardon me for asking, but I wonder if this man is a salesman of some sort. If that's the case, he may have come here and I had simply forgotten what he looked like."

"No. He's not a salesman."

Midori cocked her head to one side and took a deep breath. "This is odd, isn't it? I certainly have no recollection of this person."

"I don't suppose there's any chance that you've heard your husband mention his name?"

"No."

"When do you expect your husband to return from his trip?"

"Around the eighteenth."

"In that case I'll go to his office to see him around that time."

"Yes. That would probably be best."

"Please excuse me for bothering you."

"No, no. It's quite all right. I'm afraid I didn't help you at all." Midori was a model of politeness to the very end.

And yet, there was something peculiar about that house, Taki was sure of it. Or perhaps it would be more accurate to say there was something not quite right about that woman. As he opened the gate of the Sato home, Taki was assailed with doubts and suspicions. Perhaps it was just that the woman's demeanor had been too perfect. Or perhaps it was her obvious good looks that made him suspicious. In short, he felt sure that she held the key to the riddle of Tanaka's disappearance. The woman was clearly keeping something from him, but as long as her husband was away on a trip, he could think of no way to penetrate her defenses.

That night he again stayed at his sister's house, but he did not tell her in any detail what he had learned. He was afraid that if he mentioned anything about Midori, Reiko would assume that she was her husband's earlier lover and would be mad with jealousy. And even if she were able to control herself, she would imagine the affection between Tanaka and Midori, and would feel that Midori had taken her husband from her.

Taki also chose not to reveal his findings to the police officers who were conducting the search for Tanaka. He was afraid that if he told them, they would send someone around to Sato's house to interrogate Midori. Midori would only have to deny everything and they would get nowhere with her. He was also uncertain about how well the people at the liquor store would cooperate with the police since the Satos were good customers.

Taki decided that before he alerted his brother-in-law and gave him a chance to disappear, he wanted to get firmer evidence. The evening of the day following his meeting with Midori, he returned secretly. The neighborhood where the Satos lived was normally quiet, and by ten o'clock it was as still as late night.

With great caution and staying in the darkest shadows of the trees and fences, he approached to a point where he could observe the gate of the Sato house. He quickly made a discovery that increased the tension he already felt. He was standing in the shadow of a gate, but across the street directly opposite him he could make out the shadowy figure of a person who was also waiting. It was a rather thin, small man in a suit.

This man had already concealed himself in the shadow of a tall hedge by the time Taki had come along. It appeared that this other man was also watching the Satos' gate. At first Taki supposed it was just a figment of his imagination, but later he realized that they were actually watching the same gate. The other man occasionally moved about, going to the nearby streetlight to look at his watch, but he always returned quickly to the shadows. He seemed to be watching the gate with great intensity.

At ten-thirty he seemed to give up his vigil, shrugging his shoulders and turning on his heel to walk wearily away. Apparently he had decided nothing would be gained from further watching since there was no sign of any movement there.

On the spur of the moment Taki began to follow the other man. He watched from behind as the young man, who appeared to be a youth of about twenty, descended the sloping street, then turned right down a narrower, steeper path. Taki paused at the corner to watch. The man in front of him was walking slowly, as though very tired, and since the street was narrow, Taki was afraid that his presence might be detected if he went farther, so he turned to walk away. But suddenly another figure appeared in the steep, narrow street where Taki and the other man had just been. This new figure moved quickly and silently. In a flash Taki spun around and returned to the corner to watch.

The first young man was already halfway down the hill; the second man was rapidly gaining on him from behind. This second man was wearing a suit and what looked like a hunting cap. He was a tall man with a heavy build. The pursuer appeared to grab the first young man by the arm and slam him viciously against the stone wall. The two struggled in silence, but the sound of their labored breathing could be heard in the silent street.

For a long moment Taki just stood and watched. The difference in strength between the two men quickly became apparent, and as the pursuer pressed the attack, it was clear that he had the advantage. Still, Taki had no way of knowing what the trouble was between these two men, and he was not eager to get involved in someone else's fight. He was spurred to action, however, the moment he saw the gleam of a blade in the attacker's hand.

Taki raced down the street, grabbed the hand that held the knife, and held it down. Taki was clearly the most powerful of the three. Besides, since he mixed daily with the brawny manual laborers at the construction sites, he had confidence in his own strength.

The man he grasped grunted and released the one he had held against the stone wall. At the same time he turned to confront Taki. It was clear, however, that his intention was not to attack Taki, but to break free of Taki's grasp and flee. He fought with the strength born of desperation.

Taki's attention was diverted when the man's knife clattered to the ground, and at that moment the man broke free. He fled down the hill and Taki started in pursuit, but stumbled and fell. Meanwhile, the other man raced quickly down the hill, turned the corner, and disappeared.

The first young man was leaning heavily against the stone wall, and it was only when Taki noticed the torn sleeve and bleeding arm that he realized that this was actually a girl.

Had the man who fled away been Tanaka? The question lingered in Taki's mind. Had the attacker come out of Sato's house? Even this was unclear. Still, this girl named Yaeko Onoda had been watching the Sato house and the man had attacked her when she started to leave, so he must have some connection with Sato. Then there was the question of why Yaeko had been hanging around spying on the house in the first place. Why would she be interested in the comings and goings of the Satos? Taki realized that he had forgotten to ask her to explain what she was doing there. It was hard, however, to accept the girl's simple, innocent charm at face value. The fact that she was dressed as a man suggested a disguise. On top of that there was the matter of her refusal to go to the police to report a life-threatening attack.

Taki's head was reeling with unanswered questions and he was not sure how he was going to go about finding answers to them.

After emptying his third glass of whiskey, Taki headed unsteadily for home.

7

The Pill

Fumiyo Chino was reading the morning papers while her daughter played happily by herself. With mild curiosity she remarked, "Look at this, they have found someone stabbed to death at Amagi."

"Oh?" Yoko said, trying to sound as casual as possible, but her heart was beating so wildly she could almost hear it. This was the second day after she had been attacked in Aoyama. Fumiyo's husband had already gone to work, and she and her daughter had enjoyed a late breakfast together while Yoko was rearranging the bandage on her left arm.

"You say a body was discovered at Amagi?" Yoko spoke slowly, trying to keep control of her voice.

"Yes. It was found in a cedar grove at the foot of the mountain. The man had been stabbed to death and the body was maybe three or four days old."

Fumiyo handed the newspaper to Yoko. There on the bottom, left-hand side of the page was a two-column article. It was no accident that the article had caught Fumiyo's attention and become a topic of discussion. Both women had graduated from Shizuoka High School near Amagi, and Fumiyo's family had long lived in that area. In fact, her grandparents owned a farm near Amagi. Consequently she was interested in affairs concerning Shizuoka and especially Amagi, and had even done some hiking on Mount Amagi. Meanwhile Yoko kept her head bent low over the article.

There was no mistake about it. According to the article, two hikers who had lost their way between Mount Amagi and Shimoyama discovered the man's partly decomposed body in a cedar grove at about nine o'clock on the evening of the sixteenth. It was past ten o'clock by the time they made their way out to the highway and reported it to the police station. The station contacted police headquarters, who immediately sent officers to the scene. The victim was in his late thirties and had been stabbed in the back with a knife that had pierced his heart. In the back of his suit coat they found the name Sato. They were trying to establish the man's identity and had already begun the search for the murderer.

So, at last Sato's body had been discovered.

The moment she had been dreading had now come and Yoko suddenly felt cold. At the same time she felt she would willingly give her life for Sato's sake. Ever since that fatal night Sato's body had lain there beneath the damp shrubbery decomposing. She had known the body was there and now felt vaguely afraid about her effort to conceal the matter. But she wasn't just trying to protect herself; she also felt a responsibility to Takashi to find the real killer.

The newspaper account did not state the victim's identity, nor did it say much about any evidence found at the scene of the crime. Apparently those details had not yet been released for publication. But if the body had been discovered, it was only a matter of time before the police learned his identity. For one thing, he must have had some of his business cards with him, and for another, he had used his real name and address when he had registered at the inn where he and Yoko had eaten dinner that night.

When skilled investigators examined the scene of the crime, surely they would detect the fact that another person, "the woman who had disappeared," had lain next to the victim. They would also find the empty bottle of sleeping pills, and when they looked in the pockets of Takashi's coat, they would find the farewell notes she and Takashi had placed in an envelope bearing the name of the inn where they had stayed.

The conclusions reached by the investigating officers would be swift and sure. A love suicide, woman stabs man, woman doesn't die but runs away.

Suddenly the whole experience came back to Yoko: she vividly remembered the difficulty she'd had breathing, and she remembered how dry and parched her throat had been.

The police would surely be able to figure out the victim's name and address as well as his position. Then, using the envelope as a guide, the officers would be able to go to the hotel where they had stayed and would be able to verify the fact that on the thirteenth of September a man named Takashi Sato had stayed there in the company of a woman, and that as night came on they had left the hotel and climbed toward the summit of the mountain. According to the farewell note, they would know that the woman's name was Yoko. They would get a description of her from the people at the hotel. Only four days had elapsed and already they would have an accurate description of her, which they would surely distribute widely.

Once they had this, they would surely be in touch with Takashi's wife. Yoko also wondered whether or not Midori had received the letter Takashi had sent from the hotel. No. She had sent her own letter to Fumiyo at the same time and it had not arrived yet, so Midori probably hadn't received the letter yet. Perhaps the mail was delayed for some reason. In any case, at least until the police contacted Midori she would not officially know that anything was wrong. If I'm lucky, I may have two or three days left, Yoko thought, and at the same time she could see in her mind's eye Midori's pale face and her sad, downcast eyes. This image gave her a cruel pleasure and an oddly superior feeling of satisfaction, but it only lasted for a moment.

Judging from the newspaper article, she could assume that the police had found the body around eleven o'clock last night. They probably learned Sato's identity right away, but would wait until this morning to inform Midori. In fact she might be at the police station at this very moment being interviewed by the officers responsible for the case.

Whether or not Midori was directly involved in a conspiracy to kill Takashi, she would surely remember Yoko Noda, who had come to her house suddenly two days ago dressed as a man and saying things about Takashi being at Amagi. Yoko had to assume that Midori would tell all of this to the police. The search for the woman who had killed the man and disappeared would gradually gain momentum. In a case such as this the local police would surely ask for the cooperation of the Tokyo Metropolitan Police. Yoko assumed they would launch a search for Takashi's girlfriend and that they would spend most of today interviewing employees at Sato Metal Industries. No doubt someone would know that the president made a practice of drinking at the Jugon. Once an investigator was sent to the bar with a description of Yoko, he would be led directly to the women's college where she studied and to her apartment in Shibuya. They would probably also send someone to Shizuoka to talk to her father.

If she had bad luck—no, there was a strong possibility that when the detectives talked to her acquaintances at Jugon or at school, or to her father, about the places where she hung out, one of them might mention the name of Fumiyo Chino. The police had the knife that had been used to kill Takashi and her fingerprints were on it; eventually the police would be led to Yoko and at that point Yoko could kiss her future good-bye.

She shivered involuntarily and looked up at the clock on the dresser. It was ten-fifteen. She quickly removed her bandage.

"What are you doing? Doesn't it hurt?" Fumiyo clearly didn't understand what Yoko was going to do. From the look on her face it seemed Fumiyo had already forgotten about the incident at Amagi; all her attention was focused on the slightly soiled bandage on Yoko's arm. Yoko's story to explain the wound was that she had slipped and fallen on a gravel road and had hurt her arm, and that she had had it attended to at a nearby clinic.

"It's all right." Yoko's face was rather pale as she stood up, but it was impossible to read any emotion in her expression. "The doctor asked me to come back in a couple of days so he could make sure it's not getting infected. I think I'll drop in there today."

Even though she said this to conceal her real intention, she had decided that she would indeed stop in to see the doctor. She was afraid that if Fumiyo somehow linked her with the murder, she'd have to leave her friend's house. If Fumiyo found out, Yoko did not know where she would go but in any case thought it would be just as well to go and have her arm looked at before her name and face were being widely searched for. Besides, it suddenly occurred to her that as long as she was going to the clinic to see the doctor, she might as well stop by and take a look at the Sato house and see what was happening there.

It was a chilly, overcast day just before the autumn equinox. Yoko left Fumiyo's house wearing a blue jersey and slacks. Today, too, she dressed in a rather masculine manner. She was also wearing sunglasses.

The residential street in Aoyama was quiet even at midmorning, and since the husbands of all the families were at work, there were virtually no cars parked along the street.

As she approached the Sato house, Yoko felt the tension bringing goose bumps to her skin, and her feet seemed to become sluggish as she walked. Nevertheless, if a policeman called out to her or started to come after her, she intended to take off running. But nothing seemed unusual or out of place as she walked along the quiet street. She reached the corner from which she had observed the Sato house two days earlier. The gate in the stone wall was as deserted as it had been that night. Under the leaden gray sky the flesh-colored walls of the house seemed darker and more sinister than ever. All the windows on the second floor were closed and draped with light brown curtains.

There was no car parked in front of the house, although diagonally across the street she could see the front end of an ivory-colored Mercedes Benz; there was no sign of any police about.

It was not long before Yoko found that the iron gate in the stone wall of the Satos' house was closed. It was hard for her to see into the yard because of the closed gate and the shrubbery behind it. When she was there two nights ago, she had realized that the gate had been left open until late. No doubt Midori had already been notified of her husband's death. Didn't the fact that the gate was closed now in the middle of the day provide ample testimony that no one was at home? Yoko was sure of it. Yet once the household had been notified of the murder, it was possible that investigators were keeping the place under surveillance. Yoko suddenly felt endangered, the fear was like a physical presence. She resolutely turned on her heel and headed for the clinic. She had already begun to feel like a fugitive. Suddenly she was beset by a bewildering variety of emotions that included desperation, sadness, and anxiety.

Her previous visit to the clinic occurred late at night and the waiting room had been deserted, but now a number of patients were waiting in line. A sign announced that the clinic closed at noon for lunch and it was almost noon by the time Yoko arrived. It turned out that she was the last patient to be seen that morning.

Ever since reading this morning's newspaper Yoko felt a slight thrill of fear each time she met someone face-to-face, though, of course, both the doctor and the nurse merely looked at her professionally, and their expressions did not change at all.

"Come back in about a week and we'll take out the stitches. In the meantime it will be all right to take a bath as long as you don't get your arm wet." The same middle-aged doctor who had seen her before gave her this advice as he swabbed antiseptic on the wound.

By the time she returned to the waiting room, the clinic was closed for lunch and there were no other patients around. As she waited for her bill, Yoko stood in the bay window and looked out. She could hear the nurses behind the counter chatting casually. "There was a patrol car down the street this morning."

"Yes. I saw it, too. It was in front of the Satos' house, wasn't it? I saw it on my way to work. Mrs. Sato was just coming out of the house when I walked by."

"I wonder if something happened?" The nurse at the counter had completed the bill and counted out Yoko's change. Fortunately she continued to write some sort of notation on the bill, so Yoko merely stood by unobtrusively so she could overhear more of the conversation.

"Mrs. Sato is really a very beautiful woman, don't you think?" said the other nurse.

"Yes, she is, but always in a very fashionable sort of way. I don't care much for that type myself," the older nurse replied.

"They don't have any children, do they?"

"Apparently they can't," said the senior nurse, eager to supply the details. "I heard all about it recently from a friend of mine who works at the Ishikawa Gynecological Clinic over on Third Avenue. Mrs. Sato has been getting a prescription for birth control pills from that clinic for a long time now. She uses them for treatment of a menstrual problem.''

"Oh, speaking of pills . . .'' The conversation continued, but they began discussing patients who were unknown to Yoko. Still, she continued to stand there.

So, Midori Sato was a user of birth control pills. Hearing them mention the pill in connection with Midori set Yoko to thinking. She recalled the night that Takashi had suggested they commit suicide together and had become unaccountably furious when he learned that Yoko was taking the pill. She had wondered at the time why the mention of birth control pills should produce such a strong reaction.

Yoko remembered reading in a popular magazine that the Ministry of Welfare had proscribed the use of birth control pills for preventing pregnancy but permitted their use for menstrual problems. Despite this, many people continued to use them for contraception, and now that Yoko heard that Midori was a regular user, she wasn't sure if it was because of menstrual problems or if, in fact, Midori and Takashi didn't want to conceive a child. If it were for the first reason, there was no problem, but if it were for the second, then there was a good chance that Midori had a secret lover. If she had a lover and Takashi had suspected this, his angry feelings about the pill became less odd.

Yoko suddenly felt intensely jealous. She wondered how hurt Takashi had been by his wife's adultery and rejection. Normally he had rarely shown his feelings, but he had certainly exploded that one time. There was still a knot of emotion in Yoko's breast that she could not dispel. Perhaps some greater discord had existed between Takashi and his wife that had been brought about by her use of the pill. A vague suspicion began to form in the back of Yoko's mind and for a time she was oblivious to her surroundings.

8

Fugitive

YOKO WALKED OUT OF THE CLINIC ONTO AOYAMA BOULE-vard in search of a taxi. Her watch read past one o'clock and she was in a hurry to return to Fumiyo's house in Kitazawa. She would have to pack her things and leave in the same desperate way she had arrived several days earlier; she had to be gone before Fumiyo linked her with the murder. If her luck was bad she would get back to find that one of the neighboring housewives was visiting Fumiyo, and it would be difficult to break into their conversation with a suitable excuse for leaving suddenly.

With great caution Yoko got out of the taxi some distance away from Fumiyo's house. This, too, was a residential street, but it was very different from the one in Aoyama. The narrow, winding street was lined with small shops and old houses. Yoko looked carefully about but could see no signs of the police, and nothing seemed out of the ordinary. All she could see were a couple of mothers walking hand in hand with their small children. Yoko hurried tensely toward her destination.

Fumiyo's house was locked, but Yoko had borrowed a key, so she was able to get in. Fumiyo had probably gone shopping for groceries with Masami in tow. It was better this way, since she could make her preparations in solitude. She swiftly gathered her clothing and toilet articles while planning a note to leave for Fumiyo. She wondered if it might be better just to telephone later.

Just then Yoko heard one of the sliding doors open and whirled around. There was Fumiyo standing in the doorway to the eat-in kitchen. It occurred to Yoko that Fumiyo had not been out, after all, but only taking a nap in the other room with Masami.

Fumiyo's normally plump, ruddy face was pale and haggard. Her eyes were puffier than normal and she stared silently at Yoko, as if she had found a stranger in her house.

"Oh, you're here after all. I thought you were out shopping." Without thinking about it, Yoko gave her friend an ingratiating but artificial smile and pushed her overnight bag aside. "Is Masami still sleeping?"

"You had better hurry with your packing," Fumiyo said bluntly. Her expression remained hard and her voice sounded like that of a stranger.

"What?"

"I saw the noon news on television. They gave your name and description. They say you are the woman who holds the key to solving the murder at Amagi."

Yoko sucked in her breath.

"Yoko! Is it really true?"

Slowly Yoko let her breath out while Fumiyo stared at her incredulously. Suddenly all her plans and stratagems seemed pointless. All she wanted was for her friend Fumiyo to believe in her innocence. She realized that this was the first hurdle she had to leap in order to straighten out the wreckage of her life. And yet, she just didn't feel up to trying to explain everything right now. Yoko looked back at Fumiyo, her eyes full of emotion, and slowly shook her head.

Fumiyo suddenly dissolved into tears. "You're telling the truth, aren't you? You didn't really do it?"

"That's right."

"Then you're innocent?"

"Yes. But I had better get away from here anyway." Yoko indicated the overnight bag.

"Yes, you'd better hurry. But where will you go?"

"I don't know yet, but I can't stay here. Under the circumstances, it just wouldn't be fair to you."

"Oh, don't say that!" Fumiyo's voice had suddenly become shrill and her outburst startled Yoko. She looked at Fumiyo's pale face and weeping eyes and realized that she had never seen her friend so upset.

"Ever since I heard it on the news, I've been thinking," Fumiyo said at last as she sat down on the tatami-mat floor. "If you don't want the detectives to find you, you could just stay here in the house."

"No. I can't do that. In the first place, I would be a nuisance not only for you, but also for your husband."

Fumiyo looked down at her knees. "Maybe I could talk to my husband and he would understand. But I suppose it might be dangerous for you even if you stay here. If the police come looking around in this neighborhood, there are a number of housewives around who know you're staying with us."

"That's right."

"But if you leave, do you have anyplace to go?"

"I don't have anyplace in mind at the moment."

"Wherever you go, I think it's dangerous for you to stay in Tokyo. I expect the police will concentrate on searching the city."

Yoko suddenly felt empty and tired. When she had said she didn't know where she might go, it had not occurred to her to leave the city.

"Are you saying I should go back to Shizuoka? Perhaps to my dad's place? You know as well as I do that's the first place the police will look."

"Yes, of course, but I was wondering how it would be if you went to Kannami for a while. My grandparents live there. The police might go and ask questions at my parents' home, but they surely wouldn't think to check at my grandparents' place. Besides, my grandparents never pay any attention to the news; they won't have heard anything about this."

Yoko made no reply to this suggestion, so Fumiyo continued. "You take the Bullet Train to Atami. You know where the tunnel goes through the mountain there? Well, they live just on the other side of the tunnel in a small farming village. It's just north of Amagi. I'm sure you'll be welcome to stay there until we can get all of this straightened out. I've got it all planned for you and I even called my grandfather a little while ago. I told him you need to get away for a while so you can concentrate on writing your graduation thesis. I said you might stop in and stay with them."

Yoko's throat felt constricted; she opened her mouth, but no words came out. Instead, tears of gratitude came to her eyes, streamed down her face, and fell into her lap.

Time and again she looked out the train window into the distance, where she could see the sweep of tall mountains near Kannami.

She was fleeing.

She was a fugitive.

These were the thoughts that occupied her mind.

Fumiyo had said that if she could just lie low for a while, the truth would finally come out. While it was reassuring to think so, the situation was hardly that simple. After all, wouldn't her flight prove that she was guilty? And if she was apprehended empty-handed like this, all her efforts up to now would have been in vain.

Yoko felt dizzy.

She had decided to follow Fumiyo's advice. It was ironic that she was following the same route—the Bullet Train to Atami—that she and Takashi had taken on their way to commit suicide.

At Atami she transferred to a local train that went though the tunnel, and got off at Kannami, the next station. It was early evening on September 17. The mountains pressed in, right to the edges of the platform, and just in front of her she could see the mouth of the tunnel. The station building had a slate roof and was surrounded by a shabby wooden fence along which bloomed yellow canna flowers. It was only about an hour's travel time from Tokyo, but it seemed like a different world.

As she came out of the station, the green mountains towered before her. The station was situated fairly high on the side of the mountain and clustered around it were small houses belonging to commuters, but traveling down the slope a short distance through the fields, one had a wide open, spacious feeling.

Fumiyo had drawn a map showing the way to her grandparents' home. It was a two-story farmhouse sitting all alone at the foot of a slight elevation. Fumiyo's grandparents appeared to be in their sixties, and were pleasant, rather taciturn people. It was actually early in the year for a student to be thinking about a graduation thesis, but that was the pretext they had decided to use, and since Yoko did not want to be seen by people, she spent virtually every day in the small, second-floor room that had been provided for her. She passed the time looking out at the green fields and the mountains behind them.

The one thing she did follow with great interest were reports of the murder at Amagi, which she found in the local newspaper that was delivered at the house and on the transistor radio she had borrowed from Fumiyo. Since the murder had happened nearby, the local media were reporting it in full detail. In the tearoom downstairs was a black-and-white television set, but the hardy old couple spent their days working in the fields, and at night would watch maybe one program, then go to bed. Yoko was relieved that they rarely watched the news.

According to the local newspaper, Midori had gone to the police station near Amagi on the day after the body was discovered and identified her husband's remains. Beside the article was a blurred photograph, presumably taken inside the police station, of Midori dabbing at her pale cheeks with a handkerchief.

It was determined that Takashi Sato had died of a stab wound to the heart made by a hunting knife. Given the point where the knife had entered his back, it was virtually impossible that he had stabbed himself. The body was partially decomposed and it appeared that he had been dead for three or four days. This was verified by the discovery in his pocket of a dated suicide note. A check at the hotel confirmed that he had died on September 13, three days before the body was discovered. An autopsy revealed a small amount of sleeping medication in his stomach.

The police were able to ascertain that on the evening of the thirteenth, Sato, in the company of a woman, with whom he spent a few hours at a hotel in Amagi, set out on foot toward the mountain about ten o'clock. One police theory was that the couple had gone into the mountains intending to commit suicide together. Having first taken a small dose of sleeping medication to make themselves relaxed, the woman had stabbed Sato and then intended to kill herself. But, having failed to do so, she fled the scene. According to another theory, they had at first intended to take an overdose of sleeping medicine, and both of them had swallowed a large quantity, but they had vomited most of it up. (Traces of vomit were still discernible at the site of the murder. Sleeping pills are often prepared in such a way that a lethal dose will induce vomiting.) Having failed with the pills, they had decided to kill themselves with the knife, but at this point the man had changed his mind and wanted to live after all. Feeling betrayed, the woman killed him and then fled.

Yoko's name, address, and university had all been made public by the morning editions of the eighteenth. The media used such statements as, "This woman is an important witness who holds the key to solving this case," but it was clear to anyone who read these articles that she was really being sought as a prime suspect in the case.

The situation was developing more and more in the direction Yoko had feared. Nevertheless, on that fifth day after the murder, Yoko made up her mind to leave the house in Kannami. When she left Tokyo Fumiyo had assured her that she should stay in the country for two weeks or even a month, however long it took until it was safe for her to return, but Yoko felt uneasy about imposing on the old couple for that long, and besides, she was afraid that at some point they might learn the real reason for her being there. That could only lead to unpleasantness for everyone. Besides, the greater the danger became of her going out, the greater became the impulse to do so.

After leaving Kannami, she spent the night in a small, shabby inn at Hakone. She had intended to go directly to Tokyo, but no sooner had she gotten on the train than she had the terrified feeling that everyone in the car was looking at her, so she got off at Hakone instead of going back to Tokyo. She had not seen the Tokyo newspapers or the television reports, but she had a feeling that they had published a picture of her. She felt she had to have some way of diverting people's attention from her. She was wearing sunglasses but had been reluctant to dress as a man in front of Fumiyo's grandparents.

In any case, Yoko felt much more self-assured after spending the night at Hakone. It was impossible, however, to go on being a fugitive in this manner. She had already spent almost all the cash she had with her. The police might pick her up at any moment, and the worst possible thing would be to be arrested while trying to flee. There would be no way she could satisfactorily explain her attempt to flee the law. The only course open to her now was to return to Tokyo, where she would be in maximum jeopardy, and hope that she could discover Takashi's real murderer before she was caught by the police.

When she got on the train from Hakone to Tokyo, Yoko was wearing the gray suit she had brought with her from Tokyo, as well as a wide, red necktie she had bought the previous day. Recently it had been fashionable for women wearing pant suits to also wear a tie. This rather strange attire made Yoko feel a good deal more comfortable. Oddly enough, she found that disguising herself in men's clothing not only made her inconspicuous, it also gave her a curious sense of comfort and reassurance. Perhaps she had an inherent desire to change herself that made her feel better being disguised as a man. Perhaps there is hidden deep within the psyche of all of us a secret desire to change our sex, a desire that we ourselves usually refuse to recognize. Just as this thought came to her, Yoko flipped open the weekly magazine in her lap and was surprised to find there an article about sex-change operations in America with a photograph of a woman who had become a man.

According to the article, the woman had been raised as a girl, had even been married, and was the mother of two children, but she had always been conscious of both male and female urges within her, and when her urge to change sexual roles reached its peak after she had passed the age of thirty, she went to a university hospital in Baltimore to have an operation. The surgeons were able to transform her into a man.

The article described the details of the surgical procedure, but Yoko was most interested in the end of the article, which theorized about those who wish to alter their sex. "Although this desire is evidence of sexual deviance, in recent years, in America and the leading European countries, the number of such operations is increasing. The desire to change one's sex is beginning to be seen as a cultural illness as well as a psychological one. At first the patient is treated with a number of psychological techniques, and if he or she does not respond, then it can be argued that an actual sex change is the only way to restore the patient's emotional stability.

"In Japan this procedure is still in the research stage, but at the Johns Hopkins Medical Center in Baltimore where the operation was first carried out, doctors have formed a sex-change study group composed of specialists in many subspecialties of psychiatry and medicine." A public statement released by this group was included in the article. It said, "If the mind cannot be altered to fit the body, then perhaps we should consider changing the body to fit the mind."

Yoko trembled slightly; without realizing it, she had come face-to-face with her own feelings. At this moment, dressed as a man, she definitely felt a wave of tranquillity and pride that she had never experienced as a woman. This was not due to an abnormal psychological condition; its cause was in the serious traumatic experience she had undergone.

Yoko had maintained a very pragmatic relationship with Takashi, but it had ended in tragedy. When she thought back over what had happened one day at a time, the feelings that rose up within her ranged from pity to something that was vaguely dirty, and ended with a meaningless sense of emptiness. Overall, how much did I really love him? she wondered. Could it be that I really had doubts about loving him and only agreed to die with him so that I could prove to myself that I loved him? If that were the case, then it was not so much her relationship with Sato that was empty and impure, it was she herself. It was this female self she was rejecting now as she transformed herself into a man and a stranger.

Such were the thoughts that came to Yoko as she gazed

out at the drizzle that swirled against the train window like smoke. She was not sure why she had fallen into this reverie.

It was still drizzling when the train arrived in Tokyo. Yoko set out for Aoyama without hesitation. She was suspicious of Midori.

According to old man Sakura's story, Midori had a lover. Yoko supposed that Midori had joined with her lover in increasing the psychological pressure on the already desperate Takashi, and in the end they had finally driven him to commit suicide. And further, wasn't it possible that they had some doubts about whether Sato would be successful in killing himself, and so Midori herself, or perhaps her lover, had tailed them, and when Takashi had started to revive, attacked and killed him? And what other reason might Midori have for wanting Takashi dead? It could be that there was more to it than merely the existence of a lover.

For the time being Yoko decided to use the name Tanaka for this lover of Midori's. She would assume that he was the man who had telephoned Takashi at the Jugon. And what about the man who had slashed her on the hillside near Sato's house, wasn't he also this same Tanaka?

It was two o'clock in the afternoon. Yoko had been on this street in Aoyama many times before, but she was surprised to see it as busy as it was now at midday, with people walking by under their umbrellas and cars going back and forth. She knew that if she was going to wait at the corner of the street where she could keep an eye on Sato's gate, she had best be vigilant.

Concealing her face with a black, man's umbrella she had bought at the station, she walked past the house. She was only able to get a brief glimpse of the place but could see that the front gate was closed and appeared to be locked, just as it had been the other morning. The only thing that was different was that the curtained windows on the second floor had their shutters closed as well. The first-floor windows were hidden by the shrubbery and the garden wall, so she was not able to get a good look at them. From the outside, at least, the house appeared to be deserted.

Yoko resolutely quickened her pace as she walked past the house. Even though she was walking on the opposite side of the street, she did notice one change. The nameplate was missing from the gate. She remembered the brass nameplate very well, but now all that remained on the dark, rain-washed gatepost was the oblong cement fitting where the nameplate had been. No doubt the front door was locked and the first-floor windows were shuttered just as the second-floor ones were.

The moment she noticed the nameplate was missing, Yoko felt an unpleasant feeling in the pit of her stomach caused by an uneasy suspicion that Midori had escaped.

She continued walking along the street and, after passing several more houses, came to the liquor store. A middle-aged housewife was just coming out of the store, and on the spur of the moment Yoko decided to make inquiries.

"Excuse me, I'd like to ask you something."

The woman raised her eyebrows and looked at Yoko questioningly.

"Do you know if Mrs. Sato has moved away?"

"Why, yes, as a matter of fact she has," said the woman, still looking at Yoko with surprise but making no comment on what she saw.

"Do you know when she moved?"

"It was two or three days ago. After that terrible thing happened to her husband they had a private funeral and she moved away right afterward."

"I don't suppose you know where she moved to? You see, I'm a friend of the family."

"I believe she moved to a condominium in Meguro. The people living next door might be able to tell you the exact address of her new place."

"So she moved to a condominium."

"Yes. After all, her husband was dead, and I believe his company had folded. It was taken over by one of the larger companies."

I should have known it, Yoko thought with a sinking feeling.

"I suppose the house will be sold to someone else," said the housewife. "Apparently Mrs. Sato had been thinking for some time of moving into a condominium. Still, it was a terrible thing that happened."

9

A Chance Encounter

THE FLORAL HILLS CONDOMINIUM WAS LOCATED ABOUT five minutes by taxi from Meguro station in the western part of Tokyo. It was a new six-story building with pale pink walls decorated in an arabesque pattern.

Immediately after her husband's funeral, Midori Sato quietly moved into Apartment 102 on the ground floor. Yoko obtained this information by telephoning the people who had lived next door to the Satos in Aoyama.

As evening approached, the drizzle turned to a steady rain, making it darker than usual for that time of day. This, too, was a quiet, residential district, but its appearance was in many respects quite different from Aoyama. Some of the buildings were company dormitories and day-care centers, but mixed in with them were a few tenement buildings with sloping roofs reminiscent of old-fashioned mansions. The pink walls of the modern condominium building seemed out of place here.

There was a spacious parking lot in front of the condominium building, and four or five cars parked there were being soaked by the rain. Yoko loitered under her umbrella in the parking lot in a place where she could see by the fluorescent lights in the lobby both the elevators and the first-floor corridor. She had been hanging around there for some time.

Yoko knew, of course, that it was dangerous for her to be here. Sandwiched between the parked cars as she was, she could easily be spotted either from the street or from within the condominium building itself. It was also quite possible that police detectives were still visiting Midori from time to time in connection with her husband's murder, and for another thing, there was always the chance that she might be attacked for a second time by her unknown assailant.

The likelihood of this, however, was less than in Aoyama. Because there was a parking lot in front of the condominium, and because she was within view of the entrance and the first-floor corridor, there was really no place for an assailant to conceal himself. Opposite the building was a tennis court belonging to some company's dormitory, and there's no place to hide in a tennis court.

So here it was, late in the afternoon on a rainy day, and there was virtually no sign of anyone moving in the building's corridor, nor were there any cars going in or out of the parking lot. Several times Yoko considered leaving, but each time she decided to stay put. During this time she often thought how difficult it would be to carry out her plan, and this gave her an uneasy feeling in the pit of her stomach.

Her suspicions about Midori were strong, but to prove those suspicions she had no choice but to remain in this rather dangerous and exposed position and wait. Still, even on the slim chance that Midori's lover should enter or leave the building, what then? How could she prove that this Tanaka person was the one who killed Takashi?

Just then she thought she saw the door of Apartment 102

opening. Yes. Even though the hall was only dimly lit, she could see the door opening. Her heart beat wildly as she held her breath and watched. Yet even though the door seemed to be moving, it didn't open. It was just an optical illusion, a figment of her imagination. Probably she had just been staring at it for so long that she finally persuaded herself that it was opening. Yoko felt dizzy and suddenly very tired. An icy chill had crept up from the tips of her shoes up throughout her body and she realized she was shivering.

At that moment a heavy hand clasped her left shoulder. This was no figment of her imagination. The hand and fingers grasped her from behind and dug painfully into her shoulder. Her only thought was to escape, but she could not. Her umbrella trapped the man's smell, a mixture of sweat and tobacco.

A cold thrill of terror shot through Yoko, and there flashed through her mind a vision of the headlines: MURDERER CAPTURED. Suddenly, unthinkingly, she turned to attack her assailant. He was a tall man who hadn't used his umbrella, and she could see the drops of rain glittering on the shoulders of his dark brown suit. He looked down at Yoko with strong, clear eyes. It was Osamu Taki, the man who had saved her that night when she was assaulted in Aoyama.

Yoko gasped as she recognized him and was filled with tension and panic. For her, the police were not her only enemy just now, and again the thought came to her that she had to escape. But Taki quickly saw what was in her mind and moved his hand from her shoulder to her arm and held her lightly.

"Excuse me, I was afraid you might try to run away," he said. "What are you doing in a place like this?" There was a direct, almost savage tone in his voice.

"What am I doing here? Nothing really. I just happened to be walking along the street."

"Oh yeah? I happen to know you have been standing here for at least twenty minutes."

When Yoko made no response, he let go of her arm and opened his own umbrella, which he had been carrying folded up in his right hand. "Shall we walk together? It seems you are always hanging around places like this. You should be careful; people might start asking questions. It's no joke," he said, giving her an urgent look as they walked slowly along.

Yoko seemed to have no choice but to go along with Taki and leave the parking lot.

"I immediately thought of you when I read about the murder in the newspapers. After all, the name they gave in the papers was similar to the name Yaeko Onoda, which you gave me, so it could hardly have been a coincidence. The other evening I didn't know the background, but it seems to be a pretty risky thing you did." There was no stress or urgency in his voice as he spoke. It was clear that he already knew something of Yoko's role in the murder of Takashi Sato. Did his calmness come from the fact that he felt confident that he had Yoko well within his control? "Anyone familiar with the circumstances would understand why you had dressed yourself up as a man." Once again he gave Yoko an appraising look. "What I don't understand is this: if things happened the way the police think they did, then why am I always finding you in these risky situations hovering around Mrs. Sato?"

Taki continued to walk and spoke as though he were talking to himself, but there were overtones in what he was saying that raised some very direct questions. Somehow the directness of his voice reminded Yoko of the clear depth of his eyes. Suddenly she, too, felt a sense of release.

"You're right. I did not do what the police think I did."

"Then why are you spying on Mrs. Sato?"

After a short pause Yoko finally put into words all the feelings and suspicions she felt in her heart and concluded by saying, "But I have no hard evidence to prove my innocence."

Taki stopped and turned to her, "Don't you think you could tell me about it? I might be able to help."

"What could you do even if I told you?"

A smile bloomed on Taki's darkly complected face. "I guess I'll never have a chance to believe you if you don't try telling me. But remember, I don't want to hear your story just because I'm curious; I want to help you."

His words struck home.

At that point something else occurred to Yoko. It was something of great importance, but since she had not been sure of her memory, she had submerged it in the back of her mind. "Tell me something, Taki. That night when we first met—when the man who attacked me ran away, you called out a name. Tanaka, wasn't it? Do you know someone named Tanaka?"

This time Taki seemed to withhold a reply. His continued silence strengthened Yoko's beliefs. "I think you do know such a person. Tell me about this Tanaka. Please, it's very important. If you'll tell me who he is, I'll tell you my story."

A little over an hour later the two sat facing each other in a tearoom in the downstairs part of a small business hotel near Meguro station. They had come here in Taki's car, which he had parked some distance away from the Floral Hills condominium.

The tearoom was very quiet because of the rainy weather. The waiters looked at the couple as though they were an intrusion and a nuisance. The lights were dim and it was an ideal place for them to talk privately. The context was reassuring for Yoko and she told Taki everything just as it had happened since the time of her love suicide with Takashi. Even though she was reassured by his presence, her account was naturally told with desperate intensity. She had the same feeling as when she had told Fumiyo Chino her story, a feeling of wanting the other person to believe her, but in the case of a close friend of many years she felt she was entitled to unquestioning support. It was different with Osamu Taki, whom she had only just met after the murder, but he seemed supportive. Still, if he wished to, he could walk out of the hotel, go to the police phone across the street, and report her.

Taki had a look of mild astonishment on his face as he heard about the events that had taken place at Amagi, but when Yoko finished her story, he simply sat with his arms crossed and said, "I see." A look of disappointment appeared on his face. He seemed uncertain about whether or not to believe the strangely moving story he had just heard. Yoko was frightened by the silence that seemed to last forever after she had finished telling her story.

"Taki, now it's your turn to tell me. We made a promise, remember? You seem to have a special interest in Mrs. Sato yourself. It was no accident that I first met you hanging around her house in Aoyama, and then at her condominium in Meguro."

Taki seemed to rouse from his reverie and looked at Yoko. He continued to gaze at her for a time in silence, then replied in a gloomy voice, "This man Tanaka, about whom you have some vague suspicions—well, it's not necessarily the same person, but I expect it is. Anyway, Shuji Tanaka is my sister's husband. He's disappeared and I'm looking for him."

Taki briefly explained the circumstances of Tanaka's disappearance as he had heard it from his sister.

"Just as I was about to make inquiries about my brother-in-law at the Sato house, the killing at Amagi occurred, so I, too, have been trying to find out what connection, if any, there is between the murder and my brother-in-law. Tanaka disappeared on the eleventh, and the murder at Amagi took place on the night of the thirteenth. Now that I have heard your story, it seems probable that he was involved with Midori romantically and with Takashi murderously, and now I think he has hidden himself away somewhere. That's why you heard me call out the name Tanaka, but it makes no difference that he's my brother-in-law, I still have a feeling that something fishy is going on here." Taki made a habitual gesture of stroking his chin with one of his thick fingers. "I have no doubt that Midori is somehow involved in the riddle of Tanaka's disappearance because shortly before he disappeared he was seen leaving the Sato home in Aoyama. I figured the only way to find out the truth of the matter would be to figure out Midori's motives, so after she moved to the condominium, all I could do was try to keep the place under surveillance."

"That's still true; there's not much else we can do but watch the place."

"I guess so. I asked her directly once if she knew Tanaka, but she denied it. If we were characters in a television drama, I'm sure we'd know exactly what to do, but as it is, this is the first time I've ever been involved in something like this."

"I'm going to try to keep watch on the place anyway. No matter what we do, it's liable to involve a certain amount of danger." Yoko bit her lip and looked down as Taki gazed steadily at her. After a moment he shrugged his shoulders slightly, and with a complex look on his face, he took a pack of cigarettes from his jacket pocket and lit one. In the rather extended silence that ensued, Yoko had a feeling that Taki was coming to some conclusion regarding her.

"I will do as much as I can to help you maintain the surveillance," he said quietly, exhaling smoke from his mouth. "It's probably impossible to check out everyone who goes in or out of Apartment 102, but we can follow Midori's movements to some extent. No matter what sort of relationship she has with Tanaka, if there is anything between them at all, she must be meeting him someplace."

"Right."

"But to carry out a thorough investigation will be a very big job indeed. And there's always the danger something might happen as it did the other night." Reminded of the incident by his own statement, Taki gazed at Yoko's left arm. "How's your arm?"

"Thanks to you it's just fine." Through the cloth of her jacket Yoko stroked the spot where the bandage still wrapped her arm. Then she suddenly remembered that today was the eighth day after she had been wounded. The doctor had told her to come back in about a week so he could remove the stitches.

Having explained this, Taki said, "It's probably a good idea not to leave those stitches in there too long. I had a friend who didn't bother having some stitches removed, and it became infected and they had to reopen the wound."

"But that clinic is awfully close to the house where the Satos used to live."

"You're right, it would probably be better to go to a different clinic. Any doctor can take out the stitches." Taki smiled bitterly, but he seemed open and relaxed the whole time they had been sitting there in the tearoom. Was that because he had already made up his mind about Yoko?

He glanced at his watch and said, "Where do you plan to go from here to spend the night?"

A bewildered look appeared on Yoko's face. Since her return to Tokyo, she hadn't had a moment to consider that. One thing she was sure of was that she could not impose on Fumiyo again.

Yoko looked down at her overnight bag and said, "I'm on foot with just what I have here. I guess I can find a suitable hotel."

"Can you afford the expense?"

"I'll worry about that when I run out of money." Suddenly the interior of the Jugon came to mind. Of course she couldn't go back there to work, and it would be very dangerous to do the same sort of work in some other place.

"If you want, you can stay at my apartment. It's right near Asatani station. It's sort of messy, but it would provide you with a certain amount of security."

"Oh?" Yoko looked up in surprise, and when her gaze met his, he looked away.

''What I mean is that I am staying with my sister for the time being.'' Trying to conceal his confusion, he snatched at the check and stood up. ''After all, if you get picked up by the police, I won't be able to keep up a surveillance on Midori by myself.''

When they left the tearoom, Yoko got a ride partway in Taki's car and returned to the neighborhood of the Floral Hills condominium. They had decided that from that day forward they would continue as long as they could to observe the comings and goings at Apartment 102. Sometimes Yoko watched from the shadows of the cars in the parking lot; at other times she would move beneath the trees along the street some distance away, and from time to time she would take a break and go to a coffee shop on Meguro Avenue.

Once she even entered the building and walked as far as the door of the apartment. There was no nameplate, and the thick steel door made it impossible to hear any sound, not even that of a television, coming from within.

Every afternoon Midori went out once, usually between two and four o'clock. She always walked, so it was easy to follow her, but she only went to a nearby shopping district or to the beauty parlor, never to any place where she might be meeting someone secretly. As far as visitors were concerned, three men had stopped by in three days. One was a young man with an attaché case, but he was sent away at the door. When Yoko followed him, he met another man like himself; they turned out to be musical-instrument salesmen.

The second visitor was a large man in a gray suit who stayed about half an hour. Yoko thought he was a detective, because when the door was opened, he reached into his breast pocket and showed a small folder, presumably his badge.

The third visitor arrived on the afternoon of the second day. He wore a white turtleneck and a casual, light tan suit with a matching cap, was slightly stout, and in his midforties. He left after spending more than an hour in the apartment. Yoko tried to follow him, but he went out onto the main street and caught a taxi, and since there were no other taxis in sight, she could do nothing but watch him drive away. Nevertheless, she knew right away that he was not Shuji Tanaka, since Taki had shown her a photograph of him. She decided that this visitor might be someone associated with Sato Metal Industries.

The fourth day . . .

As usual, at around three o'clock Midori came out of the building and down the front steps, and as usual her face seemed just a little too lovely. There was one thing, however, that was different from usual. Up until now Midori had always dressed in dark clothes, whether she was wearing a kimono or Western clothing. Yoko didn't know if this was out of a genuine feeling of mourning for her husband, or whether she simply felt it was the socially appropriate thing to do. Today, for the first time since the murder, she appeared wearing a pale green, Western-style dress.

Today Yoko had borrowed Taki's gray car and had parked in an empty space in the corner of the parking lot. She slid down in the driver's seat when Midori came out of the building.

Taki telephoned Yoko at his apartment at least once a day, in the morning or in the evening, to ask how everything was.

On the first day he had dropped Yoko off at Floral Hills and had returned to his office to finish up some work, but two hours later he had come back to pick her up. He showed her the way to his apartment in Asatani, which was about a thirty-minute drive from Meguro. He explained that the apartment consisted of two small rooms and a kitchen, gave her the key, and left saying he still had some work to do at the office.

At eight o'clock this morning Taki had shown up after an absence of four days and announced that he had to go to Chiba to look at a building site, and since he would be using a company car for the trip, she might as well use his. The previous day she had explained about seeing the man in the tan suit and pointed out that it was hard to find a taxi in this part of town. By lending her his car, he was perhaps acknowledging her as an ally, who shared with him a common, urgent goal. Or perhaps he was becoming used to the idea of harboring a prime suspect in a murder case and had relaxed some of his caution. Whatever the reason, he lent her his car.

Midori held her left hand to her forehead to shade her eyes from the light of the sun while in her right hand she carried a handbag sewn with gold thread. This, too, was different from the previous three days; all the signs suggested that she was going out someplace.

Midori was a large woman, but she had a delicate profile. Yoko watched her slim figure as she walked down the narrow street to the wide avenue and turn the corner. Only then did Yoko start the car's engine. She had gotten a driver's license when she entered college, and for a time had been a member of the automotive club, so she felt comfortable and confident behind the wheel.

As Yoko had supposed, Midori was waiting at a nearby bus stop and hailed a passing taxi. The black and orange cab cruised through the quiet, residential neighborhoods and, avoiding the busy shopping districts, headed up the hill toward Aoyama.

Aha, thought Yoko. Midori's taxi was heading toward her former home. They passed under the elevated freeway and started up the steep, narrow street where Yoko had been assaulted, but at the top of the hill, the taxi turned in the opposite direction from Midori's house. When it finally stopped, it was near the clinic where Yoko had been treated for her wound. There was a traffic circle nearby, so Yoko stopped her car unobtrusively on the far side of it. She watched Midori get out of the taxi, pay the driver, and walk toward a white building. By leaning down on the seat and looking out the window, Yoko could read the lettering on the side of the building; it read, ISHIKAWA GYNECOLOGICAL CLINIC.

Yoko recalled the conversation she had overheard between the nurses at the clinic and how they mentioned that Midori regularly got birth control pills at the Ishikawa Clinic. Was Midori going there for pills today? Certainly now that she was a widow she would not need them to protect herself from becoming pregnant. Apparently she had only come to pick up a prescription, for fifteen minutes later she came out of the building and started walking up Aoyama Boulevard.

She walked along the street for a hundred yards, then crossed at a signal and walked along the sidewalk on the other side. When Yoko saw several empty taxis cruise past and Midori made no sign to hail one of them, she pulled her car over to the side of Aoyama Boulevard and parked on a side street.

Yoko trailed Midori, staying about two hundred feet behind. The slanting sun was bright, but the wind was chilly. The leaves on the plane trees lining the street were already beginning to turn and they rustled coldly in the wind. Soon they came to the large intersection at Harajuku. Without pausing, Midori turned left. On both sides the wide, gently sloping street was thronged with pedestrians, far more people than in Aoyama. The last time Yoko had been here, the street had been quiet, and at its far end she had seen the forest of Gaien Park, which looked like some sort of exotic painting. Now the streets were lined with noisy coffee shops and boutiques, and the area reflected the mood of lively, affluent young people.

Finally Midori went into what appeared to be a drive-in restaurant. The second floor had white walls decorated in a striking pattern of yellow pipes, while the ground floor had been made into a parking area. Midori appeared to be paying attention to no one as she climbed the spiral staircase to the restaurant, which was called Sunrise.

Yoko waited five minutes, then carefully mounted the same

spiral staircase. Again today she was wearing unisex clothing—a beige shirt and black slacks—and of course she was wearing sunglasses.

From halfway up the staircase Yoko could see into the bright, glass-fronted restaurant. She heard the faint sound of mood music and smelled the sweet smell of cream. The restaurant was larger than she had imagined, and was filled with people. Yoko felt the tension mount with each step she took up the stairs. Who was Midori meeting at the top of these stairs? If she were here to meet her lover, the man who had assaulted Yoko in Aoyama, then Yoko would have to spot them and hide herself before they saw her. Even though she was wearing different clothing, she was sure she would be recognized if they saw her.

Yoko stood on the third step from the top and virtually all of the slightly curved interior of the restaurant was visible to her. Midori was sitting at the very first table, at an angle to the door that opened at the top of the stairs. Yoko saw her pale profile clearly outlined against the potted plant in the background. A man sat across the table from her.

The man was looking intently at Midori and saying something. He had a short neck and it looked as though his jaw jutted straight out from the top of his white turtleneck. He had a round, red face, drooping eyelids, and narrow eyes. He wasn't wearing the sporting cap, so Yoko could see his wavy hair and his broad, high forehead, but this was definitely the same man who had visited Midori's apartment two days ago wearing a tan suit.

Evening of the following day . . .

The Western-style painter Teiji Kasai had his studio at the top of Hatsudai Hill just north of the Shibuya district of Tokyo. Taki and Yoko had climbed the hill and were now in the studio. Strictly speaking, they were in a large living room with a sofa set and some other chairs, a room that adjoined the studio itself. Three oil paintings, which they took to be

Kasai's, hung on the walls, and a dozen or so other works-in-progress were on the floor leaning against the walls. One of the paintings was a still life and the others were paintings of nude and clothed women.

The garden had been neglected and was overgrown with pink roses, asters, and dark red peonies, which trembled in the evening breeze. On the opposite wall from the oil paintings was a canvas so large it could almost be called a mural. It was a Japanese-style painting, depicting a number of people in various postures, that at first glance resembled a woodblock print. It had the name Kenzan on it, so apparently it was not one of Kasai's own works.

"Now, what sort of painting is this?" Taki looked at it curiously. "It looks like people putting on makeup."

In the painting a partially dressed person was looking in a mirror, another figure was dipping water from a small wooden bucket beside him, and in the background an indistinct figure with a cape thrown over his shoulders stood before a full-length mirror. As she looked at the painting, Yoko tried to imagine what sort of place was being depicted. "It looks like the dressing room in some sort of theater."

"Um. Maybe it's the old-fashioned Kabuki. All the people putting makeup on their faces have those exaggerated features."

In the oil paintings the women had rich, full bodies and a very feminine air, but the lines of the faces were strong and they had strong features. Clearly Teiji Kasai favored this sort of woman. Although the features of the women could not be identified as belonging to any one individual, they all seemed somehow suggestive of Midori Sato.

Yoko had learned that Teiji Kasai was the man Midori had met at the Sunrise in Harajuku. The two had left together about an hour after Midori had entered the restaurant. They had stood for a time at the foot of the staircase talking and then had gone in separate directions. From her vantage point inside a nearby boutique Yoko got the impression that Kasai had invited Midori to go someplace else, but that she had declined.

Yoko decided to follow the man. He had walked down the hill in the opposite direction from Midori, stopping from time to time to look in some of the antique shops. Presently he crossed the broad avenue and caught a taxi. This time, fortunately, there was an empty taxi right behind it. Since traffic was light and since they were not too far behind the first taxi, Yoko was able to follow him.

The house the man entered after alighting from the taxi was surrounded by neither a fence nor a wall and had a very exposed air about it. It was set in a yard of grass and flowers. Yoko had a feeling that this was the man's home. The lights had gone on shortly after he entered the house, and there was no sign that he might be about to leave. The nameplate by the front door said Teiji Kasai, so if this was his house, that must be the man's name. Apart from that Yoko had no way of knowing what sort of person this man was, but from the looks of the garden and the old, wooden house, she felt there was something distinctly unusual about him.

Yoko ended up spending an hour watching the front of the house, but no one entered or left, and she saw nothing more of the man. She had an impulse to go up to the door and ring the bell so that she might meet the man. Just as she was about to do so, however, she saw a uniformed policeman patrolling the street. He spotted Yoko loitering in the shadows of the shrubbery of the house across from Kasai's, and for a moment it looked as though he was going to question her, but he walked on past.

When the policeman had disappeared in the gathering dusk, Yoko hurried out of the neighborhood, her heart pounding. When she had calmed down after her close brush with the law, she recalled that in exchange for using Taki's car, she had promised to report the results of her surveillance before deciding what to do next.

Late that evening she received a phone call from Taki.

After hearing the name Teiji Kasai from Yoko, Taki came up with the information that he belonged to a conventional and representative group of Western-style painters. Taki himself enjoyed looking at paintings and even did a little oil painting himself, so the mention of Kasai's name immediately rang a bell, and he was quickly able to look it up and confirm that Kasai was a painter.

Kasai, however, was not all that famous an artist. Taki asked a more knowledgeable friend and learned that while Kasai belonged to one of the more powerful factions within his own group, he was not regarded as an outstanding painter. While his paintings of women were acknowledged to have a special sort of charm, he had only a small following. Besides painting, he was also a leader in artistic circles. He was in his midforties and was a graduate of a private art school in Tokyo.

After relating this information to Yoko, Taki said they should visit the man directly, so at four o'clock the couple had set out for Hatsudai with Taki driving. Unlike the previous day, Yoko was wearing women's clothing and regular glasses.

As Yoko approached the house through the garden, it turned out to be much older and more decrepit than it had appeared yesterday, seen from a distance. They went up to the front entrance, which was on a wing off the gabled main part of the house. Taki called out, asking if anyone was at home, and a full-bodied woman wearing slacks, who appeared to be in her forties, answered the door. Apparently she was the painter's wife.

Taki handed her his business card. "I'm sorry to trouble you unexpectedly like this, but I wonder if Mr. Kasai is at home?"

It had been Taki's idea that they should visit unannounced. He thought they would get straighter answers from Kasai if he did not have time to prepare himself.

The wife studied Taki's card for a moment, then looked at

his face. "He's here, but I'm afraid he's working right now," she replied in a deep, candid voice.

"We only want to speak with him for a moment." Taki spoke as though they had come to discuss some business matter.

The woman's gaze turned to Yoko, who bowed slightly.

"Come in, then, but I'm afraid you'll have to wait awhile." The woman led them across the garden to the gabled building and showed them into the living room, where they now waited. Apparently the painter's studio was in another part of this building. The woman returned to the main house and they were left waiting for nearly twenty minutes.

Yoko's gaze kept straying back to the paintings on the wall. The strong features and the mysterious beauty of the women in the paintings were surely derived from Midori. Just as Yoko was thinking this thought yet again, the door opened and the man she had seen yesterday, Teiji Kasai, entered.

10

The Painter

"PLEASE EXCUSE ME FOR KEEPING YOU WAITING." TEIJI Kasai greeted them in a high-pitched, nasal voice. As the two visitors rose quickly to their feet, he waved a hand indicating they should remain seated. He was still wearing the white turtleneck, but today he did not have on the fancy tan suit. Instead he wore a pale red shirt and loose gray slacks. He appeared older than he had on the street, and looked like someone who had devoted himself single-mindedly to painting for many years.

Kasai took a seat across the table from them and looked carefully, first at Taki, then at Yoko, with hooded eyes. He showed no sign of recognition when he looked at Yoko, and she heaved a sigh of relief that he seemed unaware that she had followed him the previous day.

"Now, what is it you wanted to talk to me about?" Kasai held in his fingers the business card that Taki had earlier given to the artist's wife.

119

Taki leaned forward in his seat. "Well, actually, we do want to talk to you, but it's not in connection with your painting. We want to ask you about Mrs. Midori Sato." They could see the look of surprise in his eyes and noticed that his eyelashes began to flutter nervously.

"I apologize for bringing something like this up unexpectedly, but will you be good enough to tell us how long you've known Mrs. Sato?" Taki had come directly to the point in order to force Kasai to give direct answers. Since Yoko had seen Midori and Kasai together twice in the past three days, they thought it possible that the two were lovers. They also hoped he'd be agreeable to their questioning as a way of protecting his modest reputation. They planned to exploit his concern for maintaining his public image.

As expected, Kasai looked at Taki with suspicion, then once again dropped his gaze to the business card he held in his fingers. He seemed afraid, and not likely, as a result, to simply dismiss them.

"I haven't known her for very long. Why do you ask?" He tried to look strong as he posed his counterquestion in a thin, nasal voice that seemed to be natural to him.

Ignoring the artist's question, Taki continued. "Do you know a man named Shuji Tanaka?" Yoko watched the artist's reaction to this question closely. He blinked his eyes rapidly several times and his lips began to tremble. It was hard to read the expression on his face, but he seemed to be thinking.

Finally Kasai said, "What is it you really came here to ask me about?" There was a note of restrained hysteria in his voice. Was it anxiety? Vigilance?

"Actually, we are relatives of this man Shuji Tanaka. He disappeared on the eleventh of September; that means he's been missing for seventeen days."

Kasai's jaw dropped and a look of surprise swept over his face.

"We have learned that Tanaka was seen coming out of Mrs. Sato's house in Aoyama just before he disappeared. We tried asking her about the matter, but she insisted that she had never heard of anyone named Shuji Tanaka.''

Kasai took a deep breath and nodded. Just then his wife entered the room from the garden. She carried a tray loaded with cups of tea. ''I'm afraid this place is filthy. No matter how often I sweep and dust, it just seems to come right back.'' The woman spoke socially as she arranged the tea-cups on the table. Having done this, she withdrew to the side, as though inviting them to resume their earlier conversation. Perhaps it was customary in this household for the wife to be a part of conversations with the guests, but Kasai looked up at her nervously and said, ''I wish you would wait in the house; I'm expecting a call from one of the art galleries.'' He turned his gaze to the main house as he spoke.

''Yes, of course.'' His wife knitted her brows as though she was not pleased with this development but turned to Taki and Yoko, saying, ''Please excuse me,'' and left.

Kasai gestured to them to drink their tea. Taki nodded but continued speaking. ''Mrs. Sato says she doesn't know Shuji Tanaka, but there is definite evidence that Tanaka was seen coming out of her house. That's when we became suspicious that their relationship might be the sort they would not want known.''

Kasai drank his tea in silence.

''We decided to check out Mrs. Sato. Pardon the intrusion, but that's when we learned that you're a familiar friend of hers, and we wondered if perhaps you might know something about Tanaka, so we came here.''

Naturally Taki made no mention of the murder of Takashi Sato. Kasai continued to fidget and kept sipping at his tea until the cup was empty. For a time he just stared at the bottom of his cup, then began to speak with great deliberation. ''As I told you earlier, I don't really know her all that well. Half a year ago a friend of mine was having a one-man show, and I saw her at the show. I asked if she would serve as a model for a painting I was planning to submit to a later competition." Partway through his explanation he paused and looked up at Taki and Yoko. "I prefer to use women with strong, elegant features as models." He turned to look at his own works that were hanging on the walls.

"Did she agree to model for you?"

"No. At first she had to decline because her husband wouldn't allow it, but I have trouble finding people with that sort of looks, so I kept asking her. It turns out she is very much interested in painting, and after I had talked to her several times, she began to want to try it once and see how it felt. It was just at that point that her husband was murdered. I was shocked at the news. But anyway, the competition for which I plan to submit the painting is not until spring, so there's still time."

"I see. It sounds as though you've gotten to know Mrs. Sato pretty well recently. Did you ever hear any mention of this man Shuji Tanaka?"

Once again Yoko watched the artist carefully. Kasai had seemed to relax while he was talking about painting, but now once again complex shadows seemed to darken his face. Painful moments passed before he finally opened his mouth and said, "I may have met him two or three times."

This was hardly a satisfactory response.

"What do you mean, you may have met him?"

"I met a man at her home in Aoyama in early August. He must have been about thirty-six or thirty-seven, but he was introduced to me as Nakayama. Midori only mentioned his name and said nothing more about him when she introduced us. Then about ten days later I happened to run into him on the street there in Aoyama. It was about eight o'clock in the evening. He invited me to a bar for a few drinks. I'm a pretty fair drinker myself, but he could really put the stuff away."

Kasai stared off into space, remembering that night, but somewhere deep in his brown eyes there seemed to be a vague glint of fear.

"Were you just drinking beer, or what?"

"That's right, all we drank was beer."

"And he always used the name Nakayama?"

"Yes. I'm not sure he's the person you are looking for at all. Now that I think about it, we were sitting at the bar and he had taken off his jacket and placed it on the stool next to him. Later he went to the rest room, and while he was gone someone passed by and knocked his jacket to the floor."

When Kasai picked up the jacket to put it back on the stool, he noticed the name Tanaka sewn in the lining. This discrepancy in the names aroused his suspicions.

"But I didn't feel I knew him well enough to ask about something like that, and later we were so busy drinking I forgot about it. In fact, it just now suddenly came back to me when you said that the name of the person you're looking for is Tanaka. Besides, when he was first introduced to me, I noticed that he didn't give me his business card."

"Did Nakayama look anything like this?" Taki asked, taking the photograph of Shuji Tanaka from his pocket. He had shown it to Yoko once; it was a small photograph used for a driver's license application, but the image was clear. The impression one got from the photograph was of a slightly neurotic businessman whose hair was beginning to thin.

"Yes. That's him all right." Kasai nodded without hesitation. Then a puzzled look came to his face and he asked, "You say this man is missing?"

By now it was clear that Taki's brother-in-law, Shuji Tanaka, definitely had some sort of connection with Midori Sato and had been using the false name of Nakayama. At this point Yoko recalled that someone named Tanaka had called the Jugon and asked for Takashi. Since it was hard to believe that two people with the same last name could have such an unusual relationship with the Satos, it was likely that Takashi and Midori both knew Nakayama's real name.

"You say you met Tanaka around the beginning of August and then again about the middle of the month? Did you only see him on those two occasions?'' Taki continued asking questions in a calm voice.

"Yes. That's right . . .''

For some reason Kasai's eyes suddenly widened and his voice trailed off. He sat for a time in silence. Early and mid-August was about a month before Tanaka disappeared; it was during this time that the clerk at the liquor store had seen Tanaka coming from the Sato house.

"What did you and Tanaka talk about when you were at the bar drinking?''

Kasai stood up suddenly and in some confusion walked over to a nearby shelf and found a pack of cigarettes. He lit one and returned to his chair, then took two or three drags before answering. "Since we were drinking, we really didn't talk about anything in particular. At any rate, nothing special sticks in my mind.'' With that he stopped talking. Yet, as he sat there looking at the glowing tip of his cigarette, Yoko had the feeling he was remembering something very clearly indeed.

"So what you are saying is that you really know nothing at all that will help us out as far as the disappearance of Tanaka is concerned.''

Kasai returned Taki's gaze and his eyes seemed to darken. "Are you sure he really disappeared?''

"Yes. He left his office on the evening of the eleventh and no one has seen or heard from him since.''

"I see. Well, I'm afraid I really can't help you with this matter.''

Taki had been watching Kasai closely the whole time, but finally, as though giving up hope, he reached for his cup of cold tea.

"Excuse me . . .'' There were several points Yoko wanted to ask about. She had intended to let Taki ask all the questions, but two or three things remained unanswered. She felt that since she was not related to Tanaka, not even by marriage, she had a different perspective on him. "Do you have any idea how Tanaka and Mrs. Sato got to know each other in the first place? One or the other of them may have mentioned something about it to you.''

For a time Kasai looked steadily at Yoko. Unconsciously she looked away.

''I really don't have an answer to that one,'' he said, stubbing out his cigarette.

''I wonder, though, if you didn't get the impression that Tanaka and Midori were lovers?''

''Well . . .''

''Excuse me for asking this, I know it's impolite, but was your own relationship with Midori limited to asking her to model for you?''

As the words left her mouth Yoko herself was shocked by her suggestion. Yet ever since the conversation had first touched on Midori, she had sensed Kasai's barely concealed panic in the way he had sent his wife away when she came bringing tea, and suddenly the question had sprung unbidden to her lips.

He sucked in his breath and looked at Yoko with astonishment. Once again he began chewing his lip as though frightened. Finally, in a strangely hollow voice, he said, ''Of course even a person such as myself felt some romantic urges in the presence of a beautiful woman like her, but Midori has very strong feelings about her role as a wife.''

Yoko noticed that even as he spoke, there was no joy in his eyes, and yet, oddly, he showed none of the anger one would expect at such a rude question. He turned to look out at the darkening garden, but now, somehow, Yoko could detect no sign of the latent fear she had noticed earlier.

Yoko walked along the noontime streets of Shibuya. When she was in college, it had been her custom once her lectures were finished for the day to come to Shibuya with her classmates to entertain themselves. She had done this mostly in her early days, when the excitement and bustle of life in

Tokyo was still new to her, so the mood of Shibuya evoked strong memories. In the old days she and her classmates would come here chattering happily, trying to decide which movie they would see, or if one of them was going to buy a blouse, they would all go along and give advice, or they might go to an ice-cream parlor and eat sundaes.

Yoko's eyes came to rest on the shop next to one of the ice-cream parlors she had frequented in those days. Back then, some two years ago, the shop had sold nice accessories, but now it had been transformed into a rather pretentious boutique. What attracted Yoko's attention was an array of beautifully colored scarves displayed in the front window. In the lower part of the window were light-colored angora sweaters that matched the scarves.

Yoko had resumed her normal style of dress. She was sick and tired of wearing gray, tailored jackets and matching trousers, and those insipid men's shirts. Not to mention the large sunglasses. Yoko quickly fell in love with the adorable and colorful clothing. She responded more intensely now to articles of clothing she liked and felt an impulsive urge to dress again in a more feminine manner. Almost in a trance Yoko approached the show window. She asked the salesgirl to take out a pink and beige sweater and a matching scarf with a floral design. Removing her sunglasses without hesitation, Yoko approached a nearby full-length mirror, wrapped the scarf around her neck, and tucked it into the V-neck sweater. Once again she saw her own lively face as it had been when she had first come to Tokyo.

''That sweater and scarf look very nice on you. I think that's really you.'' Hearing Taki's voice, Yoko whirled around in surprise and, as she did so, gave an involuntary gasp. The man standing behind her was not Taki, but a stranger. No, he wasn't a complete stranger; he had a low forehead, hooded eyes, and gaunt, hollow cheeks. She had seen his face once before in the photograph Taki had shown her of Shuji Tanaka.

''Yaeko Onoda. Now I see you as you really are.''

He lunged at her, grasping at her shoulder, and Yoko started to run. She fled through narrow back streets and alleys lined with bars and movie theaters. Other pedestrians walked by, paying no attention. All the time she could hear the sound of footsteps pursuing her, gaining on her. Not just one person either; pursuers were closing in on her from all sides. She had thought she was being chased by Tanaka, but at some point her pursuer had become the police.

A whistle sounded immediately behind her. One of the policemen had spotted her and was signaling to his comrades. The sound of the whistle was piercing.

Yoko opened her eyes. Through a gap in the pale blue curtains she could see the red band of the setting sun. The telephone on the desk was ringing.

Sitting up in bed, she reached for the phone, "Hello?" The pleasantly deep voice at the other end was Taki's.

From the background sounds she guessed he was calling from a public phone. "Hello," Yoko answered and slowly began to relax after her terrible nightmare.

"How are you feeling?" Taki asked.

It had been four days since they visited Teiji Kasai. After leaving the artist's house, Taki had taken her to a clinic he knew of to have the stitches removed from her left arm. The wound was healing rapidly and luckily there was no sign of infection, so the stitches had come out sooner than expected. That evening, however, Yoko felt like she was coming down with a cold and began running a fever, so she returned to Taki's apartment and went to bed.

For the next few days, while he was making his rounds of the building sites, Taki occasionally stopped by to bring her fruit or sandwiches. "You've been pushing yourself pretty hard ever since the incident at Amagi," he said gently. "You need to have plenty of rest to regain your strength."

"If Kasai comes up with any leads for us, we'll have to follow them up, but for the time being everything seems quiet." Because of her fever, Yoko had had neither the will nor the energy to maintain the surveillance of Midori's apartment.

"Is your fever getting any better?" Taki asked over the phone.

"Yes. Thanks to you. My temperature has come down since last night. I seem to be all right this morning." With her free hand Yoko reached out and drew aside the curtain. Since the fever had broken, the most important thing had been to get plenty of rest. It appeared, as she looked out the window, to be late afternoon.

"I'm sorry to bother you, but, uh, something has come up."

Even as he spoke these words, Yoko felt slightly embarrassed at the excessive concern Taki was showing for her.

"You see . . ." Here Taki's voice became tense. "Teiji Kasai has disappeared."

"What!"

"Well, it's not just that he disappeared, but two days ago—two days after we visited him—he just left home without telling his wife. Yesterday morning he called her from someplace and told her he would be taking a little trip and that she shouldn't worry, but he didn't tell her where he was calling from or why he was taking a trip or how long he would be away, so his wife couldn't help being worried."

Yoko held her breath as she heard this. She remembered sitting in that room surrounded by oil paintings, remembered seeing a vague look of fear in Kasai's small eyes.

"His wife seems to be a pretty stable person emotionally, not the sort to get upset easily. She said that after we talked to Kasai she noticed he was very much preoccupied with something, and she thinks his disappearance might have something to do with our visit. She got in touch with me before going to the police."

"I suppose she knew how to get hold of you because of the business card you gave her."

"No. Kasai must have taken the card with him because

she couldn't find it. However, she had looked at the card when I first handed it to her and remembered the name of my company and my first name. This morning she called me at my office.''

''I see.''

''So I just got back from meeting her at her home in Hatsudai. She wanted to talk to me about our visit there the other day.''

''Naturally.''

''Of course I gave it to her straight. I said that we were looking for my brother-in-law, Shuji Tanaka, and that since Tanaka and Kasai knew each other, I thought he might have a clue.''

''What about Mrs. Sato?''

''I didn't say anything about her. I thought it might be unpleasant for Mrs. Kasai, and besides, if I brought up the name Sato, it might have led to all sorts of explanations about the killing at Amagi.''

Obviously Taki had been looking out for Yoko's well-being.

''So, does that mean we have no idea where Kasai might have gone?''

''No. Mrs. Kasai thought she might have some ideas about that.'' It turned out that Mrs. Kasai had been a bit worried on the night of September 30 when her husband had gone out and not returned home. She supposed that he had gone drinking with some of his artist friends and having drunk too much had ended up spending the night at one of their houses. This had happened occasionally in the past when he spent the night out. By ten the next morning she still hadn't heard from him and was just about to make a few phone calls to try to locate him when the phone rang. First there was a young lady who spoke in a very businesslike manner and confirmed that she had reached the right number, then Kasai came on the line. He had hung up the phone when his wife tried to ask where he was.

As Mrs. Kasai set the telephone back down on the cluttered table, she noticed among the odds and ends an airline schedule that had been opened to the domestic timetables. When she examined it, she noticed that some numbers had been hastily scribbled beneath the telephone number used to make reservations. This led her to believe that on the previous day when she was out of the house, her husband must have called the airlines and reserved a ticket on one of the domestic flights. With this in mind, she assumed the numbers scribbled on the page were the number of the ticket he had reserved. It was easy enough to check. She simply called her nephew who worked for an airline company, gave him the ticket number, and asked him to find out who had purchased it. She had an answer within an hour. The result was that on September 30 Teizo Sakai, age forty-five, had bought a ticket for the six-o'clock flight from Tokyo to Fukuoka in Kyushu. Airline records confirmed that he had been on that flight.

"Mrs. Kasai spent the night thinking this over, and then called me in the morning. She was probably reluctant to tell all this to me because she hardly knows me, but she did so because she had a pretty good idea that Kasai's action had resulted from our visit, so she wanted to hear from me in detail what our visit had been all about."

"Do you think this is really related to our visit?"

"Uh-huh. I have a feeling it's connected." Taki's voice seemed a bit uncertain, but then he went on firmly, "The name Teizo Sakai resembles Kasai, and the age is close, so I think there's no doubt they are the same person. Since the six-o'clock flight to Fukuoka is nonstop, we can assume that Kasai flew there the day before yesterday."

"That makes sense, but why Fukuoka?"

"This is just a guess, but Shuji Tanaka was also from Fukuoka. He graduated from a private university in Fukuoka City and spent four years working in that region. He didn't come to Tokyo until he was twenty-six. When I talked to my sister, she didn't say much about his Fukuoka years, but since he has that background, I suspect that Kasai's flight to Fukuoka is somehow related to Tanaka.''

"I wonder where in Fukuoka Kasai might have gone?''

"His wife had no recollection of his having family or close friends in the area. She said he took a trip there once a long time ago but really has no idea why he might have gone there now. Now, before coming to Tokyo, Tanaka lived in the eastern part of the city near the seashore. Apparently he worked in a printing shop near his home. But since Tanaka didn't know Kasai while he was in Fukuoka, Kasai will probably be staying in some ordinary hotel.''

"What about the telephone call he made? Were there any clues there?''

"No. He didn't let anything revealing slip out, and there was no telltale background noise. But his wife pointed out that since the call wasn't direct but was handled by a switchboard operator, she assumed he was calling from a hotel.''

"Perhaps I should go to Fukuoka and take a look around,'' Yoko said, expressing the thought that had suddenly come to her. No sooner had she said it than the reality of the situation struck her. Once again she thought of the fear she had seen in Kasai's eyes when they had met four days earlier. It was quite likely that his sudden flight to Fukuoka had some hidden purpose that was both important and dangerous. Judging from his action, there must be some secret answer which could not be found in Tokyo. She also assumed that it was a matter of some urgency and that he did not want to miss his chance to solve the riddle.

"But you've been sick. Do you feel up to it physically?'' Taki asked candidly.

"I'm fine. I've had plenty of rest and I'm okay now.''

"Well, in that case, maybe it would be a good idea for you to go to Fukuoka. If you do find him, it would be killing two birds with one stone.''

"What do you mean?''

"After talking to me, Mrs. Kasai said she was going to request a police search. That's a natural action for her to take. But it means that at some point the police may come to talk to me again. Even if I try to keep you out of it, they'll probably want to know who the woman was who was with me when I visited Kasai."

"I see." This meant it was dangerous for Yoko to be staying at Taki's apartment. She suddenly realized that she had been very careless not to have realized this earlier, and she felt a chill run through her.

"Since Kasai has something of a reputation as an artist, the police may make a more serious search than they would in an ordinary case of missing persons. And because of Mrs. Kasai's story, they'll also be focusing their attention on Fukuoka. So if you stop to think about it, even though you'd leave Tokyo, you'd be placing yourself in an equally dangerous situation by going to Fukuoka."

"No, I don't think so. Besides, if I'm going to leave Tokyo, it makes sense to go to Fukuoka and try to pick up Kasai's track there. Anyway, I can't bear to go on the way I have been; all this has to be resolved somehow."

"I understand. Still, Kasai's move bothers me. Unfortunately, because of my work, there's no way I can get away today or tomorrow."

"That's all right. I'll be in touch with you from there."

Taki arranged a ticket for her on a nonstop flight to Fukuoka leaving at eight o'clock that evening. Yoko and he arranged to meet in a coffee shop at the airport.

They agreed on a simple plan of action for her to follow in Fukuoka and a method for keeping in touch with Taki. Taki saw her off at the departure gate, waved briefly, and turned to walk away. Yoko stood for a moment watching his figure recede, then walked through the passage toward her plane.

11

Fukuoka City

THE AIRPLANE LANDED AT FUKUOKA AIRPORT BEFORE TEN o'clock that evening. A light rain was falling and the air seemed cooler than in Tokyo. Yoko first took an airline bus to the train station. In the warren of narrow streets behind the station she found a modest business hotel and spent the night.

When she checked in at the front desk, she used the name Harumi Kato. Just on the off chance that she might be incredibly lucky, she inquired if they had a guest staying there named Teizo Sakai. She assumed that since Kasai had used a false name to buy an airline ticket, he would use the same false name when registering at a hotel. But the clerk at the desk consulted a list and said they had no guest by that name. She also asked if there was anyone named Kasai staying there, but again the clerk said no.

The bellhop showed her to a single room on the third floor. When she opened the window blinds, she found that she had a view of the adjacent building and a glimpse of the platform for the Bullet Train. Both were washed with rain and looked desolate. Yoko went to the bathroom, washed her hands and rinsed out her mouth, then went back down to the front desk.

In response to her query she learned that within the city of Fukuoka itself there were six hotel chains belonging to the Japan Hotel Federation and that they had between two hundred and four hundred rooms each. In addition to that there were some six hundred and fifty small hotels and traditional inns, as well as a few motels and youth hostels, making a total of nearly seven hundred small hotels. The question was, in which of these many hotels was Kasai staying? Yoko had a sinking feeling as she thought of the job ahead of her.

Yoko walked across the deserted lobby to the pale blue public telephone in the corner. She opened the Fukuoka Yellow Pages to the section on inns and hotels in Fukuoka and the surrounding area. She began with hotels that were part of national chains and started dialing. When the first hotel switchboard operator answered, Yoko asked, "I wonder if you have a guest named Mr. Sakai staying with you?"

"What is his room number, please?"

"I'm afraid I don't know which room he's in."

"What is Mr. Sakai's first name?"

"It is Teizo Sakai."

"One moment please."

After a time the voice came back. "I'm sorry, we don't have a Mr. Sakai registered here."

"I see. Well, perhaps he's already checked out. He should have arrived here a couple of days ago. Would you be good enough to check and see if he was staying with you on the night of the thirtieth?"

"Let me transfer you to the front desk."

The front-desk clerk sounded like a young man, and Yoko asked him the same thing. After some time he reported that no guest by that name had been registered with them on the thirtieth. Yoko then asked if they had had a guest named Teiji Kasai or any name similar to that, but the voice at the other end came back immediately to say that they had no name like that recorded. This time the voice was rather impatient.

Yoko dialed another hotel. This was one of the large hotels, with more than four hundred rooms, but the result was the same. She had accomplished nothing. No, that was not entirely true. After her second call she was convinced that once she learned that Teizo Sakai was not at the hotel and that he had not been there two days ago either, it was unlikely that the clerk would waste any time on her other questions.

She began to wonder if she might get better results going directly to each hotel instead of phoning them. The desk clerks might check more thoroughly if she were standing there watching them. Surely the Fukuoka police would have received a request from Tokyo by now asking them to try and locate Kasai, and there was some danger that she might bump into the police investigators, who would be doing much the same thing she was doing. This danger had to be considered, but at the same time, if she somehow missed Kasai because of a failure in her telephoning system, her trip to Fukuoka would have been for nothing.

Yoko made up her mind to begin making the rounds of the hotels the next morning. As she put away the telephone book, she felt tired all over. Even though she was young and in good health, she had been suffering from a fever until the previous day. All she had eaten was a sandwich in the airport in Tokyo, and she had forgotten all about being hungry.

Yoko returned to her room and used the telephone there to put through a call to Taki's apartment. Up until now Taki had been staying at his sister's house, but now he had decided to return to his own apartment. She had promised to let him know where she was staying in Fukuoka.

Having placed her call, Yoko sat and waited. A few minutes later the phone rang and the operator informed her in a businesslike voice, "I'm afraid your party doesn't answer."

For some reason this statement rang in her ears like a cold chill. Suddenly she felt she needed a drink. She considered going out to one of those underground bars that advertise that they stay open until two A.M. Instead she flopped down on the bed fully dressed and let her mind wander.

The next morning the rain had lifted and it was a beautiful, clear autumn day. Yoko left the hotel at about ten o'clock after having carefully perused a map of the city. This was her first time in Fukuoka. Her taxi shared the broad streets with electric trolley cars. Inside the taxi Yoko felt much better than she had the night before. In Tokyo she had always had to be on guard, but even though the danger was the same here, she felt a great sense of relief at being so far from anyone who knew her. Last night she had finally decided not to go out for a drink, had fallen into a deep sleep instead, and felt greatly refreshed this morning. The sky here was a clear, deep blue of a sort rarely seen in Tokyo. Again this morning she had telephoned Taki's apartment and just being able to talk to him had given her strength.

After jotting down the number of her hotel, he had said, "If you get a lead on Kasai, I hope you won't try to go after him by yourself." With a laugh he continued, "I know it will be hard for you to do nothing, but that would be best. Once you find him, just let him be."

Taki's words seemed to echo in Yoko's heart.

The L Hotel was a large building facing one of the city's main streets that had trolley lines running down the middle of it. Close beside it was the Nakagawa River, which flowed into Hakata Bay a short distance downstream. The surface of the water shone a flat silver under the bright sun.

Yoko approached the deserted-looking front desk. Before doing so, however, she looked around carefully to check for any police types lurking about but saw no sign of them. Since leaving Tokyo, she had been wearing a white shirt with blue stripes and an off-white pant suit. Naturally she did not remove her sunglasses.

"Excuse me," she said to the desk clerk. "I believe you have a Mr. Sakai staying here?"

"Do you know his room number?"

"No, I'm afraid I don't."

"Please wait a moment. The name is Sakai, isn't it?"

The desk clerk's response was very much the same as she had gotten last night when she had called a different hotel. But this time, while Yoko watched, the clerk took more time and searched his list more carefully than they had when she had telephoned. Still, in the end, he had to say there was no such name on his list. At this point she could think of no alternative but to say that the name she was looking for was Sakai, or Kasai, or something like that. If the answer to this last query was no, she would have no choice but to give up on this hotel.

Judging from the clerk's responses to her questions, she had the impression that the police hadn't been here making inquiries about Kasai, but of course she couldn't be sure.

If she were to walk around to each hotel asking like this, what would happen when she finally came to the place where Kasai was staying? Suddenly Yoko came to a halt, for a thought had come to her that she had never considered before. Since she would be calling Kasai from the front desk, he could hardly say he wasn't there. In such a case she would say that she had come to Fukuoka looking for Tanaka and had unexpectedly seen Kasai in the hotel. If she said something like this, it would give her an opportunity to see his response.

Yoko thought this plan over for a while, then left the lobby. She walked along the main street lined with the offices of the prefectural government and soon arrived at a large intersection. Faintly in the distance at the end of the street she could see the green band of mountains lying along the horizon. The sight of them gave Yoko a feeling of jet lag. Even though

Kyushu is in the southern part of Japan, Fukuoka is situated on its northern edge, and perhaps because of the winds that blow in off the sea, the place had a colder, more autumnlike feeling than Tokyo.

Yoko's next stop was the S Hotel, but the result there was the same. This time as she stood at the front desk making inquiries, she noticed a young man who was apparently a traveler looking fondly at her, so she quickly finished asking her questions and hurried outside.

From there she went to the Y Hotel in the southern part of the city. Here, too, her inquiries were fruitless. In this way Yoko spent the whole day at the major hotels throughout the city, trying to get a lead on Kasai but unable to turn up anything. It was shortly past three when she returned to her starting place, the plaza in front of the station. It was still early, but she felt physically and emotionally drained.

Together with the phone calls she had made the previous night, she had checked all ten of the large hotels, the six belonging to the Japan Hotel Federation and four others. Since there were far too many small hotels and traditional inns for her to go to all of them, she had to return to her hotel and telephone as many of them as possible.

Yoko reached this conclusion while sitting in a coffee shop in front of the station drinking café au lait. Having made up her mind, she felt an urge to get up and go to work. The coffee shop was on the first floor of a building that faced the plaza in front of the station, and through the plate-glass window she could see the slow-moving afternoon traffic. Above the dull red stone of the station building the cloudless, blue sky spread out as before. Gazing at the blue sky, Yoko remembered being attacked by a paralyzing giddiness one day as she stood watch in front of Midori's condominium. The trouble with trying to handle this on her own was that she was uncertain of her methods. She was equally uncertain how it all would turn out. Once again a spasm of despair seemed to well up within her. Suddenly the station building, the figures of the people on the platform, and the movement of the cars around the plaza gradually seemed to lose their reality; they all seemed to be mere figures reflected on the glass window. The symptoms of alienation which Yoko had forgotten for a time now returned. But this time the feeling was different than it had been before the events at Amagi. Perhaps this was Yoko's instinctive reaction to the condition of disbelief she had succumbed to.

Yoko turned her confused gaze away from the scene outside and looked into the corridor that led to the entrance of the coffee shop. Vaguely she noticed the elevators and some sort of announcement board. After staring at it for a time, her eyes suddenly focused. She saw a red-lettered announcement of a one-man show by the artist Kenji Suzuki. The lettering beside the announcement mentioned the sponsoring art group, the show's location—the eighth floor of this building—and its duration, for one week beginning September 28.

It was the name Kenji Suzuki that had drawn her attention to the announcement. Suzuki was better known than Kasai among lay people, and this was not the first time Yoko had heard his name. She remembered it now because Taki had said something about him recently. He had told her that Kasai belonged to the same art group as Kenji Suzuki and some others.

Teiji Kasai was supposed to have landed in Fukuoka at about eight o'clock on the evening of September 30. No matter where he went from there, however, he must have passed in front of the station at least once. And even if he hadn't, it was still quite likely that he had noticed the announcements for this show somewhere else. So if he had the slightest bit of free time, he would surely stop in for a look at his friend's exhibit.

Yoko took the elevator to the eighth floor. There in the corridor was another large poster announcing the show. The gallery itself was unexpectedly small and quiet. It was not crowded, but neither did the show look as though it had folded. Thick carpeting silenced her footsteps.

Sitting at the entrance was a young woman in a pink one-piece dress. Yoko decided she would first make some inquiries of this girl, but then she noticed a guest or visitor's book on the long, narrow table. A young man who appeared to be an art student had arrived ahead of Yoko and had just finished signing his name in the book.

Yoko's heart was beating wildly and tension gripped her. Probably not everyone who saw the show bothered to sign the book, but the names of many of the visitors were listed here. Not only did people sign their names, many of them also left messages or comments for the artist and the sponsors of the show.

Standing before the open notebook, Yoko saw that it had traditional, handmade, Japanese paper pages. Both the traditional writing brush and a felt-tip marker were laid out beside the book. Yoko chose the felt-tip pen and first signed the book, using the name Harumi Kato, which could be taken as either male or female. It was the same name by which she had registered at the hotel.

When she looked over at the receptionist, she saw that the girl was laughing and talking to a young man in a blue suit. Yoko turned back about two-thirds of the pages that had been filled with signatures. Since most of the names had been written large, they were easy to read. Suddenly she sucked in her breath and felt a jolt of emotion. On the very first page she looked at was the name Teiji Kasai. Written in his distinctive script with a traditional brush, the characters were strong and square. After the first rush of excitement, Yoko gradually calmed herself. From the very first moment she had seen the sign announcing the show, she had been sure she would find his signature here.

"Excuse me, I would like to ask you something," Yoko said, and the receptionist stopped talking to the young man.

"Can you tell me when Mr. Teiji Kasai came to see the show?" She pointed to his signature in the book.

The girl craned her neck to see the book and at the same time the young man said, "Why, he was here the day before yesterday."

The day before yesterday meant October 1, the day after he left Tokyo.

"Do you happen to know if he's still in Fukuoka?"

"Gee, I really couldn't say," the young man replied, looking somewhat abashed, but there was a smile on his face as he looked once more at Yoko.

"You see, I'm a member of the art group he has formed in Tokyo that is trying to promote his work."

"I see."

"I have some urgent matters to discuss with him, but when I called his home in Tokyo, they said he had come to Kyushu and weren't sure how long he would be here. They thought he intended to be here for some time, so I decided to come and try to find him."

"That's really too bad, but I'm afraid I don't know where you might find him." For a moment the young man looked at her closely.

"Perhaps you might have some idea where he's staying?"

"I'm afraid not."

"You said he was here the day before yesterday; about what time did he come?"

"It was shortly before noon. Mr. Suzuki had just arrived from Tokyo. Apparently they met here quite by accident. It was the first time they had seen each other in a long while."

"Well, perhaps if I could talk to Mr. Suzuki, he could help me."

"No. I'm afraid that's out of the question."

As the young man spoke, Yoko suddenly realized she was standing in front of the guest book, blocking the others who were waiting to sign their names. A group of three girls was standing behind her. The young man motioned for Yoko to follow and stepped into the corridor.

"Mr. Suzuki flew back to Tokyo that same evening. He was scheduled to give public lectures here on the twenty-ninth and the thirtieth. Judging from his conversation with Mr. Kasai, I got the impression that Kasai had other business to attend to while he was here."

"Other business?"

Without realizing it, Yoko repeated the man's words, but he went on, "I'm afraid I don't have any idea what sort of business he had in mind."

At that point the man took out a business card and handed it to Yoko. Printed on it was the name of this gallery and the man's name—Yokoyama. He explained that two days ago when Kenji Suzuki appeared at the gallery, Teiji Kasai had shown up not ten minutes later. He himself had been present at the two artists' unexpected meeting. He knew Kasai by sight and remembered that Kasai said he had come to Fukuoka on other business, but that morning he had chanced to see an announcement for the show and decided to drop in. Suzuki had completed his public lectures the previous day, and since he was free until the evening, when he was flying back to Tokyo, he had invited Kasai out to lunch.

"They were talking about where they might go to eat, and since Fukuoka is famous for a kind of fish stew, I suggested an old-fashioned restaurant that specializes in that dish. That's when the two took off."

"I see. What happened after that?"

"Mr. Suzuki returned about two hours later and said Kasai had an errand to run in Kashii, and that after they had eaten, he had called a cab and taken off."

"What is Kashii?"

"It's a district on the east side of the city near the seashore. It takes about thirty minutes to get there by car."

This was the first time Yoko had come across a definite place name, and somehow it stirred her memory.

* * *

Yokoyama also told her how to get to the restaurant where Suzuki and Kasai had eaten lunch two days ago. He said that Kasai had called a taxi at about two o'clock and set out for Kashii on the eastern side of Fukuoka. The taxi had belonged to the Toyo Taxi Company. Yoko learned this from one of the employees at the restaurant, which was called the Shinoda. The Toyo Taxi Company was within walking distance, but Yoko was too eager to get there, so she took a taxi.

By examining the taxi logs for the day before yesterday, she was able to identify the cab that had been called to the Shinoda at two o'clock as well as the name of the driver and their destination. As she had expected, the destination was only listed as Kashii.

Needless to say, Yoko wanted to know the precise address in Kashii where they had gone. The driver of the car in question was named Ogawa and he was on duty at the moment, not scheduled to go off until three o'clock in the morning. Generally he stopped back at the office around five-thirty for dinner, so Yoko decided to sit in a corner of the dispatcher's office and wait for him.

About an hour later Ogawa came in from the garage; he had been summoned by the man Yoko had talked to earlier. He drew close and looked at Yoko's face as he listened to what she had to say.

She explained that she was here on urgent business for a friend and asked to know precisely where he had taken the fare he had picked up at the Shinoda restaurant the day before yesterday.

"Well, at first he told me he wanted to go somewhere near the Kashii Shrine," Ogawa said, giving Yoko a strange look, but his voice sounded candid.

"The Kashii Shrine?"

"It's a very important historical monument."

"So he said he wanted you to take him to the shrine, but

I expect that once you got close, he directed you to someone's private residence.''

"Why yes, that's exactly what happened. We searched
around for a while, but in the end we couldn't find it, so he
finally got out in front of the shrine."

"Would you be good enough to take me there yourself?"

Ogawa looked surprised at this request and blinked several
times behind his glasses. He had returned to the dispatcher's
office to eat his dinner, but he was willing to postpone his
meal at Yoko's request.

As the taxi drove off, Yoko sat in the backseat and opened
a map of the city. The car crossed the railroad tracks and
headed east. Yoko had done a lot of walking today through
the streets of Fukuoka as she had made her rounds from one
hotel to another, but most of the hotels she had been to were
located in the central part of the city or on the western side
of town. This was the first she had seen of the eastern side
of the city.

They soon drove onto National Highway 3. The highway
runs along the northern coast of Kyushu, but the pale blue
surface of the sea is largely hidden by factories, gas stations,
and small patches of forest. What could be seen of the water
was Genkai Bay. After about fifteen minutes on the highway,
they turned off to the right. Following this new road, they
came to a stone monument that had carved in it the words
THE GRAND SHRINE OF KASHII.

"This road leads up to the shrine," said the driver.

"Is this the route you followed the other day?"

"That's right. He told me very specifically to pass in front
of the Hakozaki Shrine." The driver was referring to a shrine
whose gates they had passed shortly after they came out onto
the National Highway.

On the night of September 30 when Kasai's plane had
landed in Fukuoka, he had probably found lodging for the
night somewhere in the city. The next morning he had telephoned his wife in Tokyo. Before noon he had gone to see

Suzuki's show and accompanied him for lunch at the Shinoda restaurant. At two o'clock he had called a taxi and directed it to Kashii, but on the way he had made a detour to visit an old shrine.

Turning off to the right from the National Highway, the taxi made its way along commercial streets for a time, then crossed into the shrine grounds where the road was lined on both sides by camphor trees. The dying moments of sunlight glittered plainly over the surface of the ocean, but once they entered the tree-lined road, everything seemed much darker. Against the backdrop of the lines of camphor trees, Yoko saw an occasional old-fashioned house.

"What a lonely place," she said impulsively.

"Yes. At night it's pitch-dark in here."

Off to the left they could catch a glimpse of the red-painted shrine hidden deep among the trees.

"Did he say anything about whose house he was looking for that was close to the Kashii Shrine?"

"I asked about that, and he said a name that sounded something like Ikeda or Ikemoto. I can't recall now what exactly it was."

"Where did you search?"

"Well, I guess I don't remember exactly." Even as he spoke he turned the car to the left and came to a stop. "This here is the shrine."

He pointed to a path that led off to the left around a small pond. Yoko had a feeling that the gates to the shrine were being swallowed up as the woods that surrounded them began to fade into the growing darkness. As she turned and looked away from the grove of trees surrounding the shrine, she could see a cluster of houses beside some fields. The driver put the car in gear and started up a road between the grove and the fields. The homes were traditional farmhouses and large estates that almost reeked of history. Mixed in among them were newer houses with red and blue tile roofs.

The car made a slow turn through the neighborhood and

returned to the pond. "This is pretty much what we did the other day, although he got out of the car from time to time to look at the names on some of the gateposts. I finally let him off here and he said he'd continue to search for the house on foot."

The driver seemed perfectly sincere in his willingness to take Yoko wherever she wanted to go.

"He said he was looking for a house belonging to Ikeda or Ikemoto or something like that?"

"As I recall, it was some sort of name like that." The taxi driver did not seem to have much confidence in what he was saying.

Yoko paid the fare, giving him more than was on the meter, and got out of the cab. She had not realized how dark it had gotten. She remembered reading something about the sun setting forty minutes later in Fukuoka than in Tokyo, but the autumn twilight was surely the same in both places.

At first Yoko walked toward the lighter area outlined by the surface of the water on the pond, all the while thinking that she would have to postpone her search until morning. After all, she could only search when it was possible to see.

She assumed that the house Kasai had come to visit was located near the Kashii Shrine and that the family name was Ikeda or Ikemoto or something similar to that. It was probably profitable to make inquiries in the most logical places, and, in fact, Kasai himself may have done this. So, she reasoned, the inhabitants of those houses he had stopped at would surely remember, since it had only happened two days ago. But what if she found a family name within the neighborhood that was similar to the one she sought? She didn't have the courage to go to the police with that information.

There was a park with benches and swings beside the pond in front of the shrine, and Yoko came to a halt as soon as she reached it. No worshipers were near the shrine, but she saw a sign board that seemed to be a map of the shrine compound. As she approached it, she realized that it also listed the names of the families living near the shrine. An outdoor light fully illuminated the surface of the map.

Yoko searched for names like Ikeda or Ikemoto, but without success. Instead she found the name Ikejima. It was the only one on the map that began with the character *Ike*. To get to the Ikejima family home she'd have to backtrack along the National Highway. The road was very deserted at this hour, and as the cab driver had said, it was frightening to travel on it alone at night. However, at the end of the road the lights of the market street still burned. Yoko walked quickly with her head bent over a map of the city. For some time she walked along the tree-shaded roads and streets and, after making several turns and crossings, found herself standing in front of the Ikejima family residence. The map had been accurate, and given its size, it had not been a hard place to find. Indeed, it was a large, old estate buried in dark and gloomy foliage.

12

Words on the Beach

THE ESTATE LOOKED LIKE ONE THAT MIGHT BELONG TO AN old warrior family. On the gatepost in faded black letters was the name Ikejima. On the other gatepost was a large new plaque that said the same thing with the additional words, TRADITIONAL JAPANESE DANCE STUDIO. Of course the house looked like just the sort of place where a teacher of traditional dance would live. And yet the gate was tightly closed, and although a faint light did shine out from behind the high wall, the house seemed to be closed for the night even though it was still early.

Yoko searched for some sort of doorbell but found instead a smaller, private entrance that turned out to be open. Once inside the wall, she found a garden full of dense shrubbery; the faint fragrance of some sort of flower floated on the air. From the gate a line of stepping-stones led to the main entrance of the house. Somewhere in the back of the garden a dog howled.

Yoko approached the house where an old-fashioned wood-slat door was firmly closed. The house seemed as if it had once been very grand but had fallen into ruin, and this impression was enhanced by the neglected state of the garden.

Yoko found a doorbell beside the front door and pressed it. She supposed there was only a fifty-fifty chance that this was actually the house Kasai had visited. The question was whether he had left already or whether he was still there. She thought it most likely that he had already gone. In either case, Yoko was preparing an explanation for her own visit.

After pressing the bell repeatedly, she finally heard the sound of someone approaching the door.

"Who is it?" called a high-pitched woman's voice.

"My name is Onoda. I've come from Tokyo."

"Tokyo?" The voice sounded surprised and suspicious. "What do you want here?"

"Well, you see, it's just that . . ." As Yoko stood stammering, she heard a metallic rumble and the door opened a crack. Confronting her was a spacious, stone-paved entry hall and a forty-year-old woman wearing a crested kimono. A stout woman with narrow eyes and a tight mouth, she exuded an air of upper-class refinement.

"Excuse me, are you the lady of the house?" Yoko asked with a polite bow.

"Yes," the woman said without a trace of smile, and her eyes never wavered as she looked steadily at Yoko.

"I'm afraid I've arrived rather abruptly. My name is Onoda and I'm an associate of Mr. Kasai's in Tokyo."

Mrs. Ikejima listened to her without the slightest flicker of any expression on her face.

"I was just wondering if Mr. Teiji Kasai, the painter, is still here?" Since the woman made no response to this question, Yoko continued, "I understand that he came here the day before yesterday. I need to see him; it's a rather urgent matter."

Suddenly the woman opened her mouth as though to interrupt Yoko. Her thin, downturned lips parted and she spoke in a high-pitched voice. "I don't know what you're talking about, no one by the name of Mr. Kasai has been here." Her curt manner and totally impassive expression made it impossible for Yoko to continue the conversation.

"Oh, I see. In that case I'm terribly sorry to have bothered you." Yoko could do nothing but duck her head in a bow of apology. "I wonder, though, if there's a family in the neighborhood that has the name Ikeda, or Ikemoto, or something like that?"

"I don't know anyone with a name like that." The woman continued to confront Yoko with her curt answers. She seemed to have a dark gleam of triumph in her eyes, and showed no sign of fear.

"I see. Then I'm sorry to have bothered you."

As the lattice door closed, Yoko could hear the sound of the bolt being thrown. This was the woman's way of making sure Yoko went away and didn't bother her further. Once again from the depths of the garden came the mournful sound of a dog howling.

Yoko retraced her steps through the garden to the street. There were no streetlights on this street and she had to make her way by the dim light coming from a shopping arcade at the end of the street. As she walked away, she could still feel the weight of the woman's eyes on her, but when she turned to look back at the house, all she could see was the empty street made dark by the rows of camphor trees that lined it.

Surely that had been the house Teiji Kasai had visited two days ago. Yoko was positive of this despite the woman's denial and despite the warning look in her eyes. Despite everything, Yoko was certain that she was right. The only explanation for the woman's response was that Kasai's visit was secret and they did not want anyone to know about it. This would explain why he had left Tokyo without telling his wife, and without letting her know where he was going or for how long he would be gone. It would also explain why

Mrs. Ikejima had so resolutely driven Yoko away with her categorical denial that Kasai had ever been there. But if all this were true, where had Kasai disappeared to?

It was after eight o'clock by the time Yoko returned to the business hotel where she was staying. As usual the dimly lit lobby was practically deserted, but suddenly Yoko sucked in her breath. As she made her way to the front desk, a man sitting in a chair near the wall reading a newspaper stood up and approached her. For a moment Yoko merely stood and cowered, then she recognized his face.

"Taki, it's you!" she blurted out in a shriek. She was not only surprised, at the same time she felt a stab of loneliness in her heart. He was wearing the same dark brown suit he'd often worn before. "When did you get here?"

"I got in on the seven-o'clock airplane. I've been waiting for about half an hour."

"Sorry to have kept you waiting. Why did you come here so suddenly?"

Taki did not answer right away but took a long look at his watch instead. Then, as though talking to himself, he said, "It's late, but somehow or other we have to do it tonight." Then to Yoko, "Are you tired?"

"Yes, but that's all right. Where are we going?"

"We have a meeting with Kasai."

"We do? You mean you know where he is?"

"Yes."

"Did he call his wife or something?"

"He called all right, but not his wife. He called me directly at my office this afternoon." Taki looked down at Yoko, who stood in blank amazement. Then she returned the key she had just picked up from the front desk and went out with him.

Within minutes a taxi pulled up beside them. First Taki helped Yoko into the cab, then as he folded his own large body into the seat, he told the driver, "Take us to Kashii. Do you know it?"

"Kashii is a large district," the driver grumbled with a heavy Kyushu accent.

"We want the Unahama Hotel."

"I've heard of it. I'll see if I can find it for you." With that the taxi set out past the train station and once again headed east in the direction from which Yoko had just returned.

Yoko's gaze alternated between Taki and the dark streets outside the car. Apparently Taki had not shaved, for Yoko noticed that his jaw was lightly shadowed. She realized that she felt great affection for him. She had been with him just last night at the airport in Tokyo, and she had talked to him on the telephone only this morning, and yet she had been very keenly aware of the distance that separated Tokyo and Fukuoka.

"So, Kasai called you on the telephone?" Once again she sought an explanation.

"Yes. He called my office shortly after one o'clock this afternoon. He asked me flat out whether or not I had located my brother-in-law. When I told him I hadn't, he seemed to pause and think for a time, but it was obvious that that was what he had called to talk about. Then he told me he was in Fukuoka getting ready to depart for a trip to Hong Kong and Southeast Asia and that he would not be returning to Tokyo for some time. He asked if I would come to Fukuoka. When I told him I would come right away, he gave me the name of the inn where he's staying."

"I see. And that's the Unahama Hotel in Kashii?"

"Right. He said he'll be there all day tomorrow, but I thought we should get this taken care of as soon as possible, so I wrapped up my work at the office and headed for the airport."

Yoko then proceeded in a quiet voice to tell him of her activities during the day. She explained that after spending the day going around to hotels she had gone to Kenji Suzuki's show and from there to the Ikejima home in Kashii, and about Mrs. Ikejima's cold rebuff.

"It's the same Kashii neighborhood, so there may be a connection there," Taki said.

There was much less traffic on the highway than there had been earlier in the evening, or perhaps it was just that this was her second trip to the place, but this time they seemed to arrive at the stone monument in front of the Kashii Shrine with surprising speed.

The taxi continued straight ahead for a short distance, then angled off to the left. The street was fairly wide but completely dark. On the left was a grove of trees, and on the right the street was lined with large houses. There were a few streetlights set back among the trees.

"It's just up ahead here," said the driver as Taki showed a troubled look on his face. He bent his large shoulders and peered out the window.

At last Taki said, "There it is. There's their sign."

Sure enough, there ahead of them where he was pointing hung a sign on a telephone pole saying UNAHAMA HOTEL. The streetlight above shone directly on it and the sign had an arrow pointing to the left. Just in front of the telephone pole was a break in the grove of trees and they could see the ocean spreading beyond the grove. This surprised Yoko. Directly below the road was the rocky shore and the waves of the bay lapping gently against it. From this point on, the road turned back inland, but the sandy beach of the bay formed a gentle curve, and the black silhouettes of the pine forest cut across it.

"It's quite close here somewhere, so we might as well get out and search for it on foot," Taki said, and the taxi stopped. When they got out of the car, they could hear the gentle sound of the surf lapping against the shore.

At some point the moon had risen and the surface of the ocean spread out in a bright silver sheet. A promontory or island on the far side of the bay formed a gentle ridge line, and at the base of the U-shaped bay they could see the glittering lights of the city streets. The land sloped away on both sides.

As she walked along the soft, sandy ground, Yoko yielded to a gentle feeling of tranquillity. The moonlight, the faint smell of the sea, and the gentle sound of the waves seemed to soothe and enfold her previously shattered nerves.

Despite her tranquillity, Taki pushed ahead urgently, at last saying, "Here, this is the place."

After seeing the direction indicated by the finger on the sign, Taki pointed into the woods. Even in the depths of the lonely forest the moonlight penetrated.

After walking for some distance, they saw the Unahama Hotel, a rather large, two-story building. It was a brick building with a green slate roof and gold lettering on the front door saying the hotel offered a warm seawater bath. Most of the rooms faced the ocean.

Taki opened the door and went inside. The place seemed deserted. Besides being the off-season, it was already past nine-thirty and the whole inn was silent.

"Anybody here?" Taki called.

When he called out for the third time, there finally came an answering voice from down the corridor. A thin old man appeared wearing a cardigan sweater. "Come in, come in. Welcome." He greeted them warmly.

"I believe you have a guest staying here who is from Tokyo. His name is Sakaguchi." There was a note of urgency in Taki's voice as he spoke. Yoko had already learned from him that Kasai had registered at the inn using the name Sakaguchi.

"Yes."

"Please tell him that Taki from Tokyo is here."

"Taki is it? I'll tell him, please wait a moment." The old man disappeared down the corridor. He was back within five minutes. "He's not in his room just now. He was here earlier, though, so he may be out for a walk. Would you care to

wait?'' He indicated the chairs and sofa in the lobby. Taki
smoked a cigarette, then waited another five minutes before
he began looking at his watch with an irritated expression.
It was nearly ten o'clock. Perhaps Kasai had gone out and
come back directly to his room without using the front entrance. Since the temperature in Fukuoka is not that much
different than in Tokyo, an October night on the seashore
could be quite chilly. Yoko herself had just begun to wonder
about these things when the old man, who seemed to be the
owner of the place, came along the corridor talking to one
of the maids.

"Mr. Sakaguchi had a guest earlier in the evening. Perhaps they went out for a walk along the beach." Having said
this, the old man went to the shoe box in the entry hall. "Yes.
He must have gone out directly from his room because his
shoes are still here. He should be back shortly."

"I assume he could come and go directly from his room
without using the lobby?"

"Yes. His room is on the first floor and opens right out
onto the beach."

"You said he had a guest earlier." This time Taki spoke
to the maid.

"Yes. I noticed he had a guest when I went in to clear
away the dinner dishes." The maid was a round-faced girl
of about twenty who spoke openly and frankly.

"What time was that?"

"It must have been about eight o'clock."

"There was only one visitor?"

"Yes. A man."

"What sort of person was he?" As Taki questioned the
girl, Yoko kept her eyes on the man who owned the place,
but he merely listened impassively to the other two. It seemed
likely that the guest had not come in through the front door
but had gone directly to Kasai's room.

"When I went into the room, Mr. Sakaguchi's guest was

standing on the veranda, so I only got a glimpse of his profile," the girl said defensively.

"Nevertheless, how old would you say he was?"

"Thirty or forty maybe."

"Was he tall, short, what?"

"Well, I don't think he was all that tall."

"You say he was a man. Was he wearing a suit?"

"Yes. It looked like a blue-checked suit."

Even Yoko noticed that Taki swallowed hard when he heard this. From the woman's description of the suit, it sounded like the same man who had attacked Yoko. Certainly it was the same sort of suit Taki's brother-in-law, Shuji Tanaka, had been wearing when he was last seen.

Taki stood up from the sofa and said, "Our business with Mr. Sakaguchi is really quite urgent. Will you be kind enough to show me to his room to see if he has returned yet?"

"Yes, of course. This way, please." The owner was quite willing to guide them to Kasai's room.

The inn had a deserted air about it. The flimsy wooden floor of the hallway was lined with a narrow strip of red carpet, but on their way to Kasai's room, they met no other guests and no maids. They followed the owner down a sloping corridor and around a corner. He knocked on the door in front of them. "Mr. Sakaguchi? There are guests here to see you."

There was no response. The owner cocked his head in consternation, then with obvious reluctance, turned the doorknob. As he opened the door, he called out again, "Excuse me."

Yoko and Taki pressed into the room behind the owner. There were two rooms, with a veranda along the outside edge of both rooms. The glass doors opening onto the veranda were closed, but not locked. Stretching away from beneath the veranda were a variety of beach grasses, but there was virtually no shrubbery, and the sandy ground swept down directly to the beach.

In the corner of the bedroom was an overnight bag and a canvas shoulder bag that Kasai apparently used to carry his painting equipment. The owner slid open the glass doors leading onto the veranda. "I don't see any sandals out here, so he's probably still out walking on the beach."

"In that case, we'll go out and look for him," Taki said to the owner, and taking Yoko with him, returned down the corridor with long hurried strides.

As they rounded the corner of the building and headed for the seashore, they found that the wind was colder than they had imagined. The path along the beach was indistinct and waves were breaking on the shore nearby. Having crossed in front of the inn, they once again found themselves hemmed in by the pine forest on one side and the seashore on the other. There were no other homes or buildings near the Unahama Hotel, and no outdoor lights, only the moon to dimly light their way. The gently curving pine trunks seemed to float up whitely in the moonlight.

There was no sign of anyone around and no sound save the whispering of the waves. The beach was littered with a carpet of broken seashells, so it was impossible to make out any footprints. It was certainly not warm enough to be taking long walks on the beach. And yet, where else would Kasai have gone wearing a pair of garden sandals from the hotel rather than his regular shoes? It was not likely there were any coffee shops or drinking places in such a deserted area. Taki, who was walking in front, seemed to be in a hurry. Ever since Yoko had found him waiting for her at the hotel, he had seemed restlessly driven by some sort of urgency.

After looking along the beach in front of them to make sure there was no sign of anyone, Taki turned and headed into the forest. They had to be careful to avoid stumbling over pine roots hidden in the tall grass. Yoko began to lag behind.

Suddenly she saw Taki freeze. He stared intently for a time, then dashed toward a thick tree off to the right. Yoko heard the sound of voices muttering. She suddenly had a premonition and began running forward. Her eyes grew wide when she saw a man on his knees in front of the broad, slanting tree trunk, and Taki holding this man in his arms from behind.

"Kasai! What have you done! Kasai, listen, it's me, Taki." Kasai was sobbing for breath, the upper half of his body slumped against the tree. Both hands were pressed tightly against the side of his chest. He was struggling desperately to rise to his feet. "Kasai! Just stay still. Don't try to move. I'll call an ambulance."

Whether or not he heard these words, Kasai stopped trying to move. For a moment he even seemed to breathe easier. Then with eerie slowness he began to speak in a whisper, "Makino . . . Makino at the Yamate Clinic."

"What? What are you saying?"

"Makino . . ." His voice sounded less like an appeal to Taki than like a person speaking in a dream just before becoming conscious.

Taki supported Kasai on both sides and tried to hear what the man was saying, but Kasai's voice suddenly broke off as he struggled to breathe.

"Kasai . . ." There was no longer any sound of breathing from the injured man. He pressed his cheek against the cold trunk of the tree and stared out at the sea with glazed, unseeing eyes.

13

The Past

"HE NEVER REGAINED CONSCIOUSNESS; HE WAS ALREADY dead by the time the ambulance arrived." Taki sat slumped with exhaustion in an armchair, smoking as he talked. "He was stabbed in the left side of the back with a hunting knife. All we know is that he was stabbed, but judging from the position of the wound, it would be hard to suppose that he stabbed himself. It looks more as though he was walking along beside someone and that person suddenly pulled a knife and killed him. It looks as though the assailant was somewhat taller than Kasai, so the police are assuming that the killer was at least five foot four."

Yoko was sitting in a nearby chair listening attentively. It was already nearly three in the morning, and even in this hotel near the train station, everything was quiet. All that could be heard was the occasional sound of a passing car outside the dark windows.

"They must have questioned you very carefully." Yoko

looked steadily at Taki, who had stopped talking and was rubbing his face with the palms of his hands.

"Yes," he said with a bitter smile. "After all, I was the one who discovered the victim and I was the one who knew that Kasai was registered at the hotel under a false name. I also told the police how to get in touch with his wife."

Taki said that he had explained to the police that he was searching for his brother-in-law. Since Tanaka was acquainted with Kasai, Taki had visited Kasai's home in Tokyo some days earlier. Yesterday he had asked Mrs. Kasai where her husband had gone, then at one o'clock this afternoon Kasai had called Taki's office saying he wanted to talk about something and had given him the address of the inn where he was staying in Fukuoka. When he came to see what Kasai wanted, Taki found him on the beach breathing his last. He made no reference to the earlier Sato killing, nor did he mention that Kasai may have gone to the Ikejima home in Kashii the previous day and that Kasai had murmured "Makino at the Yamate Clinic" just before he died.

"There is no actual proof that Kasai went to the Ikejima home, and besides, the police will talk to Mr. Suzuki and the others at the art exhibit as they try to trace Kasai's movements, and they can draw their own conclusions."

Taki did not explain why he didn't mention the Yamate Clinic to the police. Perhaps he had his own reasons.

"Did the police ask anything about me?"

"No. Apparently they haven't gotten around to linking you with this. But the old man at the Unahama Hotel had a good look at you, and must have mentioned something about you to the police because they asked me who you were. I told them I didn't know your name. I said only that I'd met you by chance while searching for the Unahama Hotel, and that you happened to accompany me there. I told them you had given me some story about knowing Kasai in Tokyo, but that after we had discovered his bloody body on the beach, I ran back to the inn to call an ambulance, and you just disappeared.''

There had not been much time once they had found Kasai, but Taki had told the incredulous Yoko that she had better take off before he went to get help. This was clearly a case of murder, and needless to say, if Yoko was known to have been one of the first on the scene of the crime, she would come in for some tough police questioning.

By that time Yoko felt completely drained, but she did as she was told and fled along the beach, eventually making her way to the highway where she flagged down a taxi and returned to her hotel. By the time she got back she lacked the strength to remove her clothes but merely fell on the bed just as she was. She didn't sleep but just lay there for some hours gazing half consciously at the dim ceiling.

When the phone call finally came from Taki, she looked at her watch and saw that it was past two o'clock. He said he was calling from the Station Hotel, and that once the police had arrived at the scene he had explained what had happened. Then, after the police had searched the scene of the crime, he had been taken to the East Fukuoka Police Station where he had been questioned in detail and had been made to go over everything once again from the very beginning. When at last they released him, he had said that the only thing he wanted was a place to rest, so they allowed him to use the police telephone to call the Station Hotel. He had almost called Yoko's hotel to get a room there, but stopped himself just in the nick of time. He had been afraid that if he went to the same hotel, the police investigation might somehow stumble across Yoko.

As soon as he was settled in his room, he had called Yoko. Then, after waiting for an hour to make sure the police were not watching him, he hurried through the five-minute walk to her hotel.

''I doubt if the police will accept all my story at face value, but you ought to be all right at least for the time being, since right now their attention is focused on searching the scene of the crime and on checking out people who have some connection with Kasai. Even if they do draw you into this investigation, they won't start looking for you tonight.''

Taki took a small flask of whiskey, which he had apparently bought on his way to the hotel, from his pocket. Yoko got a couple of glasses, wiped them out with a Kleenex, and Taki poured the amber liquid into them. Handing one glass to Yoko, he drank his own with obvious relish.

Yoko sipped some of her drink. Even indoors, she felt chilled to her very bones, and it felt good when the whiskey spread its warmth through her body.

''So the killer was the man who visited Kasai before we got there.''

''Uh-huh. The police were asking the staff at the Unahama Hotel about that man. In fact the maid at the hotel got a glimpse of him, so that should be some help. If she hadn't seen him, they might have doubted my story.'' Perhaps Taki was relaxing under the influence of the whiskey, for he let out a short chuckle for the first time since all of this had begun.

''So the only one who saw the visitor at all was the maid.''

''Uh-huh. But the maid was positive she saw him. She didn't see anyone when she took Kasai's dinner in to him shortly before seven o'clock, but at eight o'clock when she went in to clear the dishes away, Kasai was sitting with his back to the bedroom and the other man was standing on the veranda looking out at the ocean, so there's a strong possibility that the two men later went out for a walk on the beach.''

''If the killer came to his room directly from the garden without going through the front entrance of the hotel, then he must have telephoned beforehand to find out which room Kasai was staying in.''

''That point is not clear. According to the people at the inn, Kasai just arrived one evening without a reservation.

Tonight, or rather, last night, the night he was killed, was his third night at the inn. In other words, he left Tokyo on the thirtieth and spent that night in some other place, and on the afternoon of the first visited that house in Kashii and afterward came to the nearby Unahama Hotel for a room. He told them he planned to stay for three or four days. They said he never went out while he was there but spent all his time on the beach sketching. He never received any telephone calls from the outside. They did say he made two phone calls to Tokyo, but they didn't keep a record of the numbers he called. The owner of the place remembers placing the Tokyo calls for him.''

"Perhaps the phone call he made to you was from the hotel.''

"I expect so. The other call may have been to his wife or to some other place—the police'll be checking that out by talking to his wife and to the telephone company—but we don't have any way to find out that information.'' Taki re filled his empty glass. "But when you stop to think about it, an ordinary visitor wouldn't call Kasai and ask which room he was staying in. It's far more likely that it happened the other way about; that Kasai called the person and told him.''

"In that case, the killer must be a Tokyo person.''

"We can't be positive of that. We know he made two calls through the switchboard, but there's a public pay phone in the lobby, so he could have called anyone in Fukuoka, and if he had enough coins, he could have called anyone anywhere.''

For a while both of them remained silent and Yoko sipped at her drink. Then she said, "When we put together everything we know about this man, all we have is that he's in his thirties or forties, is five-foot-four, and that he was wearing a blue-checkered suit.''

"Um,'' Taki muttered with a nod while his eyebrows came together in a nervous frown.

Meanwhile, Yoko continued to think out loud. "The man

we want may well be the same man who attacked me that night in Aoyama. That man was also about the same age, and also wore a checked suit.''

''Um. Naturally we have to consider that possibility.'' He stopped suddenly, then resumed. ''It's also possible that the man we are looking for is my brother-in-law, Shuji Tanaka.'' Taki himself boldly raised this possibility. ''However, we don't know enough at this point to come to any conclusions. I imagine the most useful thing we can do now is try to figure out why Kasai came to Fukuoka in the first place, and what it was he wanted to tell me.''

''Yes.''

''But I have a feeling that it wasn't Tanaka he was trying to track down.''

''You do?''

''I think he was trying to track down something in Tanaka's past. It occurred to me that perhaps Tanaka himself had said something to Kasai, and when he heard that Tanaka was missing, Kasai thought he had some sort of clue that would lead to him. In other words, I think Kasai discovered a clue that is somehow linked to Tanaka's past. You remember when we visited Kasai at his studio he told us he had met this person we assume was Tanaka maybe two or three times. But when we asked about this in more detail, he said that he had only met Tanaka once at the Sato home and that he had merely been introduced. Then he said that maybe two days later they had met by chance and that Tanaka had invited him for a drink, and that they had talked, but that their conversation had been so insignificant he couldn't remember any of it. In other words, he said he had only met Tanaka twice. But at the time something just didn't ring true in what Kasai was saying. My guess is that he met Tanaka on at least one other occasion and learned something very important from him.''

Yoko sat with her mouth closed, looking as though she, too, were ransacking her memory for a clue to the puzzle.

She tried to recall the expression on Kasai's face as he told them all this. She remembered that she had noticed what she thought was a flicker of fear in his eyes.

"Later Kasai came to Fukuoka and found something here. He decided to tell me about it because I'm Tanaka's brother-in-law and I'm looking for him. That's why he called me, don't you think? When Tanaka lived here before going to Tokyo, he lived in the eastern part of the city, in Kashii. I learned that much from my sister before leaving Tokyo."

"Well, now . . ."

"Kasai probably found out something about Tanaka's life here in Fukuoka that has some bearing on his disappearance. He decided to tell me just as a kindness to Tanaka's concerned relatives, but at the same time he must have had some inkling that this information would put him in jeopardy. Whatever he was going to reveal probably linked Tanaka somehow with something improper. After all, Kasai found it prudent to use a false name for buying his airline ticket and registering at the inn, and he had also made plans to leave the country for a while. All of this suggests that he had some idea that he was in danger."

Taki's words made sense to Yoko. "Finally, just before Kasai died, you say he mumbled the words, 'Makino at the Yamate Clinic.' Surely that must be the name of the person who stabbed him."

"A person's dying words are often supposedly the name of the person who killed them, but somehow that's not the impression I got from Kasai's. I think he was referring to someone who was more indirectly involved."

"Yes. That's the feeling I had, too."

Once they carefully analyzed their impressions and memories, they decided that this "Makino" was the person foremost in Kasai's mind as he was losing consciousness on the verge of death.

"What does it mean, 'Makino at the Yamate Clinic'? And besides that, who did Kasai come to Fukuoka to see, and what did he know? There are lots of things I'd like to hear from his lips that are gone now forever. I do believe, though, that all of this is somehow related to my brother-in-law's whereabouts, and to the identity of the person who killed Kasai. Perhaps it's even related to the killing at Amagi.'' Taki spoke in a surprisingly deep and impassioned voice; maybe it was just the effect of the liquor he had drunk.

"I expect that Kasai really did visit the Ikejima house.''

"Still, there's no way we can be sure. It'll be a different matter if the police find some evidence and follow it up, but no matter how often we try to confront Mrs. Ikejima with our suspicions, the results will be the same as you had yesterday.''

Yoko made no reply.

"In any case, Kasai knew some important information about Tanaka's past, so we have to think of some way to pursue the matter from this angle.''

Yoko nodded slowly. Although the whiskey temporarily revived her, her mind was still thick and slow-witted. Seeing her stifle an unconscious yawn, Taki stood up with a bitter smile on his face.

"Well, I think it's time we got some rest tonight. I'm a little bit out of it myself.'' He moved sluggishly to Yoko and grasped her shoulders firmly. For a moment he stood gazing at her. "We'll decide what to do tomorrow, or rather today, after we've had some sleep. I'll give you a wake-up call in the morning from my hotel.''

When she looked at the window toward which he was pointing, she saw that dawn was already beginning to break and glimpsed the upper stories of what must be the Station Hotel.

It was two-thirty in the afternoon of that same day.

Osamu Taki was sitting in the simple reception room of the Saiko Printing Company in the city of Fukuoka. Across from him was the manager, Mr. Yasuda. This was the company that had employed Tanaka before he left for Tokyo.

"I had two more years of seniority in this job than Tanaka did, but we were pretty good friends and we worked here together for three years." Yasuda's thick hair was combed straight back and he had a habit of running his hands through it. He spoke in a rich, resonant voice. He had a bit of gray at the temples, but he had a round, ruddy face, and the air of a well-established businessman from a rural city.

"My sister tells me you did a lot of favors for Tanaka while he was working here." Taki was willing to be lavish in his compliments, although he didn't know whether Yasuda had ever done anything for Tanaka or not. It was just that after he had received the phone call from Kasai and before leaving for Fukuoka, he had stopped at his sister's house and asked about any acquaintances Tanaka might have had in Fukuoka. She had given him Yasuda's name.

"Well, we helped each other out. It was a mutual thing. We were about the same age and seemed to get along well, and went out drinking together a lot. I never saw him again after he went off to Tokyo. How's he doing?" Yasuda looked down at the gift Taki had brought from Tokyo and there seemed to be a note of sadness in his voice.

"Well, actually, it was my brother-in-law I came here to talk to you about." Taki again sounded tense. From the print shop beyond the window came the ceaseless sound of the printing presses. Very briefly Taki recounted the circumstances of Tanaka's disappearance. Already more than twenty days had passed, but there had been no message from him. The reasons for his disappearance were not entirely clear, but they didn't seem to have any connection with his present job. He was speculating that it was some sort of personal problem, and that it might somehow be related to the years he had spent in Fukuoka. So, Taki concluded, he wanted to learn something about Tanaka's life while he had lived in Fukuoka.

Yasuda's eyes hardened as he listened.

"That's the situation, Mr. Yasuda, and I thought there just might be a chance that he'd been in touch with you, so I thought I'd better ask."

"No," Yasuda said curtly with a sharp shake of his head.

"You mean you two haven't been in touch at all over the years?"

Yasuda didn't look as though he were trying to hide something.

"Then maybe you can give me the names of some of the other people Tanaka was close to in those days."

"Well, let's see. Here at the shop I was probably the closest friend he had. You know he was always a very quiet person. It didn't bother me, but he didn't make friends readily, and he never really stood out very much here at the shop. He didn't seem to be cut out for this sort of work, either." With this last comment Yasuda gave a sardonic smile.

"Did he ever have any personal relationships with women, or anything like that?" Taki was recalling that his sister had mentioned another woman in her husband's life.

"Well, yes. There was something like that." Yasuda had a puzzled look on his face as he answered. When Taki returned his gaze without wavering, he said, "Hadn't you heard about that little affair?"

"Only vaguely."

Yasuda pulled a pack of cigarettes from his pocket as he recalled the past. He took his time fumbling a cigarette from the pack, and even after he had lit up, he kept his eyes fixed on the far wall.

Finally Taki broke the silence with an earnest plea. "If you know anything about this matter, please tell me about it in as much detail as you possibly can."

Knocking the ash from his cigarette, Yasuda finally gave a faint nod of assent. "If you're from Tokyo, you probably don't remember anything about that affair."

Taki grew increasingly tense as the story spilled from Yasuda's lips. "It must have been ten years ago now. Tanaka was engaged to be married. I suppose he must have been in his midtwenties at the time. She was quite an attractive girl who was trained to do dressmaking and design clothes. Tanaka was living in a boardinghouse, but the girl lived with her family nearby and it happened that she came into the shop here once to have some publicity brochures printed. That's how Tanaka first got to know her, and after that one thing just led to another."

"I see."

"But then a very nasty business happened at the home of the girl's elder sister, who was already married. Unfortunately the girl was killed."

"Killed? You say all this happened ten years ago?"

"Yes," Yasuda said, taking a long, thoughtful drag on his cigarette.

"Tell me about this 'nasty business.' What exactly happened?"

"Apparently the elder sister's husband was indifferent to his wife, and there was some trouble over that. Tanaka's girl was apparently very close to her sister."

"And Tanaka's girl, what did you say her name was?"

"I seem to recall that her name was Noriko. Yes, that's it, Noriko Yuki."

"Go on. You were saying that Noriko's sister and her husband were having some trouble. Do you mean that the husband was keeping another woman or something like that?"

"No. If there had been another woman, perhaps things would have worked out all right in the end. All of this, you understand, is just what I learned about the matter later, but it seems that the husband's friend was another man."

"Oh. He was gay."

Again Yasuda smiled bleakly. "The older sister's husband had something of a reputation as a performer of traditional Japanese dance. He had some disciples he was teaching in the Kashii district and it seems he developed a peculiar sort of relationship with one of those young men. That meant that the elder sister was a wife in name only, and after much anguish her younger sister, Noriko, urged her to return to her parents' home and break off the marriage.

"Noriko was a willful sort of person and she felt very strongly about her sister's situation. She was indignant about the whole matter and was determined to have it out with her brother-in-law, so she went to the house in Kashii. What happened after that was just fate, I guess. It turned out that the brother-in-law was out and the young man who was the source of all the trouble was in the dance studio alone."

"I see."

"There was an argument. He and Noriko quarreled, one of them picked up a letter opener from the dance teacher's desk, and it ended with Noriko being stabbed. By the time the maid decided something was wrong and went to investigate, she found Noriko collapsed on the floor in a sea of blood, and the young man had fled. So that's what happened. Eventually the family closed the dance studio and a short time later the dance teacher fell ill and died. Apparently his wife faced all sorts of difficulties after that. She chose not to return to her parents' home, and the house in Kashii fell into disrepair. Recently people have stopped talking about the tragedy, and one of the disciples from that time came back to take over the studio. I understand they're beginning to flourish a bit now."

"The family's name in Kashii where all this took place is Ikejima, isn't it?"

"Yes. That's right. You know about it, then?"

"No. Not really. I just remember hearing some rumors about it at the time."

Having learned this about the dance teacher, Taki felt it was unnecessary to ask any more. Clearly Kasai had unraveled Tanaka's past and had called at the Ikejima home. He had no way of knowing, of course, how Mrs. Ikejima had responded to his inquiry, but two days later Yoko, following

Kasai's trail, had also shown up at the house asking questions. Mrs. Ikejima's denial that Kasai had visited the house suggested that she was turning her back on an unpleasant incident that had already begun to fade into her past.

"What about the fellow who killed Noriko, was he ever caught?"

"No. He fled the house one step ahead of the police and has managed to elude them ever since." Yasuda glanced over at the printing shop, then looked back at Taki and continued, "His name was Jiro Miki. He was about the same age as Tanaka at the time, maybe twenty-six or twenty-seven. He was originally from Tokyo. He was an only child, and after his father died they moved back to Fukuoka, which had been his mother's home."

"How did they make their living?"

"His mother had a job in hospital administration, and the boy himself played the piano in a bar, produced shows for nightclubs, and competed on game shows on television and that sort of thing. They did all sorts of things like that and managed to make a living."

"I see."

"He was always hustling and never held a steady job in a company, but afterward his mother tried to protect him and never gave any clues about what might have happened to him. She burned every photograph she had of him and did everything else she could to hinder the police investigation. I heard a rumor that he might have fled to Tokyo."

"Does Jiro Miki's mother still live here in town?"

"No. As you might expect, she found it difficult to remain here and I heard that she had returned to Tokyo."

"Yes. Of course. So it was after this incident that Tanaka quit working in your shop and went to Tokyo?"

"As I recall it was in the autumn about six months later. From the very beginning, though, he had never seemed very satisfied with his work here, and he was always talking about taking off and going to Tokyo. Once this tragic event occurred, it seemed to make up his mind for him. I expect it was also difficult for him because he lived close to where his fiancée had died so pointlessly. But now you say Tanaka has disappeared. I wonder why?'' Yasuda's mind seemed to have returned to the present, and he looked steadily at Taki.

It seemed likely that in the autumn ten years ago when Tanaka had set out alone for Tokyo, he was determined to seek out Jiro Miki and take his revenge. Taki felt very strongly that this must have been the case, but he didn't say anything about it to Yasuda. Instead he asked about such details as Miki's physical appearance. Unfortunately Yasuda had never met the man directly, so all he could say was that the man had learned traditional Japanese dance, that he had had a homosexual relationship with his dance teacher, and that he was a man of delicate features.

Taki left the printing company with the final request to please let him know if they heard anything about Tanaka and his disappearance.

Kyushu is noted for its clear skies, but today the sky was obscured by scattered clouds. Taki wondered if Yoko, who had left on the first plane out that morning, had made it back to Tokyo all right. For some reason the deep blue of the sky seemed to match the color of his heart.

14

The Family Register

TEN YEARS AGO SHUJI TANAKA HAD PURSUED JIRO MIKI TO
Tokyo.

When Taki returned to Tokyo from Kyushu and told Yoko
what he had learned, she disagreed with his conclusions. He
was suggesting that Tanaka had come to Tokyo determined
to seek out Miki and get his revenge, but Yoko questioned
whether or not Tanaka had really loved Noriko that much.
That assumption was merely based on something Taki's sister
had said. Apparently Tanaka had never told his wife much
about his life in Fukuoka, so it seemed odd that he would go
out of his way to tell her about a woman he had loved even
more than he loved his wife. And yet he may have found it
difficult to displace the memory of Noriko, and thoughts of
her undoubtedly lingered in his heart.

"I wonder if Tanaka might have finally discovered Jiro
Miki just by accident after ten years?" Yoko felt she had to

say what she was thinking. "You think he discovered where Miki was hiding, got his revenge, then hid himself?"

Taki could see nothing implausible about assuming this sequence of events, but he gave Yoko a careful, scrutinizing look. They were in her room in a business hotel near Tokyo Central station. They could see the evening sky through the pattern of rain on the long, narrow window. From time to time a train would rumble past on the elevated, national railway line.

Yoko had taken a direct flight back to Tokyo, where, in obedience to Taki's directions, the first thing she did was to check in to this hotel. Taki had spent the day in Fukuoka, being questioned by the police at the hotel where Kasai had been staying. Afterward he had met with Yasuda at Tanaka's former employers, and then had flown to Tokyo in the evening.

"In any case, we can't rule out the possibility that my brother-in-law may finally have gotten his revenge." Whenever Taki was deep in thought, he rubbed his chin with his middle finger. "I wonder then if we can assume that the Jiro Miki on whom he got his revenge is the same person as Takashi Sato?"

Yoko remained silent. She felt some vague apprehension about this line of thinking, but so far there was no definite evidence linking the two men. "Jiro Miki was twenty-six or -seven at the time he murdered Noriko, so he would be thirty-six or -seven now, and the papers said Sato was thirty-eight."

"That's right."

A year or two discrepancy in age wouldn't make any real difference in this case. It was possible that they had made some error in Miki's age ten years ago, and of course there was no way to confirm Sato's age. It occurred to Yoko that even though Sato had said he was thirty-eight, he had looked older, but this didn't rule out the possibility that he might actually have been younger.

"I understand he was adopted into the Sato family seven

years ago. That means that prior to that his name was not Sato. . . ."

"And yet, even though the business has now gone bankrupt, the Sato family had been in the metal business for many generations, so they were a prominent firm. If they adopted someone into the family as heir, his background would be listed in their family register. We should try to get a look at that."

"That may be so, but he said he had married her in a love match, so the girl may have persuaded her parents to cover the matter up if they found out about his background, or she and Sato may have altered the family register themselves if there was something unsavory in his background."

"Um." Taki sat with his arms crossed, neither agreeing nor disagreeing. Suddenly Yoko had a strange feeling. She realized that somewhere in the course of the conversation she had accepted the idea that Sato and Jiro Miki were the same person. She had almost convinced herself that Takashi Sato had committed a murder in the past.

"What sort of person was Sato?" Apparently Taki was gradually coming around to Yoko's point of view.

"He was a thin man, a little over five feet tall. In terms of today's men he was not very tall. He had a narrow face with a good nose, but his features seemed very formal, even coldly so."

"Um." Taki seemed to be turning something over in his mind. "I was told that Jiro Miki was also slim and good-looking. He wasn't very tall either. On the other hand, I didn't talk to anyone who had actually seen him." Yasuda at the print shop had described Miki for him on the basis of his memory of rumors and newspaper articles published at the time of the murder. "So the theory we have now is that Jiro Miki murdered Noriko, then, avoiding his pursuers, fled to Tokyo. Three years later he fell in love with the only daughter of the family that owned Sato Metal Industries, was adopted into the family, and began life anew as Takashi Sato. Then

Tanaka came along and recognized him and got his revenge."

Once again Taki was talking to himself as he wrestled with the problem. Yoko tried to resist this idea but found that it made sense. She had been Sato's lover for almost six months. They had both known it was only a casual and temporary affair, and yet in the end the bonds between them were strong enough for them to attempt suicide together. Now that she thought about it, she realized that he had never told her anything about his life before he was adopted into the Sato family. She could not remember his ever having said where he was born. She had always just assumed that he had been born and raised in Tokyo. Now she realized that he had never told where he had been employed before, or anything like that. And in a sense this was what really attracted her to him in the first place, that vague air of obscurity with which he veiled himself. He had been changed, of course, by the stress and irritation caused by his financial troubles, and especially after he had hit the little girl. However, he had concealed himself behind this veil of obscurity even before all that happened, and even long before he had gotten to know Yoko. If this were really the case, then it probably all sprang from this secret in his past.

If Takashi Sato and Jiro Miki were really the same person, then they could suppose that he had had a homosexual experience in the past. Was there anything in his activities to suggest that he was hiding such tendencies? This thought revived memories of the many nights she had spent with Sato. Yoko stopped this depressing soul-searching before she came to any conclusions about whether or not Sato might have been a homosexual. Still, it was a powerful reason for considering the murder at Amagi to have been an act of revenge.

This would also explain the unrelenting cruelty by which Sato had finally been driven to his death. The killer had destroyed Sato's social life, had followed him as he went into the mountains with Yoko to commit suicide, had attacked and stabbed him to death when he unexpectedly started to revive, had made the murder look as though it had been committed by Yoko, and had fled. This cold, vicious method of revenge could only have been carried out by someone who was consumed by feelings of deep, deep resentment against Sato. This had been Yoko's own first thought when she had recovered from the suicide attempt and thought things through.

"If that is the case, then it means that Tanaka came to know Midori in a calculated way, and that he was successful in manipulating her."

"That's right. He got close to Midori, telephoned Sato directly and threatened him with references to the past, and pursued him in every manner."

Yoko recalled that just before she and Sato attempted suicide, a man calling himself Tanaka had telephoned the Jugon several times. There was also the question of the birth control pills. Midori's use of the pills was, for Sato, a symbol of his wife's unfaithfulness, and surely it was something that wounded him deeply.

"So the conclusion we are naturally led to is that it was Tanaka who followed you to Amagi?" This time Taki looked directly at Yoko, an intent look in his eyes, and his statement was phrased as a question.

"We have no way of knowing whether he was by himself, or whether Midori might have accompanied him."

"I wonder if he was really all that attractive to women?" Taki tilted his head to one side in puzzlement, and the sardonic smile returned to his lips. Yoko smiled, too, in response.

Taki lit a cigarette and walked over to the window, saying, "However, if Takashi Sato was really Jiro Miki, why didn't Tanaka just go to the police and report the fact? If they were the same person, a police investigation would soon confirm it. Wouldn't that have been plenty of revenge?"

If he had done this, Tanaka himself need not have become a murderer. After all, he had a wife and child to think of. There was always the possibility that Midori played a large role in the matter, but since there was no way to prove this, Yoko remained silent.

Now Taki came up with another possibility. "Even if we could prove that Sato and Jiro Miki are the same person, we still have to consider the possibility that he was not really responsible for Noriko's death ten years ago. According to Yasuda at the print shop, it was never made clear who picked up the letter opener in the first place. If it could be proven that it was Noriko, then the killing was a case of justifiable self-defense, even though he did kill her." The ash on his cigarette had grown long when Taki turned back from the window and walked to where Yoko was sitting. He took one more drag on the cigarette and stubbed it out.

"That would explain the reason, then, for killing Kasai. It seems that Kasai had some inkling that Tanaka had gotten his revenge by murdering Sato and had begun poking around. Tanaka realized this, knew he was in danger of being exposed, and killed Kasai."

Yoko nodded to indicate that she was willing to accept this argument.

"Still, there is a fallacy in this line of reasoning. Kasai might have learned a few details about Tanaka from the Ikejima family in Fukuoka, but where could he have learned the rest of it? It could only have come from Tanaka himself. Especially if Tanaka had a plan for revenge and was stalking Sato, he would keep that a closely guarded secret and it is unlikely he would tell anyone about it."

"Yes, you're right, but . . ." Yoko was running the tip of her finger around the rim of the coffee cup that had been brought by room service. "Even if Tanaka suspected Sato, he could never be sure that Sato was really Jiro Miki. Ten years had passed and his appearance had probably changed, and besides, it's unlikely that Tanaka ever knew Miki very well in the first place. So while he was trying to find out for certain about Sato, he happened to meet Kasai and decided to try to use Kasai to help him find the proof he wanted, and in the process told Kasai something about what had happened in the past. Later Kasai used what Tanaka had told him as a starting point to find out more about Tanaka himself.''

"Um." Taki's eyes were hard, but after a while he said, "My brother-in-law likes to drink, and when he does, he gets careless." There was a note of sadness in Taki's voice as he murmured this. "There is also the question of Kasai's last words—'Makino at the Yamate Clinic'—but it's probably too soon to try to follow up on that." He went on to explain that after leaving the printing company, he had looked up the Yamate Clinic in a telephone directory for Fukuoka and the surrounding area, but could find no such listing.

"Where do we go from here to follow up these leads?"

"All we have to go on are Kasai's words about this person called Makino. Is he a doctor or staff member at a place called the Yamate Clinic, or perhaps a patient? What sort of personal connection did he have with Kasai? We don't know any of this. The first step, I think, is to find out if Mrs. Kasai knows anything about this. She's in Fukuoka right now, but I'll go see her when she gets back. In the meantime, I think we ought to check and see if there are any Yamate Clinics in the city and, if so, to try and find out if any of them has a Makino associated with it.''

"Right."

"One more lead is Takashi Sato's family register. That will be the quickest way to find out whether or not his name was originally Jiro Miki."

"Leave that to me, I can check it out."

"Okay. But just remember, you're in greater jeopardy now than ever before, so be careful. Mrs. Kasai and the people at the Unahama Hotel have all gotten a good look at you, and eventually the police may suspect that there's a link between the Kasai murder and the Sato murder."

"Of course I'll be careful." Yoko made her reply casually enough, but she was already thinking of ways to make herself unnoticed, though she was unable to come up with any bright new ideas. Still, her head was spinning with plans of action.

"My first task will be to find out Sato's earlier identity and verify it." She made this statement rather forcefully in order to forestall any further advice from Taki. He had suddenly fallen silent and lit up a fresh cigarette. After a while he asked gently, "How about you? Did you really love Sato?"

Yoko's head jerked up and her eyes met his. His eyes were always very frank, but this time there was a surprising intensity in them, and she looked away.

She had loved him. She wanted to say that she had truly loved him. If she didn't make such a statement, he would surely think her too callous. And yet, somehow, she couldn't bring herself to say anything. Finally she managed to mumble, "I don't know." Suddenly her eyes were filled with tears and she was chagrined that she could not answer clearly.

At last she was able to return Taki's gaze with a steady one of her own and somehow managed to stop the flow of tears.

The following day it poured rain; it was the so-called autumn wet season. Yoko always felt depressed and gloomy when it rained, but now she was able to use the weather for her own purposes. She was able to conceal her face with an umbrella and exploit the fact that people are usually so preoccupied when it rains they rarely pay attention to others. It was about one o'clock in the afternoon when Yoko set out for the offices of the Minamiku municipal government to consult the Sato family's official register. In order to see how things went, she first asked for an official copy of Midori Sato's official register, but eventually the clerk came back and said they couldn't find such a register. It appeared that old man Sakura had been right when he said that Midori was merely a common-law wife and had not been officially registered as Sato's spouse.

According to Takashi Sato's family register, he had been

officially married on March 13, 197–. This was the listing of his original marriage several years ago. The first person listed in the register was Misako Sato. Since Takashi had been adopted into the family and had taken his first wife's name, he was listed second. Next Yoko found the column listing Takashi's vital statistics. Both his parents were dead and his family name had been Ishida. He was listed as their third son. It said that he had been born in the town of Morimachi in Shizuoka prefecture on May 13, 194–. That, at least, was when his father, Taro Ishida, had reported the birth.

The purple ink was still damp on the official transcript Yoko held tightly clenched in her hands. She went to a nearby sofa and sat down. Because of the rain, the municipal office was gloomy and nearly deserted. Under the light of a reading lamp she once again read the document carefully. When she calculated the date of his birth, it turned out that he was thirty-eight, just as he had said.

So far there were no contradictions in what was recorded, but Yoko had to admit that she was very much disturbed by his place of birth having been listed as Shizuoka. If there were not something suspicious about this fact, why had he never told her? She herself had been born in Shizuoka prefecture.

On several occasions Yoko had described for him details of Shizuoka. Her mother's family had had a farm on the upper reaches of the Tenryugawa River and she remembered telling him how, after her mother died, her father took her to the farm every summer during the summer holidays. She had told him how she and the other children would play in the river, and how she had watched her father fishing, and so on. On those occasions, Sato had kept silent and merely nodded as though he were hearing about a place he had never visited. But the Tenryugawa River flowed very close to the place where he had been born. Why had he never said something like, "Why, I grew up right near there?"

The dialect of Shizuoka prefecture is not unusual, but the

people have a special sort of intonation in their speech. When these people write, of course, they use standard Japanese, but when they speak, the intonation can be clearly heard. Certainly Yoko herself spoke that way. When she was working at the Jugon, she could tell right away if a customer was from Shizuoka as soon as he began speaking. Likewise, customers would also ask if she was from Shizuoka after they had heard her speak. In Takashi's case, however, she had not suspected it. He spoke without a trace of an accent, and for that reason Yoko had always assumed that he had been born and raised in Tokyo.

Now she was supposed to believe that he had been born in Shizuoka. Yoko told herself there was something wrong here. She couldn't accept the idea that he was from Shizuoka, and this frightened her.

She had been pondering the notion that Sato was really Jiro Miki, and even when she thought of checking the family register, she didn't expect to find right away that his original name had been Jiro Miki. Since he had married Misako for love, Yoko assumed that they'd have worked together to cover up his guilty past and would have realized how dangerous it was to simply change his name from Miki to Sato, leaving a clear record of his past in the family register. Surely they'd have created at least one buffer between the name Takashi Sato and his real name. And yet the official transcript said that he'd moved from Shizuoka to Tokyo only at the time of his marriage seven years ago.

What about his place of residence? Yoko didn't suppose that all his changes of residence were listed in the register. He probably lived in Tokyo awhile before the marriage; otherwise how would he have gotten to know Misako in the first place? The only blank space in the family register was the one that indicated his family's place of residence before his birth. Information regarding Misako was listed first, and in the column containing Sato family information, "previous official residence" was listed as Tokyo.

people have a special sort of intonation in their speech. When
these people were, of course, then sure she had become

15

The Phantom

HAVING GAINED THE INFORMATION SHE SOUGHT AT THE MU-
nicipal office, Yoko set out on foot to find an apartment for
herself. For her to continue to use Taki's apartment in Asatani
was an imposition on him and at the same time put her in
needless danger. As he had pointed out the previous evening,
she had been seen twice already, and it was possible that the
police were already keeping an eye on Taki.

Taki had volunteered to lend her money to secure a lease
and to furnish a place. "You can pay the money back once
you've cleared your name," he had said with a laugh. For
some reason this reminded her of Takashi, and though she
was unsure of her feelings, she knew that at the very least
she had grown quite fond of Taki.

He had pointed out the convenience of her having a place
on his route to and from work each day and with that in mind
had called a friend who had a real estate office in Nakano.

Yoko took an interurban train to Nakano and, following

183

the instructions Taki had written down for her, located the real estate agent. She took the first place he showed her, a place called the Asahi Apartments, about a fifteen-minute walk from Nakano station. Her apartment was on the second floor of a brick apartment building in a deteriorating residential neighborhood. Although it was quite small, the location was good, so it was surprisingly expensive. It was inconvenient in that there was a communal toilet and no telephone, but she felt she was too obligated to Taki already and decided not to consider a more luxurious place.

She moved into the apartment right away, then called Taki's office and gave him the name and address. He said he would stop by on his way home from work and have a look at it. Yoko then went to the shopping center in front of Nakano station and bought bedding, asking that it be delivered to her apartment. She also bought all the things she would need for daily life. While she was absorbed in these domestic details, she completely forgot that she was being hunted by the police, and for a time it almost seemed as if she were beginning a new life for herself.

The rain lifted in the evening. By seven o'clock it was totally dark outside her still-curtainless windows. There was a knock at the door. When she opened it, Taki cautioned her, "You shouldn't just open the door like that when someone knocks. Always ask the person to identify himself first." As he spoke, he looked quickly in the direction of the stairs he had just climbed and quickly shut the door behind him.

"Are you being followed?" Yoko asked with fear in her voice.

"No, I don't think so. But it's pretty certain that the police will be keeping a suspicious eye on me. From time to time I've spotted people who look like detectives prowling around the office or the building sites I've been inspecting."

"I'm sorry to have caused you all this trouble."

"Do you really feel you have to apologize?" With this Taki slipped off his shoes and entered the main part of the apartment. First he looked out the darkened window, then looked around the apartment. "Well, you can sleep here, but that's about all."

"All I need is a place to sleep."

"It's pretty meager, but I hope you won't have to stay here for long."

"So do I."

There was no table for them to sit at as they talked. They sat on the floor for a time in silence, and the wet wool of Taki's suit filled the chilly room with a musty smell. He sat cross-legged with a brown paper bag he brought on the floor beside him. From it he took instant coffee, sugar cubes, and a couple of Styrofoam cups.

"You see, I know what it's like to live alone. That's why I thought to bring these things for you."

Fortunately there was an ancient gas cooking ring in the apartment, so they were able to boil water for coffee while Taki lit a cigarette and used an empty can for an ashtray.

"Mrs. Kasai returned to Tokyo this afternoon, so I stopped in to see her on my way here," Taki said, sipping his coffee. "She said the words 'Makino at the Yamate Clinic' meant nothing to her. Kasai had never been hospitalized in such a place, and as for the name Makino, she thought her husband might have mentioned it occasionally, but she wasn't sure. She didn't seem to be trying to hide anything, so I suppose it was just something Kasai never discussed with her. Apparently the business with Mrs. Sato was also something he kept from her."

"That's interesting."

"I checked in the telephone directory, but the only clinics listed under the name Yamate are three animal hospitals. I called each of them, but none has a doctor named Makino. The worst possible thing would be if this Makino is not a regular employee of the clinic, but a patient Kasai just happened to meet by chance. If this is the case, there's no way we can possibly track this person down."

"Well, I don't know." Yoko stared into the bottom of her coffee cup. "It could be just a name that came into Kasai's mind as he was dying, not necessarily the name of his killer. On the other hand, even though he was losing consciousness, it was obviously very important to him to convey this name to you."

"That may be so. He called me to Fukuoka because he wanted to tell me something and he seemed to know who I was even as he lay on the beach dying."

"Then the only thing we can suppose is that it refers to something he wanted you to check out later. He was trying desperately to give you some sort of clue, don't you think?"

"In other words, you think this Makino, whoever he is, is directly related to the Yamate Clinic?"

"I think that if we can locate the Yamate Clinic, we will surely find Makino. It's probably the name of a doctor or a nurse who works there."

"Um." Taki seemed to take Yoko's opinion seriously. "But if we can't find this Yamate Clinic in Tokyo, what are we going to do, search for it all over the country? After all, there's no reason to suppose it's located in Tokyo."

Suddenly he looked up at Yoko. "I've got it. Of course. Kasai didn't say the clinic was located in Tokyo. When I didn't find such a clinic in Fukuoka, I just assumed it was in Tokyo. After all, I was born and raised in Tokyo and have never lived anywhere else, so I always assume that everything is located in Tokyo. Okay. Starting tomorrow we'll begin a wider search."

The two looked at each other and smiled, but Taki suddenly looked away. Until now they'd had many chances to be alone together, but tonight he seemed somehow stiff and awkward in her presence. No doubt this was because he was in Yoko's "place," however briefly it might belong to her. Yoko seemed to understand how Taki felt.

"How did your investigation of the family register turn out?" he asked after a time.

"Well, I found out a few things about Sato." Yoko dug out the official transcript of Sato's family register she had gotten at the municipal office.

Taki looked it over, his brow creased in concentration. "For some reason Sato never revealed the fact that he was born in Shizuoka," Yoko said. "I don't suppose he'd have been able to alter the family register, do you think?"

"It's practically impossible, but if it could be done, what do you think he might have done with this?"

Yoko felt sure that something was false or misrepresented here, but whatever it was, she wasn't able to put her finger on it.

"It's probably something very simple," Taki said, stubbing out his cigarette. "About a year before I went to work for the company where I am now, there was a case like that in one of the companies that subcontracted with us. A young lady who had graduated from a two-year college had been working for the company for three years when it was discovered that she'd been embezzling money, and there was a full investigation. They found out that she'd graduated from a rural high school and went to work in a local bank, but had been dismissed for pilfering money."

"What about her degree from the two-year college?"

"That's just it, you see, she'd never attended a junior college. After being fired by the bank, she couldn't bear to live in her hometown any longer, so she came to Tokyo and went to work in a snack bar. Eventually she became friends with a girl who had been born and raised in Tokyo and who had graduated from a junior college. This friend was from a wealthy family, and after she graduated from college she didn't have to work or anything, and eventually she went abroad and never came back. So the first girl simply took over her friend's identity and used her family register to get a job in the company she worked for."

"That's incredible."

"I don't know the details of why her ruse was not discovered when she first went to work for the company, but it was three years before she was discovered taking money, and she had gone along all that time using her friend's name and papers, and no one suspected a thing. The problem is that a person's family register doesn't have to have his or her photograph attached to it, so it's very difficult to verify that a certain set of papers really belongs to that person. This incident just occurred to me now when you suggested that it wouldn't be a simple matter to alter a family register."

"You mean you think Sato was using someone else's papers before he was adopted into the Sato family?"

"Uh-huh. That's the only conclusion we can reach if it turns out that he wasn't really born in Shizuoka prefecture. From the beginning he was using someone else's family register. There are many ways he could have done that. In his case, I wonder if he had any friends who conveniently disappeared. But there's also the problem that if he died under suspicious circumstances, his demise would be labeled as that of someone already dead."

Yoko was beginning to feel the same uneasy apprehension she had felt earlier in the municipal offices when she had first looked at Sato's family register. "But if that is the case and he married seven years ago using someone else's family register, how was he able to get away with it?"

"Hmm." As usual Taki was rubbing his chin thoughtfully with his middle finger. "I guess the only thing we can do is try to find out whose family register he was using."

"But what if that person is missing or something?" Suddenly a vague idea passed through Yoko's mind and she closed her mouth. For the time being they were working on the assumption that Takashi Sato and Jiro Miki were the same person. Thus they were assuming that Miki had killed someone in Kyushu and fled to Tokyo, where he had somehow gotten hold of the family register belonging to the family of Takashi Ishida and, using that name, had been successful in marrying into the Sato family. Consequently the real Takashi

Ishida was the biggest threat to Sato's disguise. If the real Ishida were to reveal the truth, Sato's disguise would be lost and his past crime would surely come to light. This suggested that Sato might have taken steps to silence Ishida.

For a time Taki sat watching Yoko and seemed to be reading her thoughts. As usual, a sardonic smile played across his lips. "We can be pretty certain that Sato didn't kill Ishida. If he had done that, Ishida's family register would have been canceled."

"That means the real Takashi Ishida must still be alive somewhere." With this thought, another wave of fear swept over Yoko.

Yoko was in the Koto district of Tokyo looking for the address Takashi Sato had listed as his own before moving to Aoyama. In other words, it was the place where he would have lived using the name Takashi Ishida, for he had changed his name to Sato only when he moved to Aoyama.

She remembered that the previous night Taki had cautioned her that often the place a person lists as his address may not be an actual place of residence. Still, she was walking around the neighborhood of Botan Avenue to see what she could find. The rain had lifted and refreshing sunlight surrounded her, but the streets and houses were still soaked and wet. To the east was a lumberyard stacked with freshly cut wood. Uncut logs floated in the river nearby. A couple of young men wearing traditional *happi* coats were working the logs and moving them about with long, spiked poles. This was an unusual sight and Yoko paused for a time and watched them.

Today Taki would be in Chiba all day. He had to be at a building site today, and tomorrow as well, so she wouldn't see him until the day after tomorrow. Taki thought it best if she stayed holed up in her apartment for a while, but when morning came, she had felt she just couldn't stay there any longer. If the police had begun to keep an eye on Taki as he suspected, then even her own apartment was no longer a safe place to hide. The day before yesterday she had told Taki that she wanted to verify Sato's real identity for herself. She had really felt that way, of course, but her saying it was also a way of expressing her determination to go out despite Taki's warning.

As usual Yoko had dressed in a gray suit with a dark sports shirt. She also wore black shoes and dark sunglasses. She generally wore men's clothing now when she planned to be out moving about on her own.

In this neighborhood there were many old, brick homes, and interspersed among them were lumberyards, shops that made roof tiles, and eating places. It was in the heart of the city and there were many people coming and going; no one paid any attention to anyone else. Still she hoped she could find someone who would remember a person who had once been a resident here.

Since her inquiry concerned a person who had lived here seven years ago, she decided she might as well begin with some of the older houses. Her eyes came to rest on a shabby two-story private residence with a slate roof. The door had been freshly painted, but that was all. The entrance was flanked by tubs of miniature trees and shrubbery in a way that suggested an elderly person lived there. Yoko resolutely walked up to the door and pressed the buzzer.

"Just a moment," called a clear voice, and a moment later the door was opened by a housewife who appeared to be in her forties. She seemed surprised to see Yoko.

"Excuse me. If you don't mind, I'd like to ask you something." Yoko didn't bother to try to alter her voice; it was impossible to try to imitate a man's voice all the time. She felt her disguise would be sufficient as long as she appeared to be a man at first glance.

"About seven years ago there was a man living in this neighborhood named Takashi Ishida. I wonder if you know anything about him?"

The woman tilted her head thoughtfully and replied, ''I don't recall anyone by that name. How old a person was he?''

''He's thirty-eight years old this year.''

''Oh, he was a young man then. Maybe Grandpa knows who he is, but I am afraid Grandpa's out right now. The family next door have been living here longer than we have. They might know.'' She was a surprisingly friendly woman and even pointed out the house next door for Yoko. ''If they can't help you, just go around the corner to your right, there's a police box. They might know.''

Yoko bowed in thanks and the brightly varnished door closed behind her.

The house next door was actually a small store that sold children's toys and school supplies. The clerk was a bored-looking old woman in her sixties who wore a black cap. In response to Yoko's questions the woman hunched her shoulders and listened carefully. In the end, however, she only said, ''Takashi Ishida? Never heard of him.'' Yoko had the feeling that even though the woman listened carefully to everything she had said, she only understood about half of it. This woman, too, urged her to inquire at the police box.

Just as Yoko was about to leave the shop, the old woman called her back and said, ''For something that long ago you should probably ask at the neighborhood association. They would probably know more about it than the police box.''

''The neighborhood association?''

''Turn to the left and go down the street a little way. It's the Watanabes' house.''

A neighborhood association—Yoko had lived for so long in Tokyo apartments, leading a solitary urban life, that she had forgotten that this sort of community group still existed. Remembering made her feel sad. At her home in Shizuoka a group of near neighbors had joined together to form such an association, and they had all gotten to know each other quite well. The man who had been instrumental in forming the group had been a gentle person who enjoyed helping others. Whenever anyone moved into or out of the neighborhood, they would notify the association of their change of address.

Yoko followed the directions the old lady had given. Across the street she found a mailbox with the name Watanabe painted on it. She could see the door of the house at the end of a narrow, private lane lined with hedges. The house itself was not so large, but its surroundings were most extraordinary and the whole place had an air of tranquillity about it.

In response to her call from the door, there appeared a short old man whose bald head glistened as though it had been polished with oil. It seemed as though all the houses in this neighborhood were occupied by elderly people during the morning hours.

The old man was wearing an open-neck woolen shirt and a wool vest that made him look like the sort of urban recluse who would go out to hear performances of the comic story-tellers.

"Excuse me, is Mr. Watanabe in?"

"My son has gone to mind the store. Can I help you?" the old man asked rapidly in a husky voice.

"I came to make an inquiry at the neighborhood association."

"Ah, well, I handle that sort of thing. What is it you want to know?" The old man's voice became crisp and business-like.

"About seven years ago . . ." Once again Yoko made her query about Takashi Ishida.

For a time the old man remained silent, staring off into the distance, then, "Ah yes, Mr. Ishida."

"Do you remember him, then?" Yoko suddenly felt her voice catch in her throat. She was very excited. "Do you know where he's living now?"

"Excuse me, but you haven't told me who you are."

"I'm sorry, I should have explained. I'm a distant relative of Ishida's." The lie came easily to her lips. "We haven't heard from Ishida in a long time, and I'm looking for clues to track him down. There are certain matters I need to be in touch with him about in a hurry."

"I see." The old man looked at her again, but he didn't seem at all suspicious. "Won't you come in so we can sit down and talk about it?" As he spoke, he invited her into the living room, where there was a sofa set and other furniture.

"Up until seven years ago Takashi Ishida was living in this part of the city."

"Yes. I guess it has already been seven years. Anyway, he lived here for three years prior to that. I remember that much."

"After that, where did he move to, do you know?" Yoko could hardly wait to hear the answer to this question. Confirming her theories depended on the answer she got.

"He didn't leave any forwarding address when he moved, and since that was seven years ago, we just don't have any record of it. Have you asked at the municipal offices?"

"Yes. They said he had moved from here to Aoyama, but they couldn't find a specific address in Aoyama."

"Aoyama?" The old man's eyes filmed over and he seemed to be thinking back. "No, I don't think he moved to Aoyama. I don't remember that." He blinked rapidly as he spoke. "I seem to recall that he went back to his hometown. Yes, I believe that's what he did. He's living in his hometown now."

"Hometown?" Yoko was conscious of a tightening lump in her throat. If Takashi Ishida had moved to Aoyama, there would be no talk of his having returned to live in his hometown. "You say he returned to his hometown, isn't that a rural place in Shizuoka?"

"Yes. Yes, that's right. I believe I heard that he lived

around there somewhere.'' There was a note of remembrance in the old man's nasal voice.

"Uh, do you remember where Takashi Ishida lived when he was here?''

"He was renting a small house by the river. It's been torn down, though; there's a building there now." He spoke as though he now had more confidence in his recollections.

"Was he living with his family when he was in that house?''

"Oh no. He lived alone. He was always a loner, I can tell you that.''

Yoko nodded as the old man spoke, then asked, "What sort of work was he doing when he lived here?''

"He was working in one of the lumberyards. He always seemed to be a pleasant sort of fellow, but he never said much. But you know, now that I stop to think about it, he seems to have taken an old guy like myself into his confidence on a number of occasions. He often came here to the house to play Japanese chess. I also served for a time as the district welfare officer, you see. But I was old enough to be that boy's father; maybe that's why he talked to me when he wouldn't talk to others.''

As the old man droned on with his recollections, Yoko could imagine the scene beside the river where the logs floated; the old man and the frail, gaunt, young man set up their chessboard and played.

"I don't think city life suited him very well and he was always talking about going back to his home in the country. His older brother is a farmer, but Ishida was making a living here and he didn't want to go home empty-handed.''

"If that was the case, what made him suddenly pack up and go home?''

"I guess I don't really know the details of it, but he seemed to have made up his mind to do it, so I told him I thought it was the right decision. I think he was the sort of person who would be much happier living in the country.''

At this point they heard the front door open and the voices of a child and a woman who was apparently the child's mother. The old man looked serenely in that direction, then his gaze returned to Yoko. "You mean that Ishida isn't living there in the country with the rest of your family?"

"Uh, why no. You see we sent him a letter once, but there was no reply. We just supposed that he was still living in Tokyo, and I tried to make inquiries at his old address. We're just trying to find out where he's gone."

"I see. Well, I expect that if he had come back to Tokyo, he would have made a point of dropping in here to say hello."

Yoko began to think that Takashi Ishida's family was living in the town of Morimachi in Shizuoka, and that someone using his identity, someone who knew Jiro Miki's secret, was living under cover.

16

Hometown

YOKO WAS ALONE WHEN SHE BOARDED THE BULLET TRAIN limited express which left Tokyo at ten A.M.

The clear autumn weather had continued from the previous day and the morning sunlight was fresh and bright. The wind that swirled among the tall buildings was cool to the skin. As usual in late morning the platform was uncrowded and Yoko could not help but be reminded that it had been just like this nearly a month before on that fateful and fatal day of September 13, when she and Takashi had boarded the train from this same platform.

From the very beginning there had been something false about that trip. Feeling this, Yoko suddenly realized that something within her had been restored. Even the buildings that were beginning to slip past outside the train window were different now than they had appeared when she had seen them in her earlier, alienated condition. She felt now that she had a better grasp on reality.

196

One hour and twenty minutes later they arrived in Shizu-oka. Seeing the familiar buildings and signs of the city from the train window Yoko suddenly knew that she had come home. Without realizing it, she found herself looking about to see if her father was waiting for her. She had returned home once, shortly after first going to Tokyo. When it was time to go back to the city, her father had come to the station to see her off. Tears filled her eyes as she remembered.

After getting off the train, she found a taxi and set out for the town of Morimachi. It took about an hour to get there. Having passed through the commercial district of Shizuoka, the taxi ran through open fields that were nearly ready for the harvest. Some had already been harvested and the sheaves of rice stood neatly bundled. The fields were like a sea of burnished gold bordered by the blue line of the distant mountains. Here and there in the foothills stood a persimmon tree with its ripe fruit glowing red in the autumn sunlight.

The really rugged mountains could not be seen from here, so the landscape appeared gentle. Yoko recalled that she had noticed the persimmons on their way to Amagi, but they had not been ripe then. She had been so preoccupied recently, she had failed to notice the changing of the seasons.

As they continued through the countryside, they began to see more and more hothouses. Without stopping to think, Yoko asked the driver, "What do they grow in those?"

"Melons," replied the middle-aged driver. "Melons give the farmers a more steady income than rice. All the farmers around here who have hothouses are doing pretty well." He spoke with the familiar Shizuoka accent.

Presently they began to see the yellowing bamboo plantations and tea fields, and the taxi began to slow down.

"This is the place you're looking for."

Yoko gazed around at the scene outside the car. There was a cluster of farmhouses surrounded by hothouses.

"Do you happen to know which of these houses belongs to Takashi Ishida?"

"No. But I'm sure that if you ask one of the local people, they can tell you."

Yoko thanked the driver and got out. A surprisingly strong wind was blowing. She held one hand on her head to keep her hair from blowing as she received her change from the driver. The driver smiled, saying, "It's always windy here all year round." Then, almost as an afterthought, he pointed to one of the buildings and said, "That's the farm co-op over there. Why don't you ask there?"

The co-op was a new building surrounded by a brown tile fence. It faced the dry dirt road. There was a sign on the building that read HOTHOUSE FARMERS COOPERATIVE ASSOCIATION.

It was very quiet inside the building because most people were out on their lunch break, but two or three young women sat chatting in one corner of the room. Yoko walked resolutely to one of the desks near the back of the room where a middle-aged man was looking through a newspaper.

"Excuse me, but I wonder if you could give me some information?"

The man looked up, and Yoko asked him about Takashi Ishida.

"Ah yes, Mr. Ishida," he said, nodding.

"Mr. Takashi Ishida. He does live here, doesn't he?" Yoko felt herself growing tense with excitement.

"So you've come here from Tokyo looking for him, is that it?" The man looked her over carefully, eyeing her pant suit.

"Yes. I'm an old friend of Ishida's, and I happened to be in the area today, so I thought I'd take advantage of the opportunity to drop in and see him."

"I see. Well, his house is . . ." As he talked, the man took Yoko back to the road and pointed out the way for her. He told her to go three hundred yards along the road and turn left when she came to a row of three hothouses. Takashi's house would be located just on the opposite side of the street.

"Do you know if Ishida is living alone or not?"

The co-op man looked questioningly at Yoko before he said, "Yes, he does, in a sense. His brother's family lives nearby."

Yoko remembered the story she had heard from the man at the neighborhood association in Tokyo. He had said that Ishida had wanted to return to the country, but that his brother's family were poor farmers and he didn't want to go home empty-handed.

"Is it true that Takashi doesn't get along very well with his older brother?"

"I don't think so." The man smiled bitterly at Yoko's eagerness and continued, "He's a little bit strange, you know. He seems to prefer living by himself, but he sure is a good worker. The Ishidas got involved in hothouse farming just after he returned from Tokyo. His brother is quite pleased to have him here to help."

It seemed to Yoko that what he was saying had some hidden implications, but she didn't know what they were.

"Let's see, it must have been about seven years ago that Ishida came back here from Tokyo."

"Yes. It's been about that long."

"So, he's been helping his brother with the farm work since he got back?"

"Yes. They grow melons these days."

"I guess there are a lot of melon growers in this area."

"They ship them by truck to Tokyo and even as far as Kyushu. Recently there have been a lot of problems because the farmers are short-handed and there's also the gasoline shortage, but still the hothouse-farming business has been booming over the last ten years. The farmers like it because it brings in a steady income all year long."

Yoko walked along the windy road in the direction the man had shown her. Many of the farmhouses were surrounded by hedges of black pine, which made good windbreaks. The noonday sun was bright and there was no one else on the road. From somewhere came the smell of boiling potatoes.

When she got to the hothouses that had been pointed out to her, she turned left. She found an old shrine just as the man had said, and when she followed the street that ran behind it, she came to a small, clear stream. Crossing the stone bridge, she could see a small, earth-walled house shaded darkly by the hedge and trees of the neighboring house.

As Yoko approached she could see that it was a typical, earth-floored storeroom. There was no nameplate, but she had followed the co-op man's directions carefully, so this had to be the place. A faint smell of boiling food came from this shedlike house. Apparently the people working in the fields had come back for lunch.

Yoko moved a little closer and tried to see inside the shed. She was certain now that Sato had used Takashi Ishida's papers, but if Ishida knew this, then surely he would have done something about it.

Yoko supposed that the man was already aware of Sato's murder and that he would be more than normally interested in Yoko Noda, who was a prime suspect in the case, so there was some danger that Ishida would realize who Yoko really was. She was aware of that, but she felt she had no choice at this point but to enlist his help in the matter. She had to go through with it.

"Excuse me, is anyone at home?" called Yoko at the door.

After a time a shadowy figure approached and Yoko held her breath. She had been walking in the bright sunlight and her eyes had not yet adjusted to the darkness, but if she looked closely, she could make out the figure of a person sitting on an old-fashioned, raised hearth. Now that person had stood up and was approaching her.

It was a man with a long, thin face and close-cropped hair. He wore a khaki shirt and stained trousers; clearly these were workclothes. Yoko tried to estimate his age, but he was deeply burned by the sun and it was hard to tell. At first glance she would have said he was in his forties, but they say that people in the country seem to age faster than city people, so he might be in his late thirties.

The man stood in front of Yoko and looked at her without uttering a word. His eyes were inflamed and his lower lip protruded, but there was something gentle about his childlike expression that put Yoko somewhat at ease.

"Excuse me. I wonder if Mr. Takashi Ishida is in?"

The man seemed surprised, but continued to stare at her without a word. Still, he didn't show any sign of denying that he was Ishida.

Yoko tried smiling and said, "You're Mr. Ishida, aren't you?"

"Yes, but . . ." the man finally replied, but before he finished his lips moved and his cheek twitched. He obviously had some sort of speech impediment. But that didn't matter; the important thing was that he was Takashi Ishida. At last Yoko had found the real person who belonged to the family register Sato had used.

For a moment she felt dizzy and was at a loss for words. She suddenly realized that all her energy had been devoted to searching for this person and she had not even stopped to consider what she might say once she found him. At last she managed to stammer, "Aren't you the one who lived for a while in Tokyo before you came back here?" She thought it best to verify this point first. "I heard about you from Mr. Watanabe, who is the head of the neighborhood association." Takashi Ishida moved his lips as though to say something, but no sound came. His face, however, flooded with an expression of fond recollection. At the same time, there was also a look of bewilderment, as if he were wondering who she was. Still no words came. It was as though he had been struck dumb.

"I am related to Takashi Sato." Yoko made up her mind to deliberately mention Sato's name. Ishida frowned slightly. "Actually, Sato died last month. In clearing up his affairs, it turned out that there were some irregularities concerning his family register. Especially concerning his marriage. According to his official papers, he was born here in this town and lived in Tokyo in the same district where you used to live. There were also some other irregularities, so I have been trying to check back and see the places where he lived; that's why I talked to Mr. Watanabe, as I mentioned earlier. He told me that Takashi Ishida and Sato were two different people, and that seven years ago, just when Sato married, you returned here to the country. So I'm trying to find out what is the connection between your family register and Sato's. They seem to have gotten mixed somehow. I am also trying to track down Sato's original family register. I thought you might know something about this whole matter. That's why I came down from Tokyo today to talk to you.''

There was silence for a time when Yoko stopped speaking. The only sound she heard was the stream gurgling behind her. Ishida's expression did not change; he continued to frown and look at the ground. But there was no sign of suspicion or bewilderment in the look on his face. Was it possible that he knew nothing of Sato's murder? Yoko made the point very clearly that he was already dead and that there would be no problems, that all she wanted to know was the truth.

At last she heard Ishida murmur deep in his throat, "So Eto is dead.''

"Eh, what's that? Who is Eto?''

A long moment passed.

"It's Eto,'' replied Ishida. This time, too, he mumbled the name. Perhaps this habit of mumbling everything explained his diffidence. Yoko recalled that Mr. Watanabe had said that Takashi Ishida had a speech impediment.

"Are you trying to tell me that Sato's original name was Eto?''

Ishida pondered this question for a time, then nodded solemnly.

"Eto what? What was his first name?''

"Nobuo. I think it was Nobuo.''

"Where was he born?" There was urgency in Yoko's voice as she spoke. She was determined to learn all she could from Ishida now that she had found him. One of the questions was to find out whether or not Sato had originally been Jiro Miki.

"He was from Kushiro in Hokkaido."

"Kushiro?" There was nothing unusual about this location, but somehow it surprised Yoko. "Did you ever hear anything to the effect that he might have once lived in Fukuoka in Kyushu?"

Ishida merely turned his head to one side in a manner that Yoko took to be a negative answer.

"Do you know if he ever used the name Jiro Miki?"

This time there was a pause before he answered and a suspicious look in his eyes, but he clearly shook his head negatively and eventually managed to stammer out the word, "No."

When Yoko thought about it, however, it seemed that even if Sato and Miki were the same person, it was unlikely that he would have told Ishida about it. Yoko realized that in her excitement she was just asking useless questions.

Ishida looked at her again and asked, "So Eto has died, has he?" He mumbled this in a low voice. "Are you his wife?" He seemed embarrassed when he asked this last question.

"Yes, that's right."

"I see. So you've come here from Tokyo." Ishida nodded several times as though he had satisfied himself about something. "Won't you come in?" He indicated the inside of the shed. Yoko took a seat some distance away from Ishida on the raised hearth that was littered with household goods of all sorts.

"Excuse me for asking some personal questions, but how did you first get to know Sato, or rather Eto, if that was his name before?" Yoko tried to sound casual and conversational.

"The first time I met him was when we had the accident."

"The accident?"

"He was driving his car and hit me when I was on my bicycle. He knocked me right down."

"I see."

"It dented his car a little, and I got a sprained arm."

Ishida seemed to relax some once they began talking, and the words came easier for him.

"I had just come out of a side street, so it was my fault really, but Mr. Eto paid to have my bicycle fixed and he even took time off work to come to my house and visit several times to see how I was doing. He was really a wonderful person, and smart, too; you know, he even graduated from college."

"When did all this happen?"

"Let's see. I guess it was about two years before I came back here. That would make it ten years ago."

"Do you know where Mr. Sato was living at that time?"

"He had an apartment in the same neighborhood where I lived."

"Did he live alone?"

"Yes."

"What sort of work did he do?"

"I heard that he worked for a firm of accountants in an office near Tokyo station."

An accounting firm near Tokyo station. That was not far from where Sato Metal Industries was located. Was it possible that Sato had met Miki in connection with his work? Yoko also wondered how Sato had met his first wife, Misako. Besides these, there was also the question of Jiro Miki.

"Had Mr. Sato been working there for a long time before you got to know him? Did he ever say anything about his past?"

Ishida looked down at the floor and thought about this for a while. Yoko couldn't see the expression on his face, so it was difficult to tell if he was just trying to remember, or whether he was trying to hide some information about Sato.

In the end he said he didn't know, and tilted his head, breaking into the first smile Yoko had seen on his face. Somehow his expression seemed sad when he smiled. "So you got to know each other as a result of the accident, and you became close friends, is that it?"

"We lived close to each other and sometimes we met on the street in the evening. We talked about our hometowns a lot. As you can see, I'm just a country boy, and I never cared very much for living in Tokyo. Mr. Eto had also come to the city alone from Kushiro, and he didn't seem to have any family or friends in the city, either."

"I want to ask you something that may seem a little strange, but did you ever have any reason to doubt the name Eto or to doubt that he came from Kushiro?"

"Oh, it's true, there's no question about that." Ishida was very definite in his answer to this. He looked steadily at Yoko and continued, "The very first time I met him, when we had the accident, he showed me his driver's license. It had his name on it and also a picture."

Yoko nodded. Since a person had to show proof of residence when getting a driver's license, it seemed quite likely that Sato's real name was Nobuo Eto.

"Do you happen to know why Eto wanted to use your identity papers when he was adopted into the Sato family?"

There was a long silence after she asked this question, but Yoko waited patiently. Ishida stammered briefly when he tried to answer. "It was about two years after we first met. I recall I hadn't seen him for a long time when suddenly he showed up at my house. He said he had a favor to ask, and spent a long time asking about where I was born and raised and all that."

Ishida had gone on to tell Sato/Eto that he had been born in Morimachi in Shizuoka and that he was the third son of a poor farm family. He said that he had had a problem with stuttering ever since childhood but that, nevertheless, his mother had unreasonably insisted that he attend the local high school. After he had finally graduated, he had gone to Tokyo alone, where he had worked at a variety of jobs. In response to Sato's questions, he had even divulged that he had never married and that his official place of residence was back in Shizuoka. Sato had listened intently to all this information, and when all his questions had been answered, he made a most remarkable proposal.

"Mr. Eto asked me to give him my own family register."

"Did you give it to him?"

Ever since talking to Taki about the matter, she had suspected that this was probably what had happened, but it felt odd to actually hear it spoken.

"He told me he had fallen in love with a woman who was the daughter of the president of some company, and that there was some talk of his being adopted into the family. At first the girl's parents were opposed to the marriage, but then the mother died young, and the father was quite old and was suffering from diabetes, so he was in a hurry to get someone adopted into the family. Eventually the daughter talked him into agreeing." Ishida broke off his story at this point as it occurred to him that Yoko must be the daughter he was talking about.

"Eto, of course, didn't have any particular fortune of his own, but the girl's family was primarily concerned with maintaining the family's name and bloodline. They were concerned that if he was adopted into the family and took over the company, any child he fathered would be next heir to the family name, and whether or not there was any house or fortune to be passed along, they wanted to ensure that there was a clear bloodline."

"I understand."

"But you see, this was exactly the thing Eto couldn't guarantee."

Ishida gave Yoko another appraising look. He still assumed she was the daughter of the Sato family and seemed uncertain how much he should tell her. Yoko returned his gaze but said nothing, and he quickly looked down at the floor again. With a small sigh he continued, "Mr. Eto's own family register was in Kushiro, and both his parents were dead. It turned out that his mother had murdered his father."

"Murdered?"

"It happened when Eto was still in grade school. His father was a drunken and violent man who beat his children regularly and never held a job. Eto's mother killed him with an ax while he was asleep. His mother turned herself in right away and, under the circumstances, was given a suspended sentence, but a short while later she took her own life. After that Eto was raised in an orphanage. He always did well in school and even received a scholarship so he was able to go to college. After graduation he went to Tokyo."

Yoko was so startled by all this she could only press her hands against her chest in silence.

"All these details were not written down in his family register, of course, but the story was widely known in the local community, and if the girl's family chose to make inquiries about his background, they would soon learn what had happened. It was bad enough that he had no home or fortune of his own and that he had been raised in an orphanage, but if it was known that he was the child of a murderer, they would have absolutely refused to let him marry their daughter. As I said, the girl's father was very much concerned about lineage."

"But in that case . . ." Yoko was about to ask if the girl he married knew about all this but managed to stop herself in time. Surely Misako Sato had known all this when she married Eto. They must have conspired together to deceive her parents so they would allow the marriage.

"So he asked if he could use your family register?"

"Yes. At first, of course, I was surprised to hear his story, but then I began to sympathize with his situation. After all, he hadn't committed any crime, and it was a shame to see him not able to be married to the woman he loved just because of something his parents did. I'm from a poor farm family myself, but there has been no insanity or criminal behavior in our family for many generations. Besides, I was tired of living in Tokyo and wanted to come back here to the country anyway.''

These last words were mumbled in a low voice. Ishida's sunburned face cracked into such an expression Yoko was not sure if he was going to laugh or cry.

She had already had a pretty shrewd idea of Ishida's situation from talking to the man at the neighborhood association in Tokyo and also from talking to the man at the co-op. Living in Tokyo had not suited Ishida and he wanted to return to the farm, but his brother's family was already having a hard time making ends meet, and even though they were short-handed, they couldn't afford to have him come home. By giving his family register to Sato, he had received enough money to enable him to return home. No doubt the money had been used to build the hothouses in which they now raised their melons.

''So Sato used your family register and was adopted into the Sato family under the name Takashi Ishida. Is that it?'' Yoko wanted to make sure her assumption was right.

A trace of a smile appeared on Ishida's protruding lower lip. ''I never heard him mention the name Sato. What you were saying earlier just made me think of Eto. After I gave him my family register, I came back here to the country and haven't seen him since. I figured it was best that way.''

For some reason Yoko felt a pang in her heart. It was clear to her now that Ishida was not aware that Sato had been murdered at Amagi. At the same time, she was also moved by the odd bond of brotherhood that existed between Sato and this simple, pathetic man.

''I didn't expect to live this way all my life. If Mr. Eto died first, I figured someone would come and tell me about it, and that would be the time to reveal the story. So now it turns out that Eto is dead, and I've told you the story.''

"But what about Nobuo Eto's family register? Does it still exist?"

"I reckon so. I saw a copy of it once."

"You actually saw it?"

"Mr. Eto was afraid that I might have some difficulty if he had my family register and I didn't have one, so he had a copy of his sent from Kushiro and gave it to me, but I gave it back saying I didn't need it. I didn't plan to get married anyway."

"So there really is a family register for Nobuo Eto in Kushiro." It seemed redundant, but Yoko wanted to make very sure of this point.

"Oh yes, it exists," Ishida said with a vigorous nod.

Everything he told her seemed to be on the level. Nine years ago Takashi Sato, using his real name of Nobuo Eto, had met Ishida. This Eto's official place of residence was Kushiro. His father had been murdered by his mother when he was in grade school, and his mother had taken her own life a short time later. What about the possibility that ten years ago Eto had been living with his mother in Fukuoka under the name Jiro Miki?

Yoko was preoccupied with these thoughts when she realized that Ishida was mumbling once again. "So, Mr. Eto is dead. He was still young. That means my real family register is closed forever."

17

The Yamate Clinic

YOKO RETURNED TO TOKYO ON THE BULLET TRAIN ARRIV-
ing at five o'clock in the evening. She tried calling Taki's
office from the station, but he had been away inspecting a
building site in Chiba for the past two days and was not in
the office. Yoko walked into one of the underground shopping arcades and found a convenient restaurant. She had arrived at Morimachi at noon and had missed lunch today. She
had thought that if Taki was at his office they could go out to
dinner somewhere and she'd tell him what she had learned
yesterday about Takashi's life before he married into the Sato
family. Also, she felt lonely tonight and melancholy about
having to eat dinner alone. Still, she consoled herself with
the thought that no one in the restaurant seemed to be paying
any attention to her.

It appeared as though everyone was intent on their dinner
partner or else simply gazed at the table; no one paid any
attention to their surroundings. Everyone was totally ab-

sorbed in their own affairs, and apparently they had all long forgotten about the love suicide and murder that had taken place at Amagi nearly a month ago. Even Yoko was able to hold her head up and look about instead of always trying to conceal her face. She was no longer as frightened as she once had been of people getting a good look at her.

Suddenly, however, it occurred to her that she was still a fugitive and would have to continue to live as a fugitive for ten or fifteen years, whatever the statute of limitations was. Perhaps she'd learn to live on the run and forget the fact that she was being pursued. She was afraid that if she failed to handle life on the run, she'd break down from the strain.

Darkness had already settled over the city by the time she returned to her apartment near Nakano station. Ever since the beginning of October the days had become noticeably shorter. She left the station and walked along a narrow street parallel to the railway embankment. Most of the rush-hour commuters who spewed out of the trains made their way into the shopping district or along the wide avenues. The street where Yoko walked was virtually deserted. As she rounded a corner near the Asahi apartment building, she noticed a compact car parked in a dark, empty lot in front of a partially constructed building. With a start she realized it resembled Taki's Toyota and hurried forward with rising expectations. As she got closer she saw that it was, indeed, his car. No sooner had she observed this than she also realized that a figure was lurking in the shadows about thirty feet farther along the narrow street. A heavyset, round-shouldered man, he was leaning against the window of an English conversation school. Yoko could only see his silhouette, but it was clear that he was not Taki. The man appeared to be waiting for someone, but it was also clear that he was waiting in the shadows because he did not want to be seen.

It must be the police, Yoko thought with alarm. That man must have followed Taki without his knowing it and was now waiting for Taki to return to his car. He must be expecting Taki to lead him to Yoko.

She was pretty sure it was the police. It was almost as though this was retribution for her negligence earlier that evening in the restaurant.

Yoko had gotten almost as far as Taki's car when she turned on her heel and began to walk away. Fortunately the man gave no sign that he had noticed her approach. She turned into the first side street she came to. It was lined with old-fashioned houses of the sort that have clothes-drying platforms on the roof. She made her way through these narrow, twisting streets and finally came out behind her apartment building. She was sure no one had followed her.

Suddenly a large figure came around from the front of the building heading straight toward her. "Ah," he said.

"Taki? Is that you?"

"Where have you been? I was worried about you."

"I'm sorry. It looked like you were going to be away at work for a while, so I went to Morimachi." Suddenly the strength seemed to go out of her legs as she remembered her earlier flight. She told Taki she thought someone was watching his Toyota. "I think it may be the police," she concluded.

As she spoke, Yoko was suddenly assailed by a new fear. She remembered watching Sato's house, being viciously attacked, and Taki saving her. She also remembered the time when they had been trying to find out about Tanaka's past and Teiji Kasai had been stabbed to death on the beach in Fukuoka. Might it be that Taki was also being followed and that someone intended to murder him?

"Um. It may be the police," he murmured, acknowledging Yoko's concern. "I may have been overconfident and careless recently."

"Well, now that you're here, why don't you come in?" Yoko looked up at her second-floor window.

Taki seemed a bit uncertain, but he followed her up the stairs.

Her room had been unoccupied all day and felt chilly when they entered. Though it was still early in the fall, Yoko wished she had a heater. She put the teakettle on the gas ring and began to prepare some of the coffee Taki had brought earlier.

"So you went to Morimachi today?" he said.

"Yes. Yesterday I went out and found the place where Takashi Ishida had lived here in Tokyo. I located an old man who belonged to the neighborhood association who remembered Ishida." She told him how she had learned that Takashi Ishida had returned to his birthplace in Shizuoka at just about the time Sato had turned up with the new family register, and how this morning she had gone to Morimachi and heard the whole story from the real Ishida.

"From my impression of him and the way he talked, I think he's telling the truth. If it turns out that this isn't accurate, then I think Sato was deceiving Ishida from the very beginning."

"I'm inclined to agree with you in thinking this story is true. In the first place, this man Eto got to know Ishida when they were both involved in an accident, and even then, all the initiative for friendship came from Eto's side. In the second place, the men knew each other for some two years before there was any talk of the family register. There are also the facts that Ishida saw Eto's driver's licence as well as a copy of his family register. I think we can be pretty certain that Takashi Sato originally went by the name Nobuo Eto. That means he bought Ishida's family register for a certain sum of money in order to be able to marry into the Sato family."

"So this leaves us with the question of how Miki Jiro is related to all this."

"Tomorrow I'll get in touch with a friend who works for a newspaper, and if we can verify the murder in Kushiro, I think it'll be safe to assume that Eto's mother also died long ago. Since we know that Jiro Miki was living with his mother in Fukuoka as recently as ten years ago, we'll know that Miki and Eto are not the same person unless we make the rather farfetched assumption that Jiro Miki and his 'mother' were not really mother and son. It was nine years ago that Ishida and Eto first got to know each other. That would mean that Miki would have to have taken over Eto's identity as soon as he arrived in Tokyo, but it seems unlikely that he could have found someone on the spur of the moment who would be willing to let him use his family register.''

Taki put sugar in the coffee Yoko served and took a sip, then breathed deeply. If Jiro Miki was not, in fact, the same person as Takashi Sato, they could no longer assume that Tanaka had gotten to know Midori so that he could get close to Sato and kill him for revenge, and then, when Kasai learned the truth, had killed him, too. This line of reasoning now had to be abandoned. Using what he had just learned from Yoko, however, Taki went over his entire set of assumptions again. He was probably relieved that it now seemed implausible to link his brother-in-law with all these killings.

It had also been distasteful to Yoko to think that Sato was Jiro Miki, a killer and a homosexual, but now all the evidence brought them back to their original riddle. They sat for a time in silence, sipping their bitter coffee. At last Taki put down his empty cup and resumed speaking in a voice that was intended to cheer Yoko up. "I, too, have made a discovery. Tell me what you think of it.''

"What do you mean?''

"I'm talking about this Makino of the Yamate Clinic. I checked the whole city for such a place, and when I didn't find it, you said it might be in some other part of the country. That made sense to me, so I went back and read the obituary on Kasai that appeared in the papers. Afterward I telephoned Mrs. Kasai to make sure the information was correct. I learned that Kasai's family had moved to Yokohama when he was in grade school, and that he had lived there until about ten years ago. He attended college in Tokyo, of course, but he commuted from Yokohama. This led me to wonder if there might be a Yamate Clinic in Yokohama. There is.''

''Were you able to find out if this was the Yamate Clinic Kasai meant?''

''Uh-huh. There are three hospitals and clinics in Yokohama that use the name Yamate. The very first one I called was the Yamate Surgical Clinic, and I found that they have a doctor there named Takeshi Makino, and that he was a friend of Kasai's.''

''Ahha.''

''The clinic does both surgery and plastic surgery, and in the course of our conversation I found that Dr. Makino is the assistant director of the place.''

''Were you able to find out why Kasai mentioned Makino's name just before he died?''

''No. But I decided to go see him when I got back from Chiba, so I made an appointment with him at the clinic for four o'clock tomorrow afternoon. He knows all about Kasai's murder, of course, but I didn't tell him I was the person who discovered the killing or that the doctor's name was the last thing Kasai uttered before he died. I thought that if I told him all that, it might alert him and, in any case, would give him time to think, so I'll just go there tomorrow and see if I can lure him into talking about Kasai.''

''Do you want me to go with you?'' Yoko was thinking about the dark, shadowy figure she had seen earlier near Taki's car. It might be dangerous for Taki to go alone. But she blushed slightly as she wondered what use she would be if there was violence.

''Why don't we go together,'' Taki said. It seemed as though he had a very definite idea of what might happen.

At three-thirty the following afternoon Yoko was at the entrance to Yokohama station waiting to meet Taki. Today, for the first time since leaving her original apartment, she was dressed in a feminine style, wearing an olive-green blouse and a white skirt. Even though she acknowledged the potential danger they faced, she somehow resisted the idea of dressing as a man on a day when she would accompany Taki.

To make up for this lapse of caution, she was extra careful since leaving her apartment to make sure she wasn't followed, and changed trains a number of times along the way. She was confident when she got off the train at Yokohama that no one was trailing her.

Taki arrived at the station five minutes later. After spotting Yoko, who stood apart from the milling throng of passengers, he caught her eye, then, after pausing a moment and letting his eye flick over the crowd to see if anyone was watching, walked out of the station. Yoko followed, staying several steps behind. After they left the station and crossed a pedestrian bridge, Taki began to relax his stride, and Yoko took this as a sign to close the gap between them.

"You must be exhausted. You don't look very well today," he said as he turned toward her. Yoko had not slept much the previous night, but she didn't feel particularly tired at the moment. If she looked pale and exhausted, it was probably the result of strain and tension.

"I'm fine," she said.

After they had walked for a time, blending with the crowds of people on the sidewalk, Taki flagged down an empty cab. Yoko got in first, and as Taki followed her in, he told the driver to take them to Yamatemachi. After the cab had driven a ways, he stroked his jaw and glanced out the rear window, but presently he turned back and took out a cigarette.

"When I asked someone who lived in this area about the Yamate Clinic, they told me it was a rather pretentious place located on the bluff overlooking the harbor."

Yoko nodded and said, "Were you all right last night? What happened after you left my place?" She hadn't slept well the previous night because of her concern that Taki, who had left about nine o'clock, was being followed and might be attacked.

"Nothing much really happened. I didn't see anyone around when I went back to the car. But I did notice that the nights are getting quite chilly at this time of the year. I was surprised how cold it was." He gave a rather bored laugh as he spoke in his great, booming voice, and Yoko wasn't sure what he really felt.

Their taxi emerged beside the harbor and they sped along a road from which they could see the wharves. It was a clear, windswept autumn afternoon. The water in the harbor was a deep, chilly blue color. Triangular waves beat against the sides of the anchored ships.

Yoko had come to Yokohama harbor many times before on sight-seeing trips. She felt a certain nostalgia for the not-so-tall Western-style buildings and the tall ginkgo trees that lined the streets. Signs on the buildings, written in the exotic Roman alphabet, fluttered in the wind. Most of the leaves had fallen from the ginkgo trees and swirled along the edges of the street, blown in eddies by the wind. After passing through the waterfront area, they began to climb a steep hill. Taki leaned forward to instruct the driver. "After we get to the top of this hill, go down the other side a short way and we'll be at the Yamate Clinic."

A moment later they reached the top of a hill that was occupied by expensive homes and well-trimmed trees. "Ah, here we are," said Taki. For some time they followed a narrow, winding street lined with large, Western-style houses set in large gardens. Part way down the far side of the hill they came to a large, old vine-covered mansion that appeared to be deserted. The once high-class grounds were untended and in wild disorder, but the whole city of Yokohama lay spread below them like a painting. The place had an odd charm about it.

Far below the dilapidated house was the sun-drenched sea dotted with white sailboats. The light reflecting off the boats was so bright it hurt Yoko's eyes. The Yamate Surgical Clinic was a quiet, four-story, cream-colored building that had a dark and gloomy look about it. Yoko's initial feeling was that the building blended in well with its surroundings.

They dismissed the taxi and started through the arch in the wall, walking toward the front entrance of the building. Suddenly the slanting rays of sunlight seemed weaker and thinner, and the entry hall of the building seemed cold and dark. To enter the building seemed especially forbidding.

On the right as they entered was a small nook into which Taki looked. He announced his name to the girl who was sitting there and said he had come for a meeting with Dr. Makino.

"Please wait a moment," said the receptionist, a woman dressed in white. She left her small cubicle and quickly disappeared down a long corridor.

Some five minutes later a man wearing a blue smock emerged from that same corridor with long strides. "Thank you for coming. My name is Makino. Sorry to have kept you waiting," he announced in a candid voice, looking back and forth from Taki to Yoko. His thick mane of hair was sprinkled with white, making him look over forty, but his complexion was good, and he exuded the energetic air of a sportsman.

"Pleased to meet you. My name is Taki, I telephoned you yesterday."

Makino looked them over for a moment before saying, "Please come with me." He indicated a door located behind the receptionist's desk.

The room they entered was furnished with a dark leather sofa and chairs, and on the mantel stood a bust of a bearded man, undoubtedly the founder of the hospital. Makino invited them both to sit on the sofa while he occupied the chair opposite.

"You said you were acquainted with Kasai." The way he spoke made it clear that he and Kasai had been close friends.

There was no suggestion that he might in any way be involved in the police investigation of the case.

"That's right. As it turns out, I'm in a position to know a great deal about the circumstances of his death in Fukuoka. Kasai spoke to me moments before he died, and his final words were, 'Makino at the Yamate Clinic.' "

Makino's thick eyebrows shot up in surprise as he heard this. "Oh, really? Those were his final words?"

"Yes. It took me some time to locate the Yamate Clinic in question and you in particular, but I finally did, and that's why I telephoned the other day."

"I see. But why in the world would he have said my name?" Makino's brown eyes hardened and shone with the persistence of a slow and deliberate sort of person. "Excuse me for asking, but how was it you happened to be talking with him when he died?"

Apparently Taki had anticipated this question, for he quickly explained the circumstances surrounding his search for his brother-in-law, and how this had led him to Kasai. Taki said that he had set out for Fukuoka after Kasai had called him. But by the time he had found Kasai, he was dying on the beach, where someone had stabbed him.

In explaining the matter, Taki made no reference to the murder at Amagi, but he did seem to go out of his way to implicate Midori. Apparently he was convinced that the riddle of the relationship between Tanaka and Kasai centered around the person of Midori Sato. Taki also introduced Yoko as someone who was also related to the missing Tanaka.

Makino listened to everything they had to say with great attention.

"Our principal objective, of course, is to try to locate Tanaka, and quite unexpectedly that caused me to be present at Kasai's death. You see, I had only met Kasai once before, and when he called and asked me to come to Fukuoka, I supposed that it had something to do with Tanaka's disappearance. As it turned out, the only thing I heard from his lips was your name. So I came here today hoping you could tell me what it was that Kasai might have wanted to tell me, or hoping that at least you could make a guess."

"Well, that's perfectly reasonable." Makino nodded as though he had clearly understood what Taki had been saying. "But you see, the police haven't come and asked me about this at all. Of course they'll handle this case as they see fit, but if everything really happened the way you say it did, they would have been here asking questions."

"I don't know about that," Taki said, looking away. "The police may get in touch with you sooner or later, but I expect that we have simply gotten to you before they had a chance to."

"I see. So if the police come to me later, I can tell them whatever I please. Is that it?" Makino showed a row of white teeth with his lips pulled back in an aggressive smile. "But the fact is, I can't help you at all. I really have no idea why Kasai might have mentioned my name as he was dying. You see, I know nothing about your brother-in-law, Tanaka— didn't you say his name was Tanaka? And the woman Midori, I've never heard of her. In fact, the last time I saw Kasai was at least ten months ago." Makino seemed to be speaking openly and frankly as though he had nothing to hide.

"Excuse me for asking a personal question, but how was it that you came to know Kasai in the first place?" This time it was Taki's turn to take the initiative.

"We were classmates in high school."

"Of course," said Yoko, nodding.

"We lived quite close to each other when we were in high school. We attended different universities, however, and were not really that close as far as being friends goes. After he moved to Tokyo he would call me on the telephone whenever he came back to Yokohama, but that was about it. What it amounted to was that I was a drinking companion whenever he visited Yokohama, but even when he was drinking, he didn't talk all that much."

"So you're saying that the last time you saw him was something like ten months ago?"

"It was just after the New Year's holiday, so it has been about ten months. We had a night out on the town here in Yokohama. The time before that was almost six months earlier. Actually, he did call me about a month before that, but I was busy with something, so we just talked on the phone, and I didn't see him." The doctor's manner of speaking was quite straightforward and it didn't seem as though he were lying.

"Did you ever hear Kasai mention the name Midori Sato or Shuji Tanaka?" Taki asked the question but didn't really seem to expect an answer. They already knew that Kasai had first met Midori about six months ago at a friend's exhibition, and he had only met Tanaka in August at Midori's home in Aoyama. And after all, if what Makino said was true, he had not seen Kasai since January.

"I'm sorry, but I don't recall his ever having mentioned either of those names."

"Do you have any idea why he might have mentioned your name just as he was dying?"

After a surprisingly long silence Makino's voice seemed strained. "Well, I suppose he must have intended something."

"What?"

"When I talked to him last, just after the New Year, I recalled that he had telephoned me about a month before. . . ." Makino paused and seemed to be trying to recollect something as he folded both hands on the table in front of him. Suddenly he raised his face and said, "This may be very important, and I don't want you to misunderstand, but the reason Kasai came to Yokohama from time to time was to visit gay and lesbian bars."

"Gay bars!"

Makino had spoken the words with such precision they sounded like clinical terms.

18

Unusual Surgery

"Do you mean to say that Kasai came to Yokohama to visit gay and lesbian bars?" Dr. Makino remained silent, apparently sunk in thought, so Taki tried to encourage him to tell them more.

"Yes. Yokohama is supposed to be my territory, and I should have known more about the city than he did, but as far as that sort of place goes, he knew all of them; he always acted as my guide."

"So then you . . ."

"No. As I said earlier, I don't want there to be any misunderstanding of the situation. He didn't go to those places for fun, or because he had a taste for that sort of thing; he went there in connection with his work. You may have already figured this out from looking at his paintings. When he did paintings of women, he preferred women with strong, striking features. I'm not much of an art critic myself, but the first time I saw one of his paintings of a woman, it reminded me of a young, rosy-cheeked samurai. He told me once that he thought the most bewitching beauty and the sort of thing that moved him most was a woman dressing as a man, or a man dressing as a woman, so that the two sexual roles overlap and merge together. He wanted to capture this indescribable charm on his canvases. That's why he spent a lot of time visiting gay bars both in Tokyo and Yokohama. As far as I could tell when I was with him, he wasn't turned on by what he saw in these gay bars. I always had the feeling that he was looking at the people as an artist. If he had really just wanted to go to those places to entertain himself, he surely wouldn't have invited me along.'' By now Makino was speaking in the precise, clinical terms of a physician.

Yoko recalled the strong lines and elegant faces of the women in Kasai's paintings. There had been some sketches that looked as though they had been made in the dressing room of the Kabuki theater, and others that had reminded her of traditional woodblock prints.

"Nevertheless, I still don't understand what you meant earlier when you said you might have a clue regarding Kasai's death." Taki was clearly becoming impatient.

"Well, what I was thinking of may not be related at all. I have no way to verify it, but this year when I met him in January—no, it was earlier than that, it was last summer, I think—after we had been drinking at a couple of places, he took me to a gay bar he knew about. Naturally the subject of sexual ambiguity came up, and I told him the story of something I had experienced. Before I came here to begin my practice, I spent a long time at the university medical center in Tokyo, and at that time I'd go once or twice a week to another hospital where I had a side job. It must have been about nine years ago now that we did a sex-change operation at this other hospital. I told Kasai all about it."

"A sex-change operation?" Taki murmured.

Dr. Makino laughed, showing his white teeth. "I know this is the sort of thing the press would like to get hold of and would have a field day with, but this sort of operation is really very serious, and it's not for your average gay boy. In university hospitals or other hospitals where they have the expertise to perform this surgery, they do it for purely medical reasons. Certain kinds of illness require this treatment. In the gynecology department of the university hospital where I worked they had about one case a year that required vaginal surgery.''

''Vaginal surgery?'' It was clear from Taki's response that he had never heard of such a thing before.

''You see, if a woman lacks a fully formed vagina, it can often be repaired or rebuilt. Most of this sort of surgery that is performed in large university medical centers is not so much sex-change operations, but for patients who were born without clearly defined male or female sexual organs and who are therefore not able to live fully adequate lives. With this sort of surgery they can be helped to have one sex or the other.''

''I see. Well, I've heard of people being sexually ambiguous, but this is the first I have ever heard that the big medical centers could do corrective surgery for it.'' Taki was unable to conceal his curiosity and looked steadily at the doctor.

''It's not really all that unusual. I'm not a specialist in that area, but according to a friend of mine in the gynecology department at the university medical center, about one woman in three thousand has some sort of defectively formed vagina. The greatest number of surgeries are performed on people who are sexually ambiguous in the anatomical sense. There are, for example, cases where a girl has an enlarged clitoris that is mistaken for a penis, and she is raised as a boy, or cases where a boy has a cleft urinary opening. Such conditions can be corrected by surgery and the child can be made to physically resemble the proper sex. So according to my friend, this sort of surgery is not all that uncommon. It is even covered by most forms of health insurance.''

"I see. But tell me about the sex-change operation you mentioned earlier."

"A true sex-change operation is quite rare. You see, in a case of sexual ambiguity, the person has elements of both characteristics that can be developed. But to really make a sex change work, you have to change the person's actual physical features, such as body shape and breasts. It is a very difficult sort of operation to accomplish." There was no change in Makino's soft-spoken manner as he began to elaborate on the clinical details of the operation. Taki was listening carefully with undisguised interest, but Yoko sat with her face averted.

Perhaps Makino noticed Yoko's response, for suddenly he stopped talking and his expression changed. "I'm afraid I've gotten carried away; all this really has nothing to do with the sex-change operation I told Kasai about. That was a case where a person who was completely a man wanted to be transformed into a woman. From the average doctor's point of view this is an unnecessary operation, the kind that only serves to make the doctor rich."

"Don't they have laws that prohibit such unnecessary surgery?"

"Actually, all they really did at the hospital was to remove his penis and testicles. The next stage was to surgically create a vagina for him, but there are only five or six doctors in the whole country who can do that sort of operation, and they're all in large medical centers, and generally won't perform this sort of unnecessary operation. There are probably other doctors who could attempt such an operation, but it would be very risky. In this case the patient took the advice of the doctor and went to Europe to have the vagina done."

"It sounds like a very complicated process. Why did this fellow want to become a woman so badly? Was he gay or something?"

"No. He didn't seem to be gay. The doctor I talked to about it didn't know exactly why the patient wanted to change his sex. Although a surprising number of people secretly feel they would like to try changing their sexual role just on a whim or out of curiosity, most of the time people suppress this urge. Only in extreme cases is a sex change called for. In 1966 the University of Oregon Medical School did a study that showed that one man in every one hundred thousand and one woman in every four hundred thousand was such an extreme case. Perhaps this person was just one of that small number.''

Yoko recalled the story in the magazine article she had read on the train about the American woman who was married and had two children and who wanted to be a man so strongly that she went to a medical center in Baltimore where she had such an operation performed. The article had explained her desire as a sociological as well as a psychological phenomenon. Reading the article, Yoko had suddenly been overcome by embarrassment. On that occasion she had been wearing a suit, disguised as a man, and now she could vividly recall the joyous freedom she had felt. There had been something strangely liberating about being able to transform herself into a man. Where did this curious feeling come from? She wondered if everyone experienced feelings like this.

Makino, of course, had no way of reading Yoko's mind, but he had a thoughtful expression on his face as he said, ''In any case, this sort of thing may become more of a problem in the future. They say that in America it has almost become fashionable to have a sex change, and I read that some specialists are saying there will soon be a time when we can guarantee a child's sex before it's born, and that in the future people will probably be able to alter their sex at will. We're in the process of doing that now.''

Taki was silent for a time, then: ''So in this case you were telling us about that occurred nine years ago, is it possible for a person to have such an operation just by simply saying he wants it?''

''No, but I never heard what the circumstances were in

that case. Much later I happened to meet the head nurse and she said she had heard a rumor that the patient had gone abroad and was able to have a vagina constructed without difficulty. There was no womb, of course, but from the outside he looked completely like a woman. Apparently he returned to Japan as a woman and ended up marrying someone rather prominent. Actually, once the testicles were removed, his body stopped getting male hormones, so his male characteristics would have subsided. Even before the operation, though, he had delicate features, and once when I met him, after he got out of the hospital, he was wearing a woman's kimono and it looked very good on him. A remarkably attractive woman, in fact.'' From the dreamy look in his eyes it was clear that Makino was remembering the woman he had seen nine years ago. ''He had rather strong features even as a man, but he was not so tall, so he didn't seem like a large woman. There was a refined quality about his nose and eyes, and also a certain sort of charm. He had a feminine air about him from the very beginning. So when Kasai told me about the sort of model he was looking for, I thought of this woman, and told him the whole story.''

''I see. What happened then?''

''Kasai showed a lot more interest than I had expected and asked me for that person's name and age, but I didn't even know those details about the patient. I don't even know if he used his real name when he entered the hospital. He appeared to be in his midtwenties at the time, so I told Kasai he would probably be in his early thirties now, but I don't even have any proof of that. Still, Kasai said he was going to make every possible effort to locate that person.''

''Did he ever find her?'' Taki tried to ask the question casually, but excitement was evident in his voice.

''He may have,'' Makino said with a nod as he returned Taki's gaze. ''What I mean is, as I told you earlier, he called me about a month ago. Around the beginning of September. He told me he had found a housewife he thought might be the woman I had told him about. He said he had done some checking on her background and thought it was becoming more and more evident that she was the one. He said he wanted to get together with me so he could tell me about it, but I was scheduled to be in surgery that day, so I told him I would have to make it another time. It's too bad, really. That was the last time I talked to Kasai.'' Makino looked down at his hands, which he kept folding and unfolding on the table. Presently he looked up and said, ''I thought about this when you were telling me your story about Kasai, but you see, I don't know if this is related to Kasai's murder or to Tanaka's disappearance. In any case, if the police come and ask about it, I'll tell them the same thing I just told you. I can understand why you want to locate your brother-in-law as quickly as possible, but there's a murder involved here, so I hope you're careful.''

''Yes, we'll be careful. Kasai's last words make me pretty sure his death is somehow related to what you have just told us. I think he was trying to tell me something about the person mentioned in the story told to him by Makino of the Yamate Clinic.''

''Yes. If he was saying my name, I can only think it was in that connection.'' Makino's eyebrows came together in a frown as he pondered the gravity of the situation.

''I wonder . . .'' Yoko opened her mouth to ask a question for the first time. Makino raised his eyebrows and looked at her in surprise. ''You told us earlier that the person who had the sex-change operation later married and became the wife of a fairly prominent person.''

''Yes. That's what I heard later from the head nurse, but I don't know where she got the story. After all, I suppose it's not all that unusual since outwardly, at least, he looked like an ordinary woman.''

''Of course she looked like a woman to the world at large, but could the person who did the surgery do it so thoroughly that if she got married even her husband could not tell?'' Yoko asked the question with some embarrassment.

Makino returned her gaze steadily and said, ''That's a delicate subject. Of course there were no ovaries, so becoming pregnant was out of the question, but I suppose there's no reason why she couldn't have sex. According to my friend in the gynecology department, they have some very advanced surgical techniques now, and if the woman did not say anything, it's possible the man would not know. But in a case where a perfectly normal man is changed into a woman, there would have to be a continuous treatment of estrogen injections. Naturally once a man's testicles have been removed, his body stops receiving male hormones, and this causes the male characteristics such as an enlarged Adam's apple and facial hair to disappear, but his body would not naturally start producing female hormones. In order to produce some swelling of the breasts and other female characteristics, he needs to have continual injections of female hormones.''

''That means she would have to go to the hospital periodically for shots of the female hormone.''

''Yes. Although if a person knew how to do it, she could get a syringe and inject herself. There's also another way that I have heard of; if she took birth control pills regularly, the injections would be unnecessary. As you know, the pill is used as an oral contraceptive, but it's composed of the female hormone estrogen. When the hormone is ingested this way, it interrupts the body's process of manufacturing the hormone, and this causes ovulation to be interrupted. If there is no ovulation, pregnancy is not possible.''

Yoko was stunned as she heard this; it was as though an explosion had gone off inside her head. Her eyes lost their focus and Makino suddenly seemed very far away. At the same time, his voice suddenly seemed to become Takashi Sato's. She had heard this very same explanation of birth control pills from Sato. After explaining it, he had angrily told her, "I want you to stop taking those pills. You are barely twenty years old and you shouldn't abuse your body that way."

What had provoked Sato's outburst? Why did he know so much about birth control pills? Was it just because Midori used them? Or was it because he knew why she used them?

Yoko found Taki staring at her and an involuntary cry escaped her lips.

Twilight was just beginning to fall, but the dark blue sea that spread out beneath the hotel lounge was still bright with light. Taki and Yoko sat in silence facing each other across a table. The wind had died down and now the surface of the harbor looked warmer and more inviting than it had earlier.

The lounge was quite dark, so on each table stood a small, orange lamp that transformed the people in the room into dim, shadowy silhouettes. A small combo, comprised mostly of steel guitars, was playing a slow, Western tune.

Yoko felt the weight of fatigue throughout her entire body. Taki had ordered a cocktail for her, and she felt its warmth spread through her.

"I don't think we need to wait any longer," Taki said in a low voice. When she looked up and saw his profile against the distant sea, she noticed that his face was lined with fatigue as well. His eyes seemed filled with a melancholy gloom.

"No. I think we dare not wait any longer. I didn't tell the police about Kasai's last words, so it's not very likely that they'll link Makino with the case. But it is likely that Makino will go to them. He might even make a direct call to the investigative unit in Fukuoka and tell them all about our conversation. In fact, I suspect that's what he'll do."

"Yes," Yoko agreed. While they had been talking to Makino, the doctor had apparently realized that one of the keys to solving the murder lay in the relationship between Kasai,

Yoko, and Takashi. No doubt the doctor would quickly put two and two together and go to the police.

"If he goes to the police with his story, they'll be suspicious if they don't also hear from me, and they'll certainly want to question me again. I wouldn't mind that except this time they'll have heard about Midori Sato from Makino and they'll know that she used to live in Aoyama. Once they know that, they'll immediately link all of this with the murder at Amagi. From there it's just a short step before they realize that the woman who was seen in my company on several occasions was surely Yoko Noda."

Yoko nodded slightly. She wanted him to know that she was fully aware of the danger that faced her and said, "Please forgive me. I'm afraid I've caused you a lot of trouble."

"It's really not such a problem as far as I'm concerned. All this has given me something to do in my spare time." Taki paused for a moment to moisten his throat with a sip of water. "After what we heard from Dr. Makino today, I think we can pretty safely establish the sequence of events. The Jiro Miki who killed Shuji Tanaka's fiancée ten years ago was not Takashi Sato, but his wife, Midori Sato. After fleeing to Tokyo, Miki hit on a novel way to avoid detection by the police. Through surgery he had his outward appearance completely altered so that he looked like a woman, and even conceived of the idea of getting married. As long as the police continued their investigation, they would naturally be looking for a man, but by becoming a woman and an ordinary housewife, he was able to throw them off his track. The fact that he even considered this idea in the first place surely relates back to his earlier homosexual relationship with the dance teacher, so he probably already had a tendency in this direction. He may have blackmailed his homosexual lover before coming to Tokyo in order to get the money he needed for his expenses."

"Yes."

"A year after the murder—that would be nine years ago—

Miki went to the hospital where Dr. Makino was moonlighting to have his operation. Later he apparently went abroad to complete his transformation into a woman, and he changed his name to Midori. Eventually he met Takashi Sato and they were married three years ago.''

Yoko considered Taki's words carefully. She envisioned the elegant figure of Midori dressed in a traditional Japanese kimono. Midori had severely correct features, and some shadow of sadness on her pale face. She had a deep, gentle voice. Yoko had always thought she detected some obscure look of fear in Midori's face. No doubt she had been right. Even though they had been married, it had been a common-law marriage. After all, Midori Sato had no family register to verify her identity. No doubt her real register, which identified her as Jiro Miki, was safely hidden away.

''What probably happened was that about three months ago Shuji Tanaka somehow happened to see Midori and realized that she resembled Miki. Tanaka had come to Tokyo alone after his fiancée had been murdered. Even after ten years he still may have felt bitter about the matter, even after he married my sister, and he was determined to get his revenge if he ever got the chance. When he saw the elegant Midori, something in him must have snapped.''

As Taki spoke of Tanaka, a note of sadness crept into his voice. ''He probably wasn't sure right away that Midori and Miki were the same person. He probably found some pretext to converse with her and spent some time scouting around trying to verify her identity.''

''It was at that point, then, that he met Kasai.''

''Right. From Kasai he heard of Dr. Makino's participation in a sex-change operation and that the patient was now living as the wife of a prominent businessman. Kasai would have explained that he had met Midori at the exhibition of a friend. He had spent a lot of time in gay bars and had a special interest in that sort of woman, so I wonder if he realized that Midori was not originally a woman? In any case, he asked her to model for him, and got to know her that way.''

''According to what Kasai told us, he saw Tanaka at Midori's house on two later occasions, and once they went out drinking together. Of course, Kasai would have taken the opportunity to find out what he could about Midori's background and personal history.''

''Yes. Eventually he followed the trail to the Ikejima house in Fukuoka, and by then he must have realized he was in some danger, because when he telephoned me to say that he had learned something, he also said that he was planning to leave the country for a time. Tanaka had probably mentioned his suspicions about Midori's past in order to get him talking, and that's how Kasai knew where to look.''

Taki stopped speaking for a moment and his eyes hardened. He signaled to a passing waiter for more water. Then he resumed. ''But the question is this: if Tanaka suspected that Midori was really Miki in disguise, and if he intended to kill him secretly for revenge, why would he reveal his deepest secret to an outsider like Kasai?''

Taki had expressed this doubt on an earlier occasion; apparently he was even more concerned about this point than Yoko.

''Since Kasai had known Midori longer than Tanaka had, I wonder if he asked Kasai whether Midori was really Miki? If he did, he would have had to reveal his own intentions to some degree,'' Yoko commented.

''Yes. That's the way I figured it, too, at first, but it might be explained just as simply some other way. Tanaka may just have been drunk and let something slip about his plans. But I've been thinking; there may be another way to look at this whole thing.''

There was a melancholy look on Taki's face, and he dropped his gaze to the glass of water that reflected the changing patterns of darkness and candlelight that surrounded them.

"Suppose Tanaka originally got to know Midori because he wanted to get his revenge, but what if he later became allured by her beauty and it turned out to be a case of the biter getting bitten? Surely he'd have struggled in his heart and might eventually have regained his old hatred, which would then have led him to tell the whole sordid story of the beautiful Midori's background to Kasai."

"I see." This view explained some of the things that had happened after the murder. "You're suggesting that he wasn't able to stop himself physically and emotionally from falling in love with Midori. And she encouraged his advances. In the end he lost all desire for revenge and joined Midori in getting rid of Sato." Yoko continued the logical line of reasoning aloud.

She thought of the brutal tenacity of a killer who could see that Takashi had been defeated in the so-called struggle to live, had turned his back on the world and set out to commit suicide with his lover—and still not be satisfied. He had to wait and make sure that Takashi died. When Yoko had suspected Takashi of being the missing Jiro Miki, she had envisioned Tanaka as a man so determined to get his revenge even after ten years that he could commit so casually brutal an act, but now this was no longer the case. On the other hand, if Tanaka had been captivated by Midori's charm, and if he wanted to take her for his own, then perhaps he felt jealousy and hatred for Takashi. In that case it made sense for him to have watched and made sure Takashi died, and to strike him down when he showed signs of reviving.

It would make sense, too, as far as Midori was concerned, for if she hoped to have Tanaka for a lover, the only way she could be sure her unusual physical condition could be kept secret was to get Takashi out of the way.

The waiter brought fresh water and changed the ashtray.

Taki took a sip of the water and, as though suddenly expelling his breath, said, "I really don't think we can explain it that way." Watching his profile, Yoko saw his eyebrows draw together in a frown, and once again she read a faint look of defiance on his face. Yet it seemed clear that he had no other alternative solutions to propose that would explain the facts as they now knew them.

"If Tanaka worked with Midori to kill Takashi, then made it look as though I killed him, he must have later fled and hidden himself somewhere."

"Yes. He's hiding for the time being, but someday he intends to come back and live with Midori." Suddenly Taki gritted his teeth and sat staring at the table, his water glass clenched in his fist. At last, very emphatically, he said, "Yes, I'm sure he's hiding someplace. I've always felt that somehow there was a man behind Midori. When you showed up at her house in Aoyama unexpectedly after returning from Amagi, she must have had a terrible shock, like seeing a ghost. Next she would have realized that if you were still alive, you would see through the crime, so she had the man try to kill you."

"So you do think it was Tanaka who attacked me that night?"

"That was all sort of like a dream," Taki said. "Even now the sequence of events isn't very clear to me. Actually I think I was only conscious of about half of what happened." His last words had a bitter note in them.

"And you think he's also the one who killed Kasai?"

"Probably. I expect it was either Tanaka or Midori."

"But how could he have known where Kasai was staying that night?"

"Well, I have a theory about that, but of course I can't be sure. I think both Kasai and Tanaka were in love with Midori; the only difference was a matter of degree. I think Kasai was attracted to her both as a painter and as a man. So perhaps he went to Fukuoka and found out about Midori and Tanaka's past and used that as a weapon to make Midori take notice of him. On the one hand, he knew he was putting himself in danger, but on the other hand, he was eager to manipulate her. It may seem like a paradox, but I think it's possible.''

"Yes."

"If that was the case, I can see that Kasai might have telephoned Midori from the inn where he was staying. Conceivably he told her what he had found and invited her to meet him somewhere. Midori, however, would have insisted on her innocence and refused. I expect it was after being rebuffed by her that Kasai finally decided to call me and say he had something to tell me. Nevertheless, Midori would have set to work right away to contain the situation. Either she went to Fukuoka herself, or she sent Tanaka. Whoever it was got there ahead of us and managed to silence Kasai. When Kasai mentioned Dr. Makino's name as he was dying, he intended for us to find out about Midori.''

"The maid at the inn said the person who visited Kasai's room was a man of medium height wearing a checked jacket.''

"Uh-huh. That suggests Tanaka is the one.''

"Apparently the idea is to be relentless in getting rid of anyone who sniffs out Midori's secret.'' Once again Yoko felt her skin crawl with fear. It suddenly struck her as curious that she had been able to move about unharmed even though she, more than anyone else, knew the truth about Takashi's death.

Taki seemed to be reading her thoughts, for he said, ''You were attacked that one time, but after that, it seems they changed their mind about you. Even though you know the truth about what happened at Amagi, they probably figure the police will consider you the killer and are pursuing you. And you're stuck as long as you're in a position where you can't find any evidence that will exonerate you from the false charge of murder. Once you're arrested by the police, they'll let the case drop, so Tanaka and Midori are probably counting on you being captured. That must be why they gave up their plan to kill you; they're just waiting for the police to catch you.''

Yoko felt the tension grip her once again as soon as he mentioned the word ''police.'' If Dr. Makino told the police about their visit, they would be after her in full pursuit, and surely her capture would only be a matter of time.

''As you said earlier, we can't afford to wait.''

''Yes. Somehow we have to make sure the police capture either Midori or Tanaka and make them confess before they catch you,'' Taki replied harshly. ''There was the murder at Amagi, there was Kasai's murder, there was Midori's sex change, and yet even with all this we don't have even one piece of firm evidence. At this point we have no choice but to go after them ourselves while we still have the freedom to move.''

''What, specifically, do you have in mind?''

Taki looked steadily at Yoko and said, ''Midori is the key. We have to concentrate on exposing her secret.''

19

The Challenge

IN APARTMENT 102 OF THE FLOWER HILLS CONDOMINIUM the telephone began to ring. Once, twice, three times.

The apartment was furnished with a white table and matching tea cart, and a long, heavy-looking, Victorian mirror framed in white with gold trim. The walls were white and the curtains at the windows were ivory. This was Midori Sato's fortress, decorated all in white. Given her own dark past, she seemed determined to fill her new life with light, and she wanted to be able to reaffirm this continually with her own eyes. Though she had never seen Midori's apartment, this was what Yoko envisioned as she listened to the telephone ringing.

Five times, six times. Still the phone was not answered. It was two in the afternoon. Had Midori gone out? Was she sleeping? Or perhaps she had a premonition and was reluctant to answer.

Seven times. Suddenly someone picked up the receiver

238

and Yoko heard faint breathing, then a rich, mellow voice said, "Hello." It was Midori.

"Hello?" she said once again as Yoko paused to take a breath before plunging in.

"Is this Midori Sato I'm speaking to?"

"Yes, it is. Who is this please?" Just from the tone of her voice Yoko could imagine Midori's faint, old-fashioned eyebrows drawing together in a frown. "My name is Yoko Noda."

There was a gasp and silence at the other end of the line.

"I am Yoko Noda," Yoko repeated, gaining control of herself at last. "I went to Amagi with Takashi Sato with the intention of committing a lovers' suicide, but I survived, remember? I came to your house in Aoyama once. It turns out that was a very dangerous place for me and it was only by good fortune that I escaped dying there."

Midori made no reply. Perhaps she was in shock, holding the telephone rigidly in her hand. There was no sound of breathing.

"I've done some investigating and learned a little about you since the last time we met. Yesterday I went to a certain hospital and found out all about a certain operation that was performed nine years ago."

"What are you talking about?" This was Midori's first response. She seemed calm and her voice was still gentle.

"It was at the Meiji Clinic nine years ago. The fact is that you transformed yourself from Miki Jiro into a woman named Midori. That was the first step."

The Meiji Clinic was where Dr. Makino had been moonlighting in those days. Taki had learned this from one of the nurses at the Yamate Surgical Clinic, as well as the name of the doctor who had been in charge of the clinic.

"The Meiji Clinic no longer exists, so it was real hard to check on things, but the man who was director of the clinic at that time and the man who performed the operation on you was Dr. Fujimori. I found that he is now the associate director of another clinic. I visited him and we had a long and detailed talk. They say a doctor will never reveal anything about his patients, but Dr. Fujimori was willing to appreciate the gravity of the situation as well as my position, so he agreed to tell me everything except the patient's name. The doctor said he remembers your face—excuse me, the patient's face—very well, and since the operation was of a rather unusual nature, he has preserved all the records. He felt that it would be a good precaution so that if there was ever any crime involved with this, he could make the records public.''

''You say if there were ever any crimes committed—what's that supposed to mean?'' Midori whispered softly.

''You know perfectly well what I mean. I'm talking about Takashi Sato's death, and Teiji Kasai's death, not to mention the murder of Noriko Yuki some ten years ago.''

''Why, you . . . What are you talking about?'' Now the voice at the other end of the line was nasty and hateful. But though the words were charged with unconcealed emotion, there seemed to be a trace of fear in her voice as well.

''Shall I spell it out for you more clearly? You see, I have ample proof, should I care to use it, that you were once a man named Jiro Miki. When I reveal that, it will be easy to solve three murders, and I will be free to live my normal life again. But there's something else in this that's even more important than that.''

Midori made no reply.

''You see, even if I'm able to prove my innocence, I don't really want to go back to school, and now Takashi is no longer alive. I am all alone in the world; there's nothing here for me. What I want most of all to do is to flee to a foreign country where no one knows me. I want to have the pleasure of starting over a new life. In a sense I want to do what you did nine years ago when you decided to make a new life for yourself.''

Still Midori made no response.

"I have the evidence, and before I went to the police with it, I wanted to talk to you on the telephone. I think you understand what I'm saying."

Again there was silence for a time, then Midori said, "Is it money you want?" Her voice was flat and toneless.

Yoko's cheeks burned, but she was determined to forge ahead. "After all, by going abroad I would be relieving you of facing up to your crimes."

"How much do you want?"

"I'd like to meet with you and discuss it directly."

"I'm sure you know that my husband's company went bankrupt. All I got from his estate was this apartment, but there may be a few other assets that were left lying about."

"We can talk about that when we meet. Otherwise I'll just go to the police and tell them all I know. Shall I do that?"

"No. I don't mind meeting with you." Midori's voice seemed to waver. "When would you like to meet?"

"Anytime is fine with me, but I think it would be best if we do it as soon as possible. The only problem for me is that I might be picked up by the police at any moment, and if that happens, I'd have no choice but to reveal your secret to them. I can meet you anytime; I can even meet you right now if you wish."

"No. Not right now. Wait a while." Midori seemed to be desperately racking her brain for a plan. "How about tomorrow? Could you come to my apartment tomorrow?"

"I'm afraid that's out of the question." At last Yoko felt she had gained the advantage. "You see, I might disappear just as Kasai did."

"In that case, where would you suggest we meet? We could hardly carry on a private conversation in a public coffee shop or someplace like that."

"You're right. How about if we meet in a car? At noon tomorrow I'll be waiting in a gray Toyota parked just outside that restaurant, the Sunrise, where you used to meet Kasai. I'll be in the driver's seat, so you should get in from the passenger side. We won't go anywhere; we'll just sit in the parked car and talk. That way we won't have to worry about eavesdroppers. I think that would be the best place for us to talk privately. Besides, if you decide to alert the police, I can always take off in the car. I have confidence in my skill as a driver.''

Midori seemed amenable to these arrangements. She breathed softly for a time, then said, ''All right, we'll do it your way.'' A note of determination had entered in her voice as she spoke. Yoko made no response, and a moment later she heard the phone being hung up.

Yoko replaced the receiver, and Taki, who had been standing silently beside her, switched off the tape recorder he had placed next to the telephone receiver. Yoko let out a deep breath. She could feel the sweat in the middle of her back and in her armpits.

''Good job,'' Taki said with his usual sardonic smile. He lit a cigarette and stood up, opening the aluminum sliding window. In swept the dry, autumn air, and with it the rumble of the city like a great earth tremor.

They were in a room on the twelfth floor of a clean, new building in the heart of the city. It was the architectural office of a man who had attended school with Taki. Yoko wasn't sure what Taki had said to the man, but they had gotten his permission to use the place, and since it was a holiday, the office was deserted. The choice of offices had been important since the telephones in this one were ordinarily equipped with recording equipment.

They rewound the recording and played it back, listening carefully all the way through. At last Taki spoke. ''It looks like she took the bait. This proves that something fishy's going on there, but we still don't have enough proof to do anything about it.''

''Yes.'' Yoko had intimidated Midori by saying she had met with the former director of the Meiji Clinic, but it had been a complete bluff. After half a day searching, all Taki had been able to turn up were the name of the clinic where Midori had had her operation and the name of the doctor who had been its director.

In fact it was most improbable that the doctor had kept the records of that time at all, and they couldn't be sure the doctor would be able to provide any proof even if they'd located him. Now they had this recording of Midori's conversation, but she had neither admitted nor denied the charges. Thus, even if they pursued Midori and ensnared her, if she didn't actually confess, and if they failed to turn up some incontrovertible proof while they held her, their cause would be lost.

"So, it's set for tomorrow at noon. Good." Taki looked at his watch, then turned to Yoko. "Nevertheless, we'll have to be careful now that we're about to take the last step. We have to be sure we don't blow it here. I've had lots of experience on building sites where, even though everything is laid out right in front of you, there are still plenty of things that can go wrong."

Midori appeared on the steps in front of the Floral Hills condominium at six-thirty the following morning. She made a striking figure in a rich, silver-gray, three-quarter-length coat and a dark purple pant suit.

The sun shone on the street, and occasionally the clatter of footsteps from a suited businessman on his way to work were heard, but in the apartment building itself, all the windows remained curtained, and all the cars were lined up in the parking lot, their owners still asleep at this hour.

When Yoko had observed Midori at close range at the house in Aoyama, she had worn her jet black hair swept up, but today it was tied back with a pearl ribbon and hung in a gentle curve along the line of her jaw. She wore a pair of thick Dior sunglasses and carried a shoulder bag that matched her coat. She also carried a small, white suitcase. Everything about her suggested a smart young lady off on a pleasure trip. But Yoko was not fooled for a moment. A single glance had been enough to assure her that Midori was fleeing.

Coming down the front steps of the condominium, Midori stopped halfway and took a long, slow look along the street beyond the parking lot. Suddenly the appearance of a carefree young lady on a trip disappeared. Midori was watching her surroundings with great intensity and vigilance.

Yoko had parked her Honda among the cars in the parking lot, and now slid her body below the dashboard and held her breath as she waited for Midori's gaze to sweep over her. The car she was using belonged to Taki's elder brother. Taki had borrowed it the previous morning and she had used it ever since.

Over the telephone, Midori had promised to meet Yoko today at noon at the coffee shop in Harajuku. But it seemed less than likely that she would live up to that agreement. One possibility Yoko and Taki had considered was that Midori would not come to the meeting alone. Another was that she'd try to flee before the meeting or try to get in touch with Tanaka, wherever he was hiding.

Taki had cautioned Yoko not to take her eyes off Midori even for an instant. He warned her that if she let Midori give her the slip now, there would probably not be another chance.

They had set up their plan before making the telephone call to Midori, and Taki had already borrowed his brother's car. The gray Toyota was the one Yoko had promised to have parked in Harajuku, and besides, Midori may have remembered seeing it before. For that reason Yoko was now driving the blue Honda, and was determined to keep Midori in sight day and night. Keeping track of her was Yoko's job, for Taki had to go work as usual.

Up until the previous evening the two had kept watch on the apartment together. In fact, Taki had stayed on watch until two o'clock in the morning while Yoko got some rest at a nearby inn. When she returned at two o'clock, Taki had moved from the street corner where he had been watching and slid the blue Honda into an empty space in the parking lot. He reported that up to that point there had been no sign of Midori trying to leave the place. The lights in her apartment had gone out shortly after midnight and everything had been quiet since then.

As they changed the guard, Taki had told her that he would be sleeping at his sister's house, which was less than a ten-minute drive away. Yoko was to keep watch for the rest of the night, and no matter what happened, she promised to call him at eight o'clock.

By now, however, it was clear that Midori was on the move even though it was only six-thirty in the morning. Suddenly the sluggish weariness that had engulfed Yoko disappeared.

Midori came down the steps and began to walk directly away from Yoko. As she disappeared around the corner of the street, Yoko started the car. She slowly nosed it forward to the corner until she could see around it. Some thirty yards away she saw Midori standing at a bus stop along with two or three men on their way to work. Since it was early morning, she had apparently given up trying to catch a taxi and decided to take a bus. But before the bus arrived, a hired car appeared and pulled to a stop a short distance in front of Midori. She took a few steps toward it and signaled.

Midori got into the car and set off up the street. It was not yet rush hour, so the streets were not congested. They went straight through the intersection in front of Meguro station without stopping, and presently came onto the freeway at the Meguro interchange. Traffic was still moving smoothly on the freeway. The sunlight was growing brighter and was beginning to shine in Yoko's eyes, making vision difficult.

The driver of the hired car appeared to be heading in the direction of Haneda airport, their apparent destination. Midori was carrying a suitcase, and was no doubt prepared to travel. The question was, where did she plan to go? Maybe she was just fleeing with no particular destination. Who would be there waiting for her when she arrived at wherever she was going?

Yoko wanted desperately to get in touch with Taki, but here on the freeway she could do nothing. On the other hand, now that she knew Midori was going to the airport, she felt that she and Taki would be able to figure out a plan.

Without hesitation they now followed the route Yoko had predicted and merged into the traffic heading toward the airport. They would be there in less than thirty minutes.

Once there, the hired car stopped in front of the domestic terminal. Seeing this, Yoko heaved a sigh of relief, for she had been afraid that Midori might be trying to flee the country. Suddenly Yoko realized she had to find a parking place—and fast. Eventually she found a space in a lot adjacent to the terminal building. Luckily it had not taken too much time.

Yoko raced into the lobby and looked about frantically. Some distance away she caught sight of Midori walking away from her, scanning the airline counters. There were more people in the lobby than Yoko had expected, but not much confusion, so Yoko would have to be careful that Midori didn't spot her. Midori had been very cautious when she left the apartment, but now she seemed more relaxed and less intent on her surroundings. While they had been on the freeway, Yoko had made a point to stay some distance behind the hired car and had allowed other cars to come between them, so she was pretty sure Midori had not noticed her following. And yet, each time she caught a glimpse of Midori's strong features, she couldn't help but notice that since her arrival at the airport, the woman's face was grim with tension, the tension of someone concentrating entirely on what she is doing.

Midori paused and scanned the counters of various airlines, examining the travel posters and the timetables. At last she went up to the ticket counter of Japan Airlines. Three or four people were ahead of her. Midori waited her turn, but just as the girl at the counter was about to help her, Yoko hurried forward and took the place right behind Midori. She was so close she could smell Midori's perfume.

"I would like to book a seat on flight 503 for Sapporo."

"One moment, please." The attendant consulted her schedules for a moment before saying, "Yes. We have seats available on that flight."

"Thank you. I'd like a single ticket, please."

The attendant began to write up the ticket and asked, "Your name, please."

"Michiko Yasukawa."

"Age?"

Yoko moved away as Midori answered, hurrying to a board some distance away that listed Japan Airlines time schedules. Flight 503 for Sapporo was scheduled to leave at 8:10. It was now only 7:05. Next she hurried to the coffee shop located in the Number One concourse, where she had earlier spotted a public telephone beside the cash register. Yoko uttered a prayer as she dialed the phone, hoping that Taki would still be at his sister's house. The phone rang one and a half times before Taki came on the line, and Yoko felt her throat grow tight with relief.

"What's happening? I was just about to come around and see you."

"I'm at the airport right now. Midori is taking the eight-ten JAL flight to Sapporo." Yoko also reported that Midori had bought a single ticket.

"The departure is at eight-ten? I might be able to make it if I'm lucky." There was urgency in Taki's voice. "I'll leave right now. You buy two tickets on the same flight and take care of the check-in and all that. If you can only get one ticket, that'll be all right, too. If the flight is fully booked, get standby tickets. If I don't get there in time, you go ahead and make sure that you get on that plane."

It would be touch and go for Taki to make it to the airport on time, so they decided to meet at the departure concourse, and Yoko hung up.

20

An Airport in the North

FLIGHT 503 BOUND FOR SAPPORO WAS SCHEDULED TO TAKE off at 8:10, but it was fifteen minutes past that time when the Jumbo SR climbed into the clear October sky. Inside the plane about eighty percent of the seats were occupied. Taki and Yoko were seated near the front exit, a fellow passenger on one side and the aisle on the other. Taki had raced from his sister's house as soon as Yoko called, caught a taxi, and by urging the driver to hurry, had arrived at the airport shortly before eight. Meanwhile, Yoko had bought two tickets, checked in, and was waiting for him in the boarding area in the Number Two departure concourse. Luckily it was a jumbo jet so there were seats available even at the last minute, and they had thought ahead about Taki giving Yoko money so they would be able to respond to any sudden change of plans. This precaution had paid off now.

Yoko could not see Midori from where she was sitting. In fact, after telephoning Taki from the coffee shop, Yoko had

248

returned to the ticket lobby, but Midori was no longer in sight. Relieved, Yoko bought the tickets and checked in.

When the boarding call was announced, she concealed herself beneath the stairs leading to the International Terminal and watched the check-in gate. Presently she spotted Midori. She appeared to be talking to one of the attendants at the TOA Domestic Airways counter, then she hurried across the lobby, showed her boarding pass to the man at the gate, and started up the escalator toward the boarding area. She seemed to be traveling alone.

Luckily Yoko and Taki were able to slip aboard the plane at the very last moment. Though they had not seen where Midori was sitting, they were confident that she was on the plane. The Jumbo SR could hold up to five hundred passengers on two levels, so it wasn't surprising that they did not locate her right away.

Yoko looked over at Taki, but he seemed untroubled as he read the morning newspaper. They had agreed it would be best to be as inconspicuous as possible while on the airplane. Of course they needed to ensure that Midori didn't spot them, but even so, Taki didn't seem concerned that anything would go wrong. By now Dr. Makino might have gone to the police and told them about the visit she and Taki had made to his office. If he had, a renewed search for them would already be under way. Perhaps Taki had this in his mind, for, although he was wearing the same dark suit he had worn the other day, he was also wearing a large pair of sunglasses, which was unusual for him.

For the moment, at least, the mood inside the airplane seemed tranquil, and after the seat-belt light went off, the flight attendants began to move along the aisles, handing out hot towels.

Below they could see the ragged coastline. There were few clouds, and on their right the Pacific Ocean spread out in a bright silver sheet that made them squint to look at. Yoko lay back in her seat, closed her eyes, and began to doze. Her mind kept working, however, turning over various thoughts.

Midori had broken her promise to meet Yoko by boarding this plane. Apparently she had taken seriously Yoko's threat that she had definite proof of Midori's former identity. This fact was the key to unraveling the crimes that had been committed. Even if Midori had been able to silence Yoko by giving in to her demands, it was only common sense to assume that eventually the blackmail demands would increase, and in the end she would no longer be able to escape. No doubt she had decided to get out now through what she considered to be her blackmailer's carelessness.

What was not so clear, however, was why Midori had chosen Sapporo in Hokkaido as her destination. Was there some special significance in the place? Yoko remembered that Takashi Sato had been born in the town of Kushiro in Hokkaido. Somehow that information kept nagging at her, and it seemed related to the pursuit of Jiro Miki. This train of thought reminded her of the tragic events surrounding the death of Takashi's parents and how he had tried to flee his past by obtaining a phony family register. The dark gloom that always seemed to surround him had sprung from this tragedy and from his knowledge of Midori's dark secret. By the time he had begun his love affair with Yoko, things must have been completely dismal for him, and Yoko had glimpsed a look of real tragedy in his eyes.

On the night he had invited her to accompany him to Amagi, she had been conscious of the deep anguish in his features. At first he had thought he could resolve his problems, but in the end they had overwhelmed him, and Yoko recalled the pity she had felt. With these thoughts in mind, she drifted off to sleep.

She suddenly came awake with the announcement to fasten their seat belts for landing. Looking over at Taki, she found him gazing forward with no particular expression on his face.

It was 9:55 when they arrived at Sapporo's Senzai airport. Yoko only looked at Taki once as she got up from her seat. As they moved into the aisle, he whispered, "You go out the front exit and wait for me in the lobby. I'll go out the rear exit and see if there's anything there."

Somehow Yoko felt unexpectedly warm as she exited the airplane. Perhaps they had heaters on inside the terminal building. The passengers debarking from the Jumbo SR formed a line as they silently made their way through a labyrinth of corridors into the terminal building. Since Yoko had been sitting near the exit, she was near the front of the line. She could see no sign of Midori by the time she finally reached the main lobby of the terminal building.

The terminal itself was quite new. Above the forest of steel towers and antennas the sky was clear and cloudless. All around them at the end of the wide runways stood forests of trees.

The small lobby was soon thronged with people. Most of the passengers clustered around the baggage-claim area. Yoko joined this crowd but kept her eyes turned in the other direction, watching the stairs the rest of the passengers were descending. Suddenly tension gripped her as she saw Midori among them. She was wearing sunglasses and clutched her shoulder bag with one hand. Reaching the bottom of the stairs, Midori paused and looked around the lobby, then began walking away from where the rest of the passengers were clustered. Midori was carrying her small suitcase and had no need to wait at the baggage counter. She was heading for the exit.

Just at that moment someone tapped Yoko on the shoulder. She whirled around to find Taki standing next to her. "Quick!" he whispered. She saw that he, too, had his gaze fastened on the retreating Midori.

As they shoved their way through the glass doors, they suddenly found themselves chilled by the surprisingly cold air outdoors. The day was bright and sunny, but the air was cold with the chill of late autumn. Thirty feet away stood a single taxi and Midori was heading straight for it. There were several taxis in the line, but only the first one was occupied by a driver. Since the arriving passengers had not yet received their luggage, the drivers were lounging around, in no hurry to occupy their cabs. With a sinking feeling, Yoko realized that the taxi behind the one Midori was getting into was empty, but at that moment a young man wearing a sweater and sandals approached Taki and asked, "You want to go into town?" No doubt he was the sort of unlicensed cabby you always find in tourist areas.

A look of relief spread over Taki's face and he asked, "Can you follow that cab?" With his jaw he indicated the taxi Midori was just climbing into with her suitcase.

"Sure," the young man said with a faint smirk as he slid quickly into the driver's seat of his own car.

The two cars set off down the road, the second maintaining a fixed distance between them. The road was lined with cool, green acacia trees. Presently the lead car entered a freeway ramp. There was little traffic on the freeway and their speed quickly increased to sixty miles an hour as they passed between a pair of hills and ascended a slope. Yoko and Taki's car clung tenaciously to the car ahead.

"They're obviously heading for Sapporo," Taki muttered, keeping his eyes on the car ahead.

"Are you familiar with Hokkaido?" Yoko asked, for this was her first trip to the north country.

"No. Not really, but I've been to Sapporo two or three times."

The wide, grassy prairie around them was yellowed with autumn. The fields had already been harvested, and the dry earth was visible through the stubble. Here and there they saw a silo or the galvanized roof of a farmhouse.

Outside the car the wind was blowing strongly, and they could imagine how cold it must be. Yoko was suddenly reminded of the highway at Amagi. Had Midori and her accomplice been following her and Takashi just as they were now following Midori?

After about fifteen minutes they left the freeway and found themselves in the middle of Sapporo. Yoko was disoriented, had no clear idea of the direction in which they were heading, but she sensed that they were getting close to the center of the city as the streets became more congested. There was a relatively large number of cars on the streets of the city.

The farther they fell behind the car in front, the more difficult it was to follow. Wherever Midori was heading, she showed no sign of getting out of the taxi anytime soon. They followed through the streets, always keeping one car between them and Midori until at one intersection they got cut off by a changing stoplight.

"Damn!" said Taki. "We don't know where she was heading, and now we've lost sight of her."

"Wait," Yoko said as she suddenly thought of something. Taki looked at her questioningly. "TOA Domestic Airways."

"What?"

"At the airport in Tokyo before she boarded the airplane I saw Midori talking to someone at the ticket counter of TOA Domestic Airways, so maybe that's where she's headed."

"TOA uses Okadama airport instead of Senzai," said the driver. "Shall I take you there?" He was clearly tired of chasing other taxis.

"Yes," Taki said with some uncertainty, but in the meantime Midori's taxi was lost. "Let's do that."

The taxi abruptly turned into a side street.

"Okadama airport is east of the city," Taki explained. "All of TOA's local flights originate there."

Where could Midori be going? All they could do now was gamble that she was going to the other airport. As they passed through the streets, the landscape began to change to open fields and factories. Tall poplars, their pretty yellow leaves fluttering in the breeze, lined the road.

It was 11:50 when they arrived at Okadama airport. The terminal was a small, low building compared to Senzai airport, and few people were around. When they got out of the taxi and entered the lobby, there was no sign of Midori. Taki looked at Yoko, gave a small, uncertain nod, and led her to an inconspicuous corner near a newsstand.

On the wall was a timetable of flights for Hakodate, Kushiro, and Memambetsu. A sign on the counter said CHECK-IN FOR THE 12:45 FLIGHT TO MEMAMBETSU.

"Memambetsu?" Yoko said without realizing she had spoken aloud.

"It's near Abashiri on the northeast coast of Hokkaido," Taki said, but suddenly he was clutching Yoko's shoulder.

Midori was approaching the counter, taking a ticket from her handbag as she walked. She seemed to be preparing for boarding and soon joined a small group of waiting people. About thirty feet away on the parking apron outside stood an orange and white YS-11.

"You wait here," Taki said, heading for the counter. After talking to the attendant for a time, he drew a wallet from the pocket of his overcoat. After he had bought two airplane tickets and completed the check-in procedures, he returned to Yoko.

"Let's board," he said, and they went to the boarding exit, which was deserted by now except for the attendant.

It was a small, propeller-driven airplane with a capacity of no more than fifty or sixty passengers, so there was a considerable risk that Midori might spot them this time. Taki had to stoop to enter the low door, and since there was no assigned seating, he quickly found a seat in the third row. Yoko found a seat across the aisle, one row behind him. Having just gotten off a jumbo jet, this plane seemed very small and cramped.

"Did you see where she is sitting?" Yoko asked.

"I thought I caught a glimpse of her way at the back," Taki said, without turning his head. He nervously turned his attention to the window. Yoko had been concentrating on following Midori, but apparently Taki was also worried about the chance that the police were following them.

The airplane took off without incident and on schedule. Yoko rummaged in the seat pocket in front of her and found a map of their route. Sure enough, there on the southern shore of Lake Abashiri was the town of Memambetsu with a red mark beside it, indicating it was one of the airline's stops. According to the route marked on the map, the plane would first head south from Sapporo, then turn back north.

Was Midori's destination really Abashiri? This seemed odd. Earlier, when she had perused the schedule in the airport, Yoko had supposed that Midori would take a flight to Kushiro. Why would she be going to Abashiri instead?

A short time later she saw the deep blue wall of the mountains from the window. As they followed the line of the mountains, she noticed that they were bright with snow. Presently the plane began to descend. Some fifty minutes after takeoff, the plane made a lazy circle over the deep, green water of Lake Abashiri and landed at Memambetsu.

The landscape was quite different here. The runway was surrounded by dry wheat fields and brown pastures. Everything bespoke the changing of the seasons, and there was no trace of summer lingering here.

As the plane rolled to a stop, the cabin's audio system began playing "Stardust." Of all the passengers, Taki was the first out of his seat. Even before the exit was opened he was heading for it with long strides, and Yoko hurried to follow. As they went down the steps from the airplane, they could feel the dry wind. The sunlight seemed to make the air extraordinarily clear.

Taki hurried across the apron to the terminal. Somewhere among the thirty or forty passengers debarking behind him was Midori. It would not do for her to notice them now. If she did, she would surely change her plans, even if she intended to meet Tanaka here. Somehow Yoko had a hunch there was a man waiting for Midori at the end of her journey.

When they entered the terminal, Taki paused for a moment to get his bearings. A small knot of people in the spacious lobby stood waiting to greet the arriving passengers, but there was no place to hide. Directly in front of them was a coffee shop with a red gabled roof. Taki went in. It was called the Okhosk, and the windows on one side looked directly out over the terminal lobby, while the windows on the other side looked out over the front of the building.

Without a word Yoko seated herself across the table from Taki. When the waitress came, Taki simply said, "Coffee, please," and held up two fingers. With his other hand he fished some coins out of his pocket and placed them on the table. The whole time he kept his eyes alertly on the crowd of arriving passengers. Yoko was sitting with her back to the baggage-claim area, so all she could do was slide down as low in her seat as possible to give Taki a clear view.

"There she is," he said in a whisper. Twisting around in her seat, Yoko looked over her shoulder in time to see Midori just entering the terminal building. She stopped at the entrance and leisurely glanced about the terminal. It was hard to tell if she was suspicious and thought something was wrong, or if she was looking for someone who might be waiting for her.

Taki was watching her intently and was just about to get up from his seat when the waitress arrived and placed two cups of coffee on the table. At the same moment something quite unexpected happened. A middle-aged man wearing a dark suit entered the coffee shop and approached their table. He looked the couple over carefully and said, "You must be Osamu Taki, and you would be Yoko Noda."

From behind his glasses Yoko could feel the intensity of the man's scrutiny. She sucked in her breath as she suddenly realized who he must be. He quietly pulled a leather wallet from his pocket. "I'm with the Abashiri Police Department.

Why don't we go downtown; there are a few questions I'd like to ask you.''

"Damn!" This time it was Taki who spoke. At the same moment he suddenly thrust his way past the waitress and raced out of the coffee shop. As Yoko turned to watch him go, she also saw a slim man in a gray coat detach himself from the crowd of people in the lobby and approach Midori, who was still standing by the entrance. Yoko knew that Shuji Tanaka had surfaced at last.

Now that the police had caught up with her just at the moment she had finally found Tanaka, Yoko was determined to prove her innocence. Suddenly she, too, darted away from the table, slipping past the short detective and following Taki.

"Hey! Wait. Stop," he called after her in a loud voice, and perhaps he managed to trip her, because the next thing Yoko knew, she had fallen heavily onto the cement floor.

As a result of the uproar, both Midori and Tanaka turned in their direction, but the man who had his coat collar turned up to conceal his face was not the man Yoko remembered from the photograph of Shuji Tanaka. The tight eyebrows and the line of the nose gave the man a look of cold formality. Yoko had seen this pale face before, but it had been different, more sunburned and more robust. Yoko stared in blank amazement from where she lay sprawled on the floor. The man's gaze met Yoko's and their eyes locked. She could not believe her eyes. It was her lover, Takashi Sato.

"Takashi!" The cry came unconsciously to her lips.

Takashi's features became strangely distorted. The pair continued to look at each other for several seconds. At last, and with great difficulty, he looked away. He took Midori by the arm and started to hurry away.

The police detective grabbed the fallen Yoko, and at the same moment Taki pinioned the fleeing Sato. Midori was the only one who remained free. Takashi shouted something to her, but she turned and fled. She shoved her way through the bystanders who were watching all that was going on with amazement. She went out the door and started across the parking lot to an old, battered foreign car parked nearby.

Midori made it to the gray Volkswagen, and they watched as she sped away.

21

The End of the Journey

TAKASHI SATO, TAKI, AND YOKO WERE ALL TAKEN BY THE police detective to the police station at Memambetsu, and from there to the main police headquarters at Abashiri.

Most of the questioning in this matter would, of course, have to be carried out by the police in Shizuoka, where the first murder had been committed, but for the time being the Abashiri police questioned all three of them individually to find out how it happened that Takashi was still alive, and how he came to be in Hokkaido.

In response to questioning by senior detectives in the Abashiri police force later that same day, Takashi calmly made the following confession:

"I got to know Midori Aikawa about three years ago when she was working in a restaurant that I often went to, and now she is my common-law wife, but I have not listed her on my family register. I met Midori about a year after my first wife, Misako, died. From the very first I knew I was in love with

259

Midori, and after having an affair with her for nearly a year, we began to talk about getting married. Midori was delighted and agreed to the plan, but said she wanted to wait a while before she was actually listed in my family register. She explained that she understood I was coming under heavy criticism by the people in my company, and for that reason she thought it would be better to wait. Frankly speaking, I, too, was pleased to keep the matter quiet for the time being. Ever since my first wife died, her relatives have been trying to force me out of the company and have treated me as an outsider. It was a very difficult position for me to be in.

"Midori told me she had been raised as an only child by her mother, and her mother had recently died, so at that time she was alone in the world. Under those circumstances she quietly moved into my house in Aoyama, and we kept the matter quiet.

"For about a year we lived together normally, but after only a few months I had noticed that there was something strange about Midori. She was physically different. Forgive me for being so blunt, but in her daily activities she seemed to be somehow different from other women. The thing that made me feel this most strongly was her hands. Midori's hands are soft, and she often wore gloves to protect them, but somehow the bones were big, and the fingernails were rounded, and they just gave the impression of being more like a man's hands. With my conscious mind I dismissed the idea as pure nonsense, but it stayed with me and kept gnawing at my mind, and soon I found that I was obsessed with the idea.

"My suspicions were confirmed when I found out that Midori was taking birth control pills. From the time we were first living together I made it clear to her that I hoped we could have a child right away. I felt that if I had a child and heir, it would relieve me of some of the pressure at the company, and I would then be able to officially put Midori on my family register. But as it turned out, of course, there was no sign of Midori becoming pregnant. Then, quite by accident one day I saw her coming out of a neighborhood gynecological clinic and asked her about it, and she told me she was going there to get injections of hormones that would ensure that she would become pregnant. She said she had kept this secret from me because she was embarrassed about it. But the hormone treatments didn't seem to be working. That fact and my recollection of how nervous Midori had been when she explained to me her reasons for going to the clinic made me suspicious.

"One day I discovered a cache of birth control pills among Midori's things. I had thought my wife was receiving medical treatment to increase her fertility, so I couldn't understand why she would be taking birth control pills. I decided to take the matter into my own hands and went to the clinic to make inquiries. I was stunned by what I learned. They said that my wife had no ovaries as a result of a surgical procedure she had undergone. Midori had been this way ever since I had known her. She had requested hormone injections, but the doctor had suggested birth control pills as a simpler alternative, and he had written a prescription for her. Of course she had told the doctor that I had agreed that she should take the birth control pills. Without telling his nurses about it, the doctor made up a medical chart for Midori that indicated the pills were needed because she had menstrual difficulties, but since I didn't know about any of this, it was a real shock when I found out the truth.

"That night I questioned Midori about it, and after a fit of weeping, she confessed everything to me. She said that nine years ago she had undergone a sex-change operation. The only explanation she could give for it was to repeat over and over that she had simply wanted to become a woman. The funny thing about it is that even after she told me about it, I didn't feel that there was anything odd or abnormal about it. Even after I learned the truth, Midori seemed unbelievably feminine to me. She was still a beautiful and wonderful wife.

"It was unfortunate that Midori was this way, but I had no intention of throwing her out of my home. All I could think of was that I wanted to do what I could to ease the burden she had to bear as a human being. In fact, I was very much moved, and as I looked back over the troubles in my own life, I could appreciate her difficulties. A person never knows how he will be moved by an experience such as this. But my body reacted differently from my emotions; it rebelled. I couldn't bear the thought of embracing Midori or of holding her in my arms. I didn't stop loving her in my heart, but physically I could do nothing.

"During that whole period, I sort of lost my emotional equilibrium. The difficulties my company was experiencing also added to the problem. Or maybe it was the other way around; perhaps the company fell on hard times because I was the president and I was preoccupied with my personal difficulties. In any case, I was caught in a vicious circle and everything seemed to be falling apart on me.

"It was in the midst of all this that I became intimate with Yoko Noda. She is the one I really feel sorry for. She has committed no crime; she's not the one who killed Shuji Tanaka."

"Does that mean you're the one who killed Shuji Tanaka?"

"No. Actually I'm not. Tanaka's appearance on the scene just made for another terrible ordeal I had to suffer. Tanaka first made contact with Midori sometime in July, but it was not until one evening toward the end of August that I met him for the first time. I had an appointment concerning the car accident, but it was postponed, so I ended up getting home earlier than I had planned. I found this man there with my wife. Midori introduced him as Shuji Tanaka. Right away I sensed something peculiar was going on. Tanaka just gave me an evil look and said some threatening things I didn't really understand and left the house. When I asked my wife about him, she said he was an acquaintance from the past, from the time before she had become Midori. Actually, she said she had not really known him too well at that time, but that he knew all about her. He had spotted her on the street in July quite by chance, and had approached her, saying his name was Nakayama, but Midori knew right away that he was someone out of her past who was using a phony name. She soon learned that his real name was Shuji Tanaka, and he began putting the squeeze on her. As soon as he admitted that his name was Tanaka, she knew she could expect blackmail.

"I knew right away that Midori was lying, or at least that she was concealing something. The question that bothered me was how on earth he had been able to recognize Midori after nine years and a sex change if he had only been a casual acquaintance. I figured that there must be some reason why he remembered her so vividly. I pursued the matter and was rewarded with the most desperate confession imaginable. In fact, I didn't believe it myself. But the story my wife told was true.

"The person Tanaka had remembered from the past was a man named Jiro Miki. In fact Tanaka and Miki had not even been friends in the past. They had only met once before and that was quite by chance. But the reason Tanaka remembered Miki's face was that Miki had killed Tanaka's fiancée and had fled the area. Once Tanaka had seen through Midori's disguise, he used that crime from the past as a means of blackmailing her.

"When I heard all this, my first response was to protect Midori. Even though she was not listed on my family register, and even though she had kept some of her most intimate secrets from me, I still considered her to be my wife. Besides, she was all alone in the world, and I was the only one she had to rely on. I felt I had an obligation to protect my wife, at least against any sort of external threat.

"When I say he was blackmailing her, it was money, of course, that he wanted. I made up my mind that I'd listen to his demands and pay him off once and for all. By that time my company was on the verge of bankruptcy, and I wasn't sure I could raise enough money, but I decided to hear what he had to say and to do the best I could to meet his demands. After I actually met Tanaka face-to-face, he stayed on me all the time wherever I went. He even called me at the bar in Roppongi and said all sorts of nasty things, and I figured I'd have to get together with him as soon as possible.

"About ten days passed in this fashion, then on the evening of September eleventh I returned home to find Midori and Tanaka together in the living room once again, only this time Tanaka was lying in a huge pool of blood with a hunting knife protruding from the left side of his back.

"Midori was standing there covered with blood; her face was white as a ghost. The story she told went like this: 'It wasn't money that Tanaka was after. No, he got close to me in the first place because he wanted to get revenge for his fiancée, and he did demand a large sum of money, but that's not what he really wanted. If revenge is really what he wanted, he could have simply gone to the police and turned me in, or he could have killed me. It turns out that it was me he wanted. Tonight he came here and told me he wanted to make love to me. I refused. I wouldn't even hold hands with another man; I'd rather die first. I knew that Tanaka liked to drink, so I fixed him Scotch and mixed some sleeping pills in it to make him sleepy. I thought that if he went to sleep, I'd wait until you came home. I wanted to say good-bye to you and then turn myself in to the police, but as I thought about it, I knew I didn't want to face all the scandal that would involve, so I decided to commit suicide. But before Tanaka passed out, he attacked me, and there's what happened.'

"Midori collapsed in tears as she told me this.

"This time I believed she was telling the truth. Suddenly, now for the first time, I made up my mind to leave her. But don't get me wrong, I wasn't trying to get away from her just because she was a murderer. I shared her agony, and I knew how very much I loved her. But at the same time, I knew that physically I rejected her. I knew that if we continued to live together, we would always have to face this reality and that we would both be hurt by it like some sort of eternal punishment.

"But even though I had made up my mind to leave her, I felt that I first had to take care of this matter of the murder she had committed, since I felt that my wife's business was my responsibility. It may sound like a funny thing to say at a time when my company was going bankrupt, but I sort of thought of it as a farewell gift to my wife."

"So you got involved with Yoko Noda and you planned to make it look like a love suicide, and you switched Tanaka's body for your own."

"That's right. That plan occurred to me because I really didn't think Yoko would live too much longer anyway. She was melancholy and had schizoid tendencies, and she often talked about death. Our thinking was much the same, so I thought I could talk her into committing suicide with me. About a month prior to that I had been driving in the neighborhood near my company, and I hit and killed a young girl. The matter was settled out of court, but the child's grandfather was half-crazed with grief, and he used to follow me around pouring out streams of abuse. I always sympathized with him, and there was nothing I could say in my own defense. Because of the anger caused by the accident, and the failure of my company, along with all of Midori's problems, I was just exhausted and had lost all desire to go on living the way I was. All I wanted to do was to wipe the slate clean and spend the rest of my life in some other country where I could start all over again. If I had been successful in doing that, I could have left here and everyone would have thought that I was dead."

"Tell us in more detail about the phony suicide."

"First I put Tanaka's body in the bathtub and packed it

with ice to keep it cold. I left the knife in place just as it was to avoid further loss of blood. The following day, on the twelfth, Midori bought a large quantity of dry ice and continued to keep the body cold. That evening I invited Yoko to a hotel with me and suggested that we commit a lovers' suicide together. Perhaps because I was already a goner as far as society was concerned, my words seemed to ring true, for Yoko agreed right away to join me. I almost abandoned my plan when she said yes to my proposal because she's still so young and has so much to live for. But I had that body to dispose of, so in the end I decided to go ahead with the plan.

"At three o'clock the following afternoon I met Yoko on the platform of the Bullet Train at Tokyo station. We took the limited express to Atami and got a hired car there and headed for Amagi Meadows. At an appropriate time Midori set out from Tokyo in a rented car with Tanaka's body concealed in the trunk and drove to Amagi. You should understand, I'm not trying to suggest that Midori was there in her rented car to follow us when we got the hired car at Atami station. After all, she knew where we were headed. When we were on the Skyline Drive out of Atami, Yoko seemed to think there was a car following us, but that was just a woman's instinctive suspicion.

"Once we arrived at Amagi Meadows, we stopped at an inn called the Amagi Hotel and waited for night to fall. This was also planned so that the people who worked at the inn would remember Yoko's and my face. Yoko told me she had left on this trip without telling anyone, but when we got to the inn, she said she wanted to send a letter to her friend named Fumiyo Chino. I was afraid she might become suspicious if I was unreasonable in trying to prevent her from sending such a letter, so I said I would also send a letter to my wife. After we had each written our letter, I said I would take them down to the front desk to mail them, but of course I didn't. The problem was that if Mrs. Chino read the letter, she'd probably turn it over to the police, and they'd quickly find the bodies, and then there'd be a strong possibility that they could tell that Tanaka's body was not mine, because even though it had been preserved with dry ice, it would have deteriorated more than Yoko's body had.

"After Yoko suggested that we write letters, it occurred to me that Yoko and I should write a last testament on the stationery provided by the inn. I dated it and put it in my jacket pocket, thinking that this would make it clear that it was Yoko and I who had killed ourselves.

"We set out about ten o'clock from the inn and walked along the crest highway. We didn't go very far up Mount Amagi, but turned off into a grove of cedars, where it would be unlikely that anyone would find us for some time. I've been going to that area since last year on frequent golfing outings and had done a lot of walking there, so I pretty well knew the area. I sat down at the foot of an exceptionally large cedar tree, and with Yoko sitting beside me, we both took a dose of sleeping medication. Actually, I only swallowed a small number of vitamin pills. We sat for a time with our arms around each other, and soon Yoko, who had taken about fifty of the sleeping pills, fell asleep. As soon as I was sure she was asleep, I hurried back to the main highway. That's where Midori was waiting with the car. I remember the mist was starting to come up.

"Tanaka's body was wrapped in a plastic sheet, and we carried it to the site of the 'lovers' suicide.' When we got there, I took off my suit and put the one I had been wearing on Tanaka. My suit was a bit narrow in the shoulders for Tanaka, and somewhat long, but the difference was not enough to be noticed. When Midori had stabbed Tanaka, he had not been wearing a jacket, only a white shirt, so we put my jacket on him and left him facedown in the bushes. I even went so far as to change shoes with the dead man, and to put my own Swiss watch on his wrist. The last thing we did was to arrange it so that Yoko's hand was clutching the handle of the knife that had been plunged into Tanaka's heart.

"So that's what we did, supposing that it would be several days before the bodies would be found even though it was still the hiking season and tourists were passing along the highway every day. Since the bodies were deep in a cedar grove and could not be seen from the road, there was every chance that we would have some respite. It was nearly the season when people would stop leaving the road at random places to ascend the peak, and also it wouldn't be long before people stopped coming down off the peak through the woods to hit the road. If everything went as we hoped and the bodies weren't discovered for several days—the plan was that if the bodies weren't discovered within a week, Midori was going to ask the police to conduct a search and suggest that they begin by looking in the area around Mount Amagi—if, as I say, the bodies remained for a week or so, by that time they would be thoroughly decomposed, and it would be impossible to detect any difference in the time of death between the two. The idea was that in the man's pocket they'd find a last testament written by both of them, and it would be on the stationery of the Amagi Hotel, and the hotel would confirm that such a man and woman had stayed there on the day in question, and that in the evening of that day they had set out for the mountain. After that, they would call Midori to come down from Tokyo, and she would make a positive identification of the body as her husband's, and after that, there would be no question that they would be disposed of as the bodies of Takashi Sato and Yoko Noda who had committed a lovers' suicide together. At the scene of the crime they would surely conclude that the woman had stabbed the man, and had then killed herself by taking an overdose of sleeping pills. It would not be unusual for the two decayed bodies to be cremated at once.

"After we left Tanaka's body there, I returned to Tokyo in the car Midori had rented. She had brought a suitcase of clothes so I could change into my own clothes in the car. By the time we reached the airport at Haneda, it was fogged in.

"It was at this point that Midori said that she hoped we could go on living together, but I declined and took the first available flight to Hokkaido. I thought I had separated from Midori permanently. That, at least, was my intention at the time. Once I was gone as president of Sato Metal Industries, it was only a matter of time until the company collapsed. I was penniless, of course, but Midori already owned a condominium in Meguro, so she was able to live there at no expense. All I could do was hope that Midori would be able to improvise on her own once I was gone. The fact is that I own a small lot here on the outskirts of Abashiri City with a little house on it. I had acquired this shortly after I had gotten to know Midori and at a time when my company was still strong, so I had bought it privately at that time. I had been raised in Kushiro, and both my parents had met their unfortunate deaths there, and I had set out for Tokyo at an early age, but always, somewhere deep in my heart, I've felt that I really wanted to return to Hokkaido. But the fact is that I had no great desire to return to the town of Kushiro, which I had known as a child. To the east was Abashiri, an area I had always liked. The city had always seemed light to me because there was nothing around it but the Sea of Okhosk. At the time I bought the house, I never really intended to live there, but had thought to make it into a sort of summer home someday, and in the meantime, I had asked the people living nearby to look after it for me. But now I wonder if perhaps I had prepared it because I really, instinctively, expected to use it this way someday. Besides, the important thing is that the property was not registered to me as Takashi Sato; rather it was in my real name, Nobuo Eto, so I had nothing to worry about in that respect. The name listed in my official family register was Takashi Ishida, so the important point is that Takashi Sato had totally disappeared from society.

"I intended to resume my original name of Nobuo Eto and to live quietly by myself on the northern island of Hokkaido. I figured that a man living alone could get along some-how.''

"But when Yoko Noda turned up alive, that sort of fouled up your plans, is that it?''

"Well, it was apparent from the very beginning that there were several weak points both in the plan I had come up with and in the way we implemented it. The first sign came three days after the event when I got a special-delivery letter from Midori—that was before the murder at Amagi had even been discovered. You see there is no telephone in my home in Abashiri, it was a house that Midori and I had just decided to buy one time when we were here traveling, so she knew the address.

"I knew something had gone wrong as soon as the letter arrived, because when we separated at the airport, we expected that we would never meet again but would each live our own lives independently. Receiving a letter from her was a violation of our agreement. But it was the content of the letter that shocked me. She had written saying that on the afternoon of September fifteenth Yoko Noda had showed up at our house in Aoyama. At first I didn't believe it and thought she must have been seeing things, but Midori went on to explain that the woman had taken off her sunglasses and had announced her name, and when Midori had said that her husband was away on a business trip, Yoko had replied that she had seen me recently at Mount Amagi. It was obvious that Yoko was alive and well and had returned to Tokyo! It seemed impossible, but I knew it was true, and I was at once filled with surprise, and also with a sense of relief. Relief that this innocent young lady had not sacrificed her life after all.

"In any case, this raised the question of how she had managed to come back to life. I had obtained the sleeping pills I had given her from a friend who worked in a pharmaceutical company, and earlier when I had tested it by taking a normal dose, it had put me right to sleep. With my own eyes I had watched Yoko consume fifty of the pills. Later I figured out what must have gone wrong when I read an article in a medical magazine. It often happens that when people take a lethal dose of sleeping medicine for the first time, it causes them to vomit. Apparently, sometime after we had placed Tanaka's body beside her and left, she had vomited the medicine and eventually regained consciousness. No doubt she had been frightened by what had happened and fled back to Tokyo.

"For some reason she had decided to present herself to Midori. I was faced with the question of what Yoko might make of this bizarre episode she had been involved in, and of what she might do next. Soon the relief I had felt earlier gave way to fear and uneasiness that I might be found out.

"Judging from the contents of the letter, Midori was even more stunned by this development than I was, and was feverishly trying to do something about it. At first Yoko had appeared and announced herself to Midori in broad daylight, then she took to watching the house at night, while Midori was staying all alone. Midori decided that Yoko must have already figured out what really happened, so wearing Tanaka's sports coat, she went out in the night and tried to stab Yoko to death. But a man passing by intervened, and she failed to kill Yoko. After that, I'm not sure what role Yoko played in what happened, but at that point a man calling himself Tanaka's brother-in-law began making inquiries about Tanaka. Midori asked in her letter what she should do to take care of him. I was careful, however, not to send a letter in reply. For one thing, I didn't have any plan to suggest, and for another, if I sent a letter, I had no way of knowing who might see the Abashiri postmark, which could lead them to me.

"After that two days passed, then I read in the newspapers that some hikers had discovered Tanaka's body. Midori had gone immediately to the site, of course, and had positively identified the body as that of Takashi Sato, and after an autopsy, he had been cremated. By the time he was discovered, the remains were in a fairly advanced state of decomposition, and it was impossible to tell exactly how long he had been dead, but on the basis of the last testament in his pocket along with the testimony of the employees at the nearby inn, it was determined that he had died on the night of September thirteenth.

"That much, at least, went according to the plan, but since they only found the one body, the police decided that Yoko Noda, the woman who had been accompanying him, had killed Sato, and then fled without taking her own life, and they began a manhunt for Yoko as a prime suspect. It occurred to me that things had turned out in a most unfortunate way for Yoko, and then on top of everything else, she had been careless enough to actually show herself to Midori.

"In any case, there was really nothing I could do but look on quietly from my refuge in the north."

"Then what about the appearance in Fukuoka of the person who murdered the painter Teiji Kasai? Was that also Midori disguised as Tanaka?"

"I learned about that in Midori's second letter, which I received about two weeks later. Apparently Tanaka's brother-in-law was investigating his disappearance, and in addition to him, there was one other problem. That was the artist, Teiji Kasai, who had recognized that Midori was not an ordinary woman and apparently had learned something of her past from Tanaka. In any event, every time he met Midori, he would ask her hard questions about her background. Midori became really alarmed about the situation when Kasai went to Fukuoka and telephoned her from there. He said he had visited the home of a famous traditional dance teacher where a murder had been committed ten years ago by Jiro Miki, and he said he could tell that there was something shady going on, and he told Midori he wanted to meet with her and talk the matter over in detail. Midori told him she didn't know what he was talking about and refused to meet him in Fukuoka, but she did take the trouble to find out where he was staying there.

"After a long night of indecision, she once again donned Tanaka's sports coat and set out for Fukuoka. She located Kasai's inn, which was on the beach, and after looking around a little, figured out which was his room. Then she waited until night and simply went in for the kill.

"Apparently Kasai was not all that surprised to see Midori dressed as a man. No doubt this was because he had already found out about her past. She had come prepared to stab him to death in his room when he least expected it, and that's what she intended to do, but the plan had to be changed after a maid came into the room. She invited him to go for a walk on the beach in the moonlight, and that's when she stabbed him and fled. She explained all of this in great detail in her letter. Each time she committed one of these crimes, she made sure she was wearing Tanaka's jacket so that in case there were any witnesses, she would have the advantage of any doubt that was cast on the missing Tanaka.

"Right after that, Midori sent me a number of letters. This was the third murder she had committed, and she was beginning to feel like a fugitive and feared detection. She wrote to me that she wanted to reconsider our relationship, that since Takashi Sato was dead, she thought we would be able to go to some foreign country where no one knew us and start life over.

"At that point I had to struggle with myself, and I forced myself to remain silent, but in the end I guess I allowed Midori's fervent pleas to move my heart. Here I was in Abashiri prepared to spend the rest of my life in seclusion; perhaps it was a mistake to give myself up to that dream she offered. Just as Midori continued to yearn for me, I found that I had to return to her.

"This morning I received a telegram from Midori saying that she would arrive here today. Since she had my address and some recollection of where the place was, I decided that it would be best if I met her at the airport. But now I can see that she must have contacted me because she knew she was being followed. I knew there was some risk that I might be caught by whoever was following her if I went to meet her at the airport, but in the end I decided to take the risk.''

"What's that supposed to mean, you decided 'to take the risk'?''

"If it turned out that Midori was not being followed by anyone, we'd have a chance to be together again with no problems, and we could simply live here quietly on our own. If we were discovered, we could always go to a foreign country. We'd have been able to forget about the past and live in our own private world. Of course we wouldn't have been able to forget entirely about the past. I'll admit that much. To tell the truth, I think that people who have committed a crime are always faced with that fact, and they continue to suffer for it in ways that can never be healed. Shortly after Midori killed Tanaka and I made up my mind to leave her, I felt that as long as we two lived together we would be faced with our wretched past. After all, we would be guilty forever of the crimes we had committed. After I had fled away and hidden in the north country by myself, I came to realize that even then I couldn't escape the fear and anxiety. Ever since Midori confessed to me about her sex change, I had felt that to go on living with her as we were would make me an accomplice in a sin against God. And yet I was determined to make the best of the situation, and despite the enormity of our crimes, I decided to go on living with her. I also decided I wouldn't make any moves unless Midori was arrested. The fact is that Midori is a woman, both physically and emotionally, and I had to come to terms with the fact that I was her husband, for better or for worse. I realized that was something that would never change, no matter what happened.''

As he completed his statement, there was a sad and poignant look on Sato's haggard face. While he was being questioned, Midori's whereabouts were being sought, but the car she had been driving had gotten away without a trace. When Sato was asked where she might have gone, he merely said he didn't know, and he refused to tell them where he had been living.

Shortly after he completed his confession, news reached the Abashiri police station that a house in the isolated hills east of the city had gone up in flames. The house had been burned to the foundations and in the ashes they found the remains of a body, but it was impossible to determine either the age or sex of the victim. When the chief detective asked Sato about this, he confessed that the house was the one he had been living in as a fugitive. He closed his eyes and murmured, "So that's where Midori's long journey came to an end, in a lonely house by the sea."

22

The Sea of Mourning

YOKO WAS A STEP BEHIND TAKI AS THEY CROSSED THE SIN-
gle set of railroad tracks intersecting the highway that ran
straight down the peninsula. They were climbing the slope
of a hill that was covered with a scattering of low bushes. It
was like a wild garden. From early summer through August
there had been a luxuriant growth of all sorts of wild grasses
and flowers of the sort that grow by the sea. Now the pampas
grass was waving with its subdued autumn colors, and here
and there they could see a cluster of dark blue berries on the
bushes. The whole scene bespoke the early winter of the
north country. The seashore was deserted, and the wind was
cool as it caressed their bare arms.

"According to the chief detective, Dr. Makino of the Yamate Clinic finally went to the police this morning and told
them of our visit and the content of our story. He explained
to them that the chief of medicine was away yesterday and
they had an emergency, which is why he had not been in

276

touch with them sooner. Whatever the case, I think we were very lucky that he waited before going to the police.''

Until a short time before, both Taki and Yoko had undergone an extensive questioning about their role in the whole affair. Taki was not under any direct suspicion, so the police were relatively easy on him. The questions they put to him were roughly the same as the ones they had asked Sato, and when they had finished questioning him, they questioned Yoko.

As it became clear that her story corresponded with Sato's, they gradually eased up on her. The detective who questioned her was in his late middle age, and his eyes, as he looked at her, were filled with a great weariness as they relayed back and forth the answers to the questions that Sato had given to see if they corresponded.

''When the report came in this morning from Yokohama,'' Taki said, ''they began a frantic search for me, and when they found that I was not at work, they went to my sister's place and questioned her. She told them she thought I had gone to Hokkaido, and they put out an alert at all the airports.''

As they climbed the slope they could hear in the distance the voices of the officials who were still at the site of the fire, and caught the scent of burning wood in the air. When they returned to Tokyo, they would surely be questioned again by the police there. But now that Sato had been found alive and as a result of his confession, there wouldn't be much suspicion on Yoko. They were, therefore, permitted to go to the site of the fire where apparently Midori had burned herself to death.

By the time they arrived on the scene, Midori's remains had already been removed. But since the body had been burned so badly it was impossible to tell either the age or the sex of the victim, it seemed unlikely that they would be able to identify any physical details. Thus Midori had held her own funeral, apparently hoping to avoid the humiliation of being arrested.

The ruined house was in the middle of a vast prairie near Lake Tototsu, where the white sea gulls flew. All that remained was a little smoking rubble, and they had to imagine what the small house might have looked like.

The house seemed forlorn and alone standing as it did on the withered prairie near the wind-whipped lake. At the far edge of the prairie stretched a large, fallow field, and on the distant horizon was a small farmhouse surrounded by a larch windbreak. All that could be seen of the farm buildings was a roof and the silo.

Presently the couple reached the crest of the hill, and from there they had an unobstructed view of the Sea of Okhosk. Beneath the overcast sky the sea spread out in a broad, dark blue, gently undulating band. No islands were visible on the watery horizon, but off to their right a peninsula thrust out into the sea. The ridge of the peninsula was composed of steep mountains whose peaks were already dusted with early snow.

They started down the slope and the wall of mountains seemed to close in on them in a lonely and isolated embrace. The stillness and loneliness of the place were somehow exaggerated by the dissonant sounds of the wind and waves.

Yoko and Taki stopped and stood for a time looking out over the sea. The gray of the landscape seemed infinitely melancholy, and for some reason Yoko thought of Midori dressed in a traditional Japanese kimono. What Midori might have looked like back when she was still Jiro Miki remained a mystery to her. She'd had a creative job and probably a slim, youthful figure, which seemed to be always a part of Midori. Probably, too, she'd had an unhappy childhood, and in the end had stabbed a young girl to death. She had undergone an excruciatingly painful and potentially dangerous sex-change operation, yet Yoko believed that the sex change had not been motivated by a fear of being caught and charged with murder. Still, somehow, Yoko doubted that Jiro Miki's life really changed all that much once he became Midori. Yoko felt this because she believed Midori's tragedy stemmed from her body and the deep wounds it had caused her.

In the end Midori had happened to meet Takashi Sato. They had fallen in love and she had asked him to marry her. Perhaps she had really found fulfillment at this point as she began a new life with Sato's help.

Sato, too, had been all alone after mourning the death of his first wife. Midori had fallen desperately in love with him, and because of their successful relationship, she herself had been given a new life and was able to go on living. All she had to believe in was the purity of her love, and if she lost that, her life would revert to darkness. That was why she wouldn't permit either Shuji Tanaka or Teiji Kasai to become intimate with her. Instead of enduring humiliation in silence, she had committed the most foul of crimes, all because she wanted to protect the absolute love she felt for Sato. Even after he had gone away to a distant part of the country, she still defined her own self through his existence. As Sato had said in his testimony at the police station, even after he had learned of Midori's physical secret, he still planned to go on living with her as his wife. Midori had abandoned her natural sex, and like any other woman, once she had truly fallen in love, she never wavered in that love.

At last Taki sucked in a long breath and said, "I guess human beings are capable of doing just about anything." There was a note of fatigue in his voice. "We've both been through a lot, but it's finally turned out all right in the end. From now on we're free to do whatever we wish; someday we may even be able to transcend our limits as human beings."

Yoko made no response to this, but in her heart she thought that what he was saying was true, and that people might even be capable of more than he was saying. There are terrible demons and deep fears inside all of us.

For some time neither of them said anything, and yet even as they lingered a little longer, the air seemed to grow increasingly chilly. The late-autumn sea breeze seemed to pierce their very bones. Soon this seashore would be buried in snow and the sea itself become a sheet of floating ice. After watching the scene in silence a little longer Yoko called to mind the lines of a favorite poem:

> In the smoldering sky,
> Devoid of light
> The sun's hiding place is clear.
>
> Without radiance
> It shines in glory
> The dark waves of Okhosk.

Somehow these lines that came to mind seemed appropriate to this setting.

"When he heard that Midori had committed suicide by burning herself to death, Sato murmured that at last her long journey had come to an end," Taki said in a tone of voice that was gentler than before.

"Both Midori and Sato had their own dark shadows they were trying to flee from. Perhaps that explains the long journey for each of them."

"Yes. And this is where it all came to an end."

Yoko wondered if perhaps her own feelings were wandering, and if she, too, wanted to flee from something.

> Smoldering sky and dark waves
> My eye follows the long sweep of the shore.

At the foot of the mountains on this northern coast Sato and Midori had wanted to live quietly together. Like tired birds of passage they would love each other and be strangers to the world. Why were they denied that? Suddenly Yoko was seized with a deep feeling of sadness. Perhaps it was caused by the sound of the wintry sea pounding desolately on the shore. There had been a poet once who had referred to this lonely northern coast as the "sea of misery." "My love is buried in a sea of misery," he had written.

Tears streaked Yoko's face. Suddenly Taki was standing in front of her, asking gently, "Do you still love Sato?"

"I don't know," she said. Yoko felt a feeling of simplicity take control of her. After the shock of learning that the love suicide had been false, and after fearing for her life, after the pain and the shock she had experienced, now, for some odd reason, all these emotions were gone. Was it because somewhere deep within her she still loved him? Or was it because she now realized that the feelings she had earlier mistaken for love were really something else?

"I understand," Taki said. "A person's feelings are never that simple. Each of us just has to get along as best he can."

Yoko made no reply but drew her face close to Taki's and closed her eyes.

As the cold wind of Okhosk swirled around them, their lips met with burning eagerness.

About the Author

The bestselling mystery writer in Japan, Shizuko Natsuki has written over eighty novels, short stories and serials, forty of which have been made into Japanese television movies. Several of her short stories have been published in *Ellery Queen's Mystery Magazine*. She is also the author of *Murder at Mt. Fuji*, *The Third Lady*, and *The Obitary Arrives at Two O'clock*. Ms. Natsuki lives in Fukuoka, Japan.

JAPAN'S
BESTSELLING
MYSTERY
WRITER
SHIZUKO
NATSUKI